A Temporary Situation
(Temporary series: Tristan and Dom #1)

H.L Day

Also, by H.L Day

A Christmas Situation (Temporary series; Tristan and Dom #2)
Time for a Change
Kept in the Dark
Refuge (Fight for Survival #1)
Taking Love's Lead
Edge of Living

Blurb

Personal assistant Dominic is a consummate professional. Funny then, that he harbors such unprofessional feelings toward Tristan Maxwell, the CEO of the company. No, not in that way. The man may be the walking epitome of gorgeousness dressed up in a designer suit. But, Dominic's immune. Unlike most of the workforce, he can see through the pretty facade to the arrogant, self-entitled asshole below. It's lucky then, that the man's easy enough to avoid.

Disaster strikes when Dominic finds himself having to work in close proximity as Tristan's P.A. The man is infuriatingly unflappable, infuriatingly good-humored, and infuriatingly unorthodox. In short, just infuriating. A late-night rescue leading to a drunken pass only complicates matters further, especially with the discovery that Tristan is both straight and engaged.

Hatred turns to tolerance, tolerance to friendship, and friendship to mutual passion. One thing's for sure, if Tristan sets his sights on Dominic, there's no way Dominic has the necessary armor or willpower to keep a force of nature like Tristan at bay for long, no matter how unprofessional a relationship with the boss might be. He may just have to revise everything he previously thought and believed in for a chance at love.

Copyright

Cover Art by
A Temporary Situation

CW01501487

Warning

Intended for an 18+ audience. This book contains material that may be offensive to some and is intended for a mature, adult audience. It contains graphic language, explicit sexual content and adult situations.

Chapter One

There he was—Mr. Fucking Perfect. I watched covertly from the interior of the elevator as Tristan Maxwell strode purposefully across the lobby floor. Numerous people, both male and female, turned to stare as he passed them. They were probably fixated on the perfect fucking hair, or the perfect fucking cheekbones, or maybe even the perfect fucking tailored suit, which probably cost more than I earned in a month. Mr. Fucking Perfect acted as if he were completely oblivious to their scrutiny. He was probably far too perfect to notice the blatant admiration and lingering looks of the everyday common person.

Against my will, my gaze moved to his lips. Like the rest of him, they were perfectly shaped. It was a shame they'd uttered such damning words in a magazine interview, giving away the true thoughts of the man behind the mask. Actually, it was good, I reminded myself. Or else I might have been lulled into believing, along with the rest of the workforce, that the inside was just as attractive as the outside.

A loud *ding* announced the imminent closure of the elevator doors. It prompted Mr. Perfect to break into a graceful trot, while politely asking for the door to be held. As the closest person to the controls, my hand hovered momentarily over the button, which with one press would keep the door from closing. I removed it with a smirk, allowing the doors to swing shut right in Mr. Perfect's shocked face. It gave me just as much satisfaction as returning Mr. Perfect's smile with a glare had, a few weeks back. Actually, strike that. It was more satisfying: shock always trumps confusion.

Exiting the elevator on the fifteenth floor, I whistled cheerfully as I made my way down the corridor, pausing to greet a few familiar faces as I passed them. The office where I'd been personal assistant to John Stone for the last year was at the far end of the corridor. John was a fairly hefty man in his mid-fifties and hardly likely to set the engineering world alight, but he was a fair boss, and I enjoyed working for him.

The connecting door between the two offices stood open, so I could clearly see Mr. Stone—as he always insisted on being called—at his desk, mid-conversation, the phone held to his ear. On noting my arrival, he gestured wildly for me to step inside his office. That was unusual. Normally if he was busy, we saved the morning pleasantries until later, and I just got stuck into the day's tasks. Dutifully, following his directive like the good and amenable PA I was, I waited patiently by the corner of his desk for the call to finish. Well, if you can classify a lot of foot tapping and fidgeting as patient. Once Mr. Stone had bidden the caller farewell, he fixed his attention on me.

"Dominic. Good morning. How are you today?"

"I'm really good, Mr. Stone. Did you need to speak to me?"

Mr. Stone peered intently over the top of his wire-rimmed glasses without speaking.

I was getting the distinct impression he was reluctant to say whatever was coming next. I wondered what could be so important it couldn't wait till later, never mind provoke this strange delay in getting to the point. "Because if not, I need to type up that report for you, the one you need for your ten-thirty meeting."

"Ah!"

He took off his glasses slowly, folding them neatly and placing them on the desk in front of him. "You're not going to like this."

I narrowed my eyes, trying to read his mind through sheer force of will. Strangely enough, given I had zero psychic powers, it didn't work. I went the old-fashioned route instead. "Not going to like what?"

"They want to borrow you. Just temporarily though."

"Borrow me? I'm not a library book."

Mr. Stone chuckled. At least one of us was finding this conversation amusing.

"You said no, right? You said I was indispensable. That you couldn't manage without me."

My boss sighed, looking slightly irritated. I wasn't entirely sure whether he was irritated with my reaction or with someone taking his personal assistant away. "If it had been anyone else, I probably would have done, but it was short notice, what with Kevin being rushed to hospital the way he was, with appendicitis, so..."

A cold dread settled in my stomach, and I found myself regretting the breakfast I'd eaten an hour earlier. "Kevin? As in Kevin Taylor?"

Mr. Stone nodded. "That's right. Mr. Maxwell's PA. Terrible business! His appendix burst, and they only just managed to operate in time. He's going to be off for at least a couple of weeks. I could hardly say no to the big boss man, could I?"

I'd heard the news about Kevin. There wasn't much, news or gossip, that didn't spread around the building like wildfire. For such a large building and workforce, there certainly seemed to be a very speedy and effective whisper network operating at all times. My friend Paul was even one of the main players. I didn't know Kevin particularly well, but he was a nice guy. We'd chatted a few times. It had never crossed my mind for one minute that his absence would impact me in any way. "But how will you manage?"

"They'll give me a temp. They won't be as good as you, obviously, but it's only for a few weeks. They can hardly give the boss a temp, can they?"

"Yeah, but...there's other people, better people than me. They should—"

The phone rang again, bringing an abrupt end to the conversation. Mr. Stone automatically reached for it, his hand pausing for a moment on the receiver "Mr. Maxwell wanted to meet you as soon as you got here, so you better go straight up."

"I should probably wait and talk to the temp. I don't want to leave you in the lurch." The delaying tactic failed miserably. Mr. Stone simply shook his head, before bringing the phone to his ear

I left the office, leaving him to his phone conversation, and spent a few minutes trying to wrap my mind around the situation. Mr. Fucking Perfect had requested—no, not requested, demanded—that I was going to be his personal assistant for the next two weeks. Mr. Fucking Perfect, who'd had the elevator door closed in his face less than ten minutes before by the man he'd requested to meet. Well, this ought to be a very short meeting, probably closely followed by my dismissal. Maybe if I wished hard enough, *my* appendix would burst.

Resigned to my fate, I headed for the office on the top floor where Mr. Fucking Perfect surveyed his empire from the comfort of his office while the minions did the hard work. His words, not mine. I still remembered every word of the double-page interview he'd given to *Fortune* magazine.

They were burned into my brain. His attitude in it had made me sick. If I'd seen it before applying for the post, I wouldn't have bothered. I'd considered quitting, but the pay was a real step up from my previous job. Besides, I'd constantly reassured myself that my contact with the egotistical CEO of the company was minimal: the occasional meeting, where I usually managed to merge into the background, and those unfortunate glimpses in the lobby. I could put up with that for a job I really liked.

Unfortunately, it seemed the minimal contact was about to come to a crashing end.

I took the stairs rather than the elevator. The longer it took me to get there, the better. If I could manage to arrive sweating and out of breath, that would be a bonus. Hopefully, he'd take one look and change his mind, go for someone with slightly better hygiene habits. I felt absolutely no inclination to whistle during any part of the journey.

"YOU!"

Tristan Maxwell stared incredulously.

I fought the urge to perform a slow twirl. "Me."

Several emotions briefly flitted across the other man's face. His perfect face. I tried my best to avoid noticing that he was even more devastatingly attractive close up. Whilst I waited for the inevitable explosion to hit, I certainly didn't admire the vivid blue depths of his eyes, or the perfectly shaped cheekbones. I didn't notice that he was clean shaven, without even a hint of stubble, and I wasn't even slightly aware of the expensive but subtle cologne he wore.

The explosion never came. Instead the look on his face settled to one of concern.

"Listen, I've been racking my brains, and I'm really sorry, but I can't remember what I've done to upset you."

I kept my face deliberately blank. "Upset me?"

"Yeah. The other week, the look you gave me."

I shrugged in a way I hoped conveyed a "paranoid much" demeanor.

"I suppose you didn't deliberately close the elevator door on me this morning, either?"

Scratching my head, I decided an out-and-out lie was the only way to go. "This morning? Were you in the elevator this morning? I don't remember seeing you."

The gorgeous blue eyes of the man stood opposite me, narrowed. "No. I wasn't *in* it. I couldn't get *in it,* because somebody closed the door on me."

Resisting the temptation to point out I hadn't *closed* the door, simply not *stopped* it from closing, I nodded sagely. "Well, I quite understand you needing to get somebody else for this position, Mr. Maxwell. What with all these misunderstandings between us. I'll go back to Mr. Stone, and you can find someone else. Someone more suitable, and the temp can be relocated to wherever they're needed."

Affecting what I was pretty sure was a weak smile at best, I began to edge my way slowly toward the door, already anticipating being safely back behind my own desk in the next ten minutes. I could make a cup of coffee and tell Mr. Stone—who would be mightily impressed, not to mention relieved—how I'd managed to extricate myself from the clutches of evil.

He frowned and took a step forward, immediately canceling out the distance I'd managed to put between us. "Not so fast. You're really good, apparently."

I shook my head and pulled a face. "Ermmm, just average really. Nothing special. Mr. Stone...you know. He likes to exaggerate."

"John? Really? I can't think of anyone less likely to exaggerate." He had me over a barrel there. I made a mental note to not stray too far from the truth in my future efforts to be persuasive. The closer I stayed to the truth, the more convincing it would be. But I wasn't ready to give up quite yet. My life's aim had become to just escape from this office. No way in hell was I going to work closely with this man, even if it was only for a couple of weeks.

Racking my brain for further reasons, I came up with one. "And I've only worked for the company for a year. Think of the fuss, Mr. Maxwell, if you choose me over someone else, someone who's worked here for years. Everybody will be talking about it. You'll look bad. I'll look bad. There'll be gossip. There'll be..." I trailed off, unable to add another reason to the argument.

Mr. Fucking Perfect regarded me steadily. Was that a hint of amusement in his eyes? I didn't want him amused. I wanted him annoyed, irritated, and desperate to get rid of me. "Tristan. Call me Tristan, please. I look around for my father when someone says Mr. Maxwell."

Christ! I was having enough problems calling him Mr. Maxwell rather than Mr. Fucking Perfect. I'd probably choke on the word if I attempted to call him Tristan.

I shuffled another step closer to the door, but he came after me again. "I don't care what people think. I've got to work with my PA, so I get to choose who it is. You came highly recommended, so I've chosen you."

I opened my mouth to protest, but in the absence of any further arguments, I closed it again without making a comment.

Mr. Fucking Perfect smirked knowingly, as if he knew he had me beaten. The smirk made me dislike him even more. He gestured over to the corner of the office. "Your desk's over there. I've written down a list of tasks I need you to get started on straight away. Give me a shout if any of them don't make sense, and I'll come and explain."

Fighting the urge to salute, I slunk over to the desk in the corner while he disappeared into the adjoining office. Deliberately ignoring the list of tasks, I glared at the wall. How the hell had the day gone wrong so quickly?

Chapter Two

Over the last twenty-four hours, I'd come up with a plan: be obnoxious enough for Mr. Fucking Perfect to decide having a PA like me was too much trouble, but not quite obnoxious enough to get fired altogether. The only problem with putting the scheme into action was it required Mr. Perfection to actually set foot in the building, and so far he'd been a complete no-show.

As if my thoughts alone had triggered his presence, the man himself strolled through the door, looking like a million dollars, and smiling broadly. "Good morning, Dominic."

Looking down, I made no effort to return the smile or the irritating cheeriness. "Mr. Maxwell."

"I told you yesterday. Call me Tristan, please."

A pair of perfectly tailored trousers halted in front of the desk, forcing me either to look up or continue to stare at the man's crotch. I looked up. It was time to put my plan into action. "I'm not comfortable calling you by your first name, so I'll stick to Mr. Maxwell. I don't remember there being anything in my contract about being forced to call senior members of staff by their Christian names, if I don't feel comfortable doing so." I silently applauded myself for managing to sound so much like I had a stick up my ass.

Mr. Perfection's smile wavered slightly. "I'm not forcing you. I just thought you'd prefer...never mind. I suppose I can put up with Mr. Maxwell, if it makes you happy." The smile returned full force, revealing his fucking perfect teeth.

Mr. Fucking Perfect was apparently Mr. Fucking Reasonable and Unflappable as well. No worries. I'd just have to try harder.

He leaned over, still smiling. "I brought you coffee."

I stared at him, wondering if I'd heard correctly. In my haste to annoy him, I hadn't even noticed the two Costa cups he held in his hands. Even if I had noticed, I probably would have assumed it was for someone else. He placed one of the cups on the desk in front of me. Bemused, I continued to stare at it. "I think I'm meant to get you coffee, Mr. Maxwell. Not the other way around."

"I know, but I pass it on the way in. It's not a big deal. Kevin used to really appreciate it. That reminds me. I need you to sort out some sort of gift for Kevin. Oh, and a 'Get Well Soon' card."

I was thinking more along the lines of a "Get Well Now" card. Maybe I could scratch out the "soon" and replace it, and then convince the hospital staff he was healthy enough to return to work. I smiled at the thought.

"I presume you like the coffee?" Mr. Fucking Perfect had clearly misinterpreted the reason for my amusement.

"What kind is it?"

"A latte."

I sighed. Of course it was. My favorite! A perfect choice, but I could hardly tell him that.

"What flavor?"

"Vanilla. I figured everyone likes vanilla."

Of course I liked vanilla, but I was meant to be behaving like a dick, so I shrugged. "It'll do, I suppose."

Quashing the feeling of guilt at the crestfallen expression that immediately appeared on his face, I took a sip and recoiled as if it tasted disgusting.

"What flavor *do* you like?"

I gave a more dramatic shrug. I'd obviously missed my calling. I should have been an actor. "Gingerbread...or cinnamon. I'm not particularly fussy."

Surely he had to take issue with *that* comment, but he simply smiled. "Excellent! I'll know for tomorrow."

I stared at his departing back. Maybe I should call him "Mr. Too Good to be True."

THE MAN IN THE HOSPITAL bed grimaced in pain as he tried to hoist himself up to a sitting position. He managed a wan smile as he looked over at the card and flowers I'd deposited on the cabinet by the bed.

"Thank Tristan for me, would you?"

"What, for his five seconds of holding a pen and scrawling his name?" I picked up the card and examined it more closely. "At least I think that's his name. It could say anything, really. Maybe next time I should help him to form his letters correctly."

Kevin started to laugh before grinding to a sudden halt, clutching his side. "Oh, God! Don't joke. It hurts to laugh."

"Who's joking?"

Kevin ignored the comment, probably interpreting it as yet another joke. "Anyway, you know the secret now?"

"Secret?"

"Yeah. How great Tristan is."

Somehow—and it took great effort on my part—I managed to avoid choking on the polystyrene cup of rapidly cooling, tasteless machine coffee. Kevin didn't seem to notice and carried on regardless.

"Because, you know, sometimes I make things up that he's done or said, just so people don't realize what a great boss he is, or they'd all be after my job. I guess I'll have to fight you for it now."

"I'd quite happily give it back to you tomorrow if I could. Actually, forget tomorrow. You can have it now. Do you need help dressing?"

Kevin's amazement was written all over his face. "Really? Wow! I didn't realize working for John Stone was that great. He always looks so dour and miserable. Whereas Tristan..."

I stopped listening while Kevin went on and on, extolling the apparently never-ending virtues of his boss. Bored, I began to consider how you went about applying for a sainthood for someone. Was there an actual application form I could fill in, or maybe it would just be easier to contact the Pope directly? It was clear he'd never read the interview where his boss had talked in such a derogatory way about his employees. Maybe I should bring him a copy in? It seemed like Mr. Fucking Perfect was able to pull the wool over a lot of people's eyes.

A sudden silence signaled Kevin had directed a question my way and was waiting for an answer.

"Hmmm... Sorry?"

Kevin's eyelids began to droop, and he yawned. "Doesn't matter. There's lots of stuff I should probably tell you, to make life easier for you and for Tristan. If you come back another day, I'll get you up to speed on stuff. I'll..." His words trailed off, the fight against drowsiness lost.

Dumping the rest of the coffee, I made my way back to the office. I spent the journey time thinking up new ways to annoy my temporary boss in the hope of making him even more temporary.

NOTHING WORKED. I'D been trying to annoy Mr. Perfect now for the last two days, but it was like water off a duck's back. Any snarky comment I made was met with unrelenting cheeriness. How anybody could put up with a PA showing the attitude I did, I had no idea.

The intercom on my desk buzzed, followed by a request to please come into his office. It wasn't a command. He didn't do commands. He did polite, reasonable requests.

Sighing, I grabbed the diary and tape recorder and did as asked. Letting myself into the office, I plonked myself noisily down on the chair, making sure I was slouching. The man opposite continued to beam enthusiastically at me.

For some reason, it was getting harder and harder not to return that smile. I tamped down on the urge, offering a curt "Mr. Maxwell" instead. I made sure to drum my fingers impatiently and loudly on the desk top while I waited to hear what he had to say. If he noticed, he didn't comment. I was just considering whether an obvious check of my watch would be pushing things too far when he started talking.

"This weekend, I have a conference coming up in Brighton. Kevin usually accompanies me. It helps to have someone there to take notes and field phone calls. Is that okay?"

I stared at him, aghast. "You want me to accompany you to Brighton? All weekend?"

He nodded. "Of course, you'll have Monday off. I'm not expecting you to work straight through. Oh, and you'll get paid overtime. That goes without saying."

Even with the promise of extra money, money I could spend a hundred different ways, I decided I'd still rather stick pins in my eyes than go to

Brighton. The thought of being stuck with him all weekend made having to put up with him during the day seem like child's play. Although maybe, I'd finally get to see a crack in this perfect-boss façade he had going on. Chances were, I'd finally get to meet the man who'd given that interview. Because the man I'd seen so far was obviously putting on a great show, but it couldn't last forever.

Chapter Three

I kicked my suitcase while I waited on the train platform at Victoria, wondering yet again why the hell I'd agreed to this. Nothing in my contract stated I had to be available to work on weekends. I could have said I had plans I couldn't possibly get out of, that it was too short notice, that I had a sick relative whose bedside I had to sit next to. There were numerous lies and excuses I could have used to avoid this. So it was beyond even my own comprehension why the hell I'd agreed.

"What did it do to you?"

I swung round to find Tristan Maxwell, standing far too close, holding out a Costa cup.

Taking a step back, I took the container and sniffed its contents. The pungent scent of cinnamon assailed my nostrils, almost but not completely blocking out the familiar and distracting scent of cologne emanating from my boss. He tended to favour the same one. Not that I noticed, of course. "Hmmm?"

He grinned, suddenly looking far too young to be the CEO of a major engineering company. "The suitcase? I wondered what it had done to deserve the poor treatment."

"Oh, nothing. I was just—"

Thankfully, I was saved from having to explain any further by the timely arrival of the train. Following my boss to our seats, I rolled my eyes at every admiring glance thrown his way. Given the sheer number of them, I was lucky my eyeballs managed to remain in my head. Within two minutes of sitting down, he closed his eyes and gave every indication of going straight to sleep.

"You're going to sleep?"

One blue eye slowly opened, closely followed by the other. "I was going to. Did you want me to talk to you?"

"No."

"Well, let me sleep then." His eyes closed again. I tried not to stare at the dark eyelashes fanned across his cheek. They were far too long and pretty for a man.

"I suppose you're expecting me to wake you up when we get there."

This time he didn't even bother to open his eyes. "No. I'll wake up."

I discovered a lot of things on the hour journey. I discovered I should have brought a book to read to make the time go faster. I'd expected to be given work to do. I also discovered that no matter how much you stare at someone, they don't wake up or even stir. Lastly, I discovered sitting opposite someone whose sleeping form was constantly ogled and discussed wasn't particularly good for my own ego. I was a good-looking guy. Normally, with my combination of platinum-blond hair and blue eyes, I was the one getting admiring looks. But I might as well have been invisible in comparison to Mr. Fucking Perfect.

Even now, two girls stood in the aisle of the train, taking covert glances and giggling. The blonde-haired girl turned to her friend and whispered, "He's so hot."

I reached the end of my tether. I was hot, irritated beyond belief, and bored. "He's just got out of prison."

The girls both turned to me, wearing twin looks of shock. "Oh, my God! Why? What did he do?"

I paused for dramatic effect. My audience leaned in closer. "Double homicide."

The girls ran away so fast, I was surprised they didn't leave scorch marks on the floor.

Less than five minutes later, the train pulled into Brighton station. I was just contemplating whether I could come up with a realistic excuse to leave Mr. Fucking Perfect on the train when the man in question's eyes slowly opened.

"Who did I kill?"

"What?"

"The double homicide. I just wondered who it was."

Short of spluttering about people pretending to sleep, I had no answer. I settled for ignoring the question altogether and busied myself with reaching for my suitcase and making sure I hadn't left anything behind.

THE HOTEL ROOM DOOR closed with a *click*, and I allowed myself the luxury of removing my jacket and tie before sprawling across the bed while I reflected on the day. I'd presumed I'd be expected to merge into the background, only leaping in when needed. But my boss had gone out of his way to include me in everything, seating me on his right-hand side, pouring me coffee, even calling a short break when he realized there was a problem with the tape recorder and I was struggling to record everything quickly enough by hand. I'd never been required to attend a conference with Mr. Stone, but I knew it would have been a very different affair. I was confused. Everything I'd seen today was at complete odds with the attitude he'd revealed in that interview.

I remembered my shock at reading it. Here was a company where I'd only been employed for a month, with the boss happy to detail how he just sat back and did nothing. He'd said he had a building full of obedient minions at his beck and call. He'd also made some sort of comment that, if he lost employees, they were easily replaced. I'd studiously avoided reading any other interviews he'd done after that, my blood already at boiling point. I didn't need any more evidence of the type of man I was working for.

But today Tristan Maxwell had done the opposite of sitting back. Where he could have left things to me as one of his minions, he'd often done it himself. He'd worked hard, been the consummate professional. I'd obtained a grudging respect for just how good Tristan Maxwell was at his job. Not that I'd ever admit that to the man himself, even under duress.

My mobile rang, the caller display showing an unknown number. Fatigued, I was almost tempted to ignore it. It was probably going to be a wrong number or some sort of sales call. I answered it with the intention of getting rid of them quickly. Then I could have a long shower, maybe watch a bit of TV before getting some much-needed sleep.

"Dominic?"

I frowned at the familiar voice on the line. "Mr. Maxwell. How did you get this number?" I'd only left the man fifteen minutes ago. Had I forgotten to do something crucial? There was a strange edge to his voice I wasn't used to hearing. Was the minion about to get a dressing down? Was he finally going to reveal his true personality?

"It's on your employee file. Anyway, never mind that. I need you to come to my room. Now! It's room thirty-four."

"What—"

The line went dead. The short walk, down one flight of stairs and along the corridor below mine, left just enough time to worry about what I'd done wrong to warrant the unusually curt command.

Before I got a chance to knock, the door was wrenched open. Tristan Maxwell was jacket-less, tie-less, shoe-less, and wearing a panicked expression. He grabbed my arm, hustling me into the room. "You need to get rid of it!"

Ignoring the feel of my boss's fingers burning their way through my shirt, I didn't even attempt to hide my confusion.

"Get rid of what?"

"In the bathroom?"

"What's in the bathroom?"

Tristan Maxwell started to pace. He gestured wildly with his arms. "A monster."

I glanced around the room, searching for any tell-tale signs of non-prescription drugs to explain this rather strange behavior. There were none I could see. It didn't mean they weren't there. They could be in his suitcase, or in the bathroom. I spoke slowly. "There's a monster in the bathroom?"

"Yes. And I need you to get rid of it."

"And this...*monster*...you've seen it?"

Tristan Maxwell shuddered. "Yes. I was going to take a shower, but I couldn't because it was just sitting there looking at me. With its *eyes* and its *legs*."

Something about his emphasis on the word "legs" made an idea click into place. "How many legs does this monster have?"

I suppressed a smirk when Tristan Maxwell shot an exasperated look my way. "The usual, I think. Eight. I didn't stop to count them. It was looking at me."

"So this...*monster*...is a spider?"

He gave another shudder at my use of the word. "Yes. I said so, didn't I? Are you going to get rid of it or just stand there?"

I was really tempted to just stand there. Watching Mr. Fucking Perfect completely unravel because there was a spider in the bathroom was too delicious for words.

"I don't think it's in my job description."

"You're a personal assistant. I need some *fucking* personal assistance!"

My eyes widened as the curse slipped out of his mouth.

Tristan Maxwell stopped dead. "Sorry. God! I'm sorry. I didn't mean to swear at you. Please help. I can't go in there till it's gone. Please!"

Worried he was going to drop to his knees and beg, I let myself into the hotel bathroom.

"CLOSE THE DOOR! In case it tries to get in here."

Laughing silently, I did as he asked. In the center of the shower floor sat a spider. It was a fairly average-sized spider as spiders go.

"HAVE YOU GOT RID OF IT?"

"Not yet."

"WHAT?"

"I SAID, NOT YET!"

I pressed the button to switch the shower on. The spider quickly lost its footing and washed straight down the plug hole. I let the water run for longer to make sure it couldn't crawl back up. I didn't fancy another phone call at midnight, should "the monster" reappear.

Walking back into the bedroom, I found my boss cross-legged on the floor drinking whisky.

"It's gone."

"Thank God! Thank you."

"I'll leave you to it."

Tristan Maxwell cocked his head to one side, a small smile playing at the corner of his lips. "You're going to make me drink alone."

"I'm not *making* you do anything."

He smiled, holding the bottle up so I could see the label. "This is seriously good whisky. You should try some."

"I should go to bed. It's been a long day."

"One drink?"

I eyed the door to the corridor speculatively. For some reason, the idea of a drink with Tristan Maxwell wasn't as abhorrent as it should have been. For that reason alone, I should head straight back to my room. Instead, I found myself joining him on the floor.

He poured a drink and held it out.

"Thanks, Mr. Maxwell."

He refused to relinquish the glass to my grasp. "No way you're going to drink with me and call me *Mr. Maxwell*."

"I—"

"Come on. It's two syllables. Tris-tan. Give it a try."

I repeated it slowly, like a child learning to read, and Tristan handed the glass over.

THREE HOURS AND HALF a bottle of whisky later, I laughed as Tristan compared the workings of the company to the hierarchy of the Death Star. I allowed my glass to be filled again.

"You do realize that makes you Darth Vader."

Tristan covered his mouth with his hands and did a perfect impression of the sound of Darth Vader's breathing.

"What am I, a stormtrooper?"

He shook his head. "No way! They're not snarky enough." He waved a drunken finger. "Don't argue it. I know! You're Han Solo. Yep. That's it. Han Solo."

"You're a secret geek."

Tristan took a large swallow of whisky. I dragged my eyes away from the sight of his tanned throat contracting as he swallowed. "Maybe."

Unfortunately, that brought my eyes back to the other thing they kept being drawn to. At some point during the night, half of Tristan's shirt buttons had either been unfastened or had come undone. Now every time he moved, I caught a tantalizing glimpse of nipple. No matter how hard I tried not to look, my gaze was irrevocably drawn back to it.

"Tristan, did you do this with Kevin?"

"Kevin doesn't drink." Tristan smiled, and I returned it. "I've finally got a PA that drinks. You're far more fun." He put his finger toward his face, almost missing his lips. "But shhhhh, don't tell him. Come here." He gestured clumsily for me to come closer. "I've got something to tell you."

Obligingly, I shuffled closer, eager to hear what Tristan had to say.

His breath tickled my ear. "I like it when you smile. I like it a lot. It makes you look different."

Heat engulfed me like a tidal wave. Was I missing something here? Was Tristan getting me drunk so he could make a move? Had he deliberately undone his shirt?

I turned, pressing my lips over Tristan's. They'd barely touched before Tristan pushed me off. "Whoa! What are you doing?"

I stared at him, suddenly feeling completely sober. "Kissing you. I thought..."

Tristan was shaking his head. "I'm not gay."

Mortification hit like a sledgehammer. Shit! I'd just tried to kiss my straight boss. I stumbled to my feet. "I'm sorry. I don't know what... I'm sorry."

I turned tail and ran, ignoring the sound of Tristan calling my name. Thankfully, I was still sober enough to find my room.

Chapter Four

Head in hands, I perched gingerly on the edge of the hotel bed. Surprisingly, I'd slept. Or maybe "passed out due to an excess of alcohol" would be a more accurate description. Memories of the previous night's events had rushed back as soon as I'd woken, contributing to the nausea. They'd remained at the forefront of my mind all the way through showering, shaving, and dressing. There was no way I could face Tristan this morning. Obviously, I was out of a job, but the question was, did I hang around and wait for it to happen or get the hell out of the hotel and postpone the inevitable to a time when I wasn't nursing a sore head? If I left the hotel now, I could buy a train ticket for an earlier train. Tristan's ticket I could leave at reception.

Mind made up, I almost mistook the knock on the door for the pounding in my head. When I opened it, my heart sank. Tristan stood outside. In my machinations to come up with an effective escape plan, I hadn't considered the possibility he would seek me out. Expecting anger, I was completely thrown by the smile on the other man's face.

His smile grew wider. "Oh, you're up. Great! I'm not going for breakfast on my own, and I'm starving." He inclined his head toward the stairs he'd obviously just climbed to get here. "Let's go."

Lost for words, I simply stared. Was it possible he didn't remember the previous night? Could he have been *that* drunk?

Tristan's smile slowly faded to a look of puzzlement. "What's wrong? Do I have toothpaste on my face?" He scrubbed at his face in an effort to remove the non-existent toothpaste.

"No. I just thought—"

"What?"

"After last night. I mean, I...I thought..." God, this was awkward. I fixed my attention on the floor as a means to avoid eye contact, watching my own feet shuffle restlessly on the thick pile of the hotel carpet. "I made a pass at you."

Whatever I'd expected to hear next, it certainly wasn't the sound of laughter. My head whipped up in shock. Tristan was apparently finding something hilarious.

The smile was back full-force. "You call that a pass? I've been more intimate with my... Well, I was going to say grandmother, but that doesn't sound quite right. But you get the picture."

I took a moment to try and wrap my head around the fact my boss was amused rather than annoyed. "I'm really sorry. It shouldn't have happened. I'd had a lot to drink, and I—" I stopped short of admitting I'd found him wildly attractive, and I definitely wasn't going to mention my drunken belief that he'd been trying to seduce me. In the cold light of day, without whisky coursing through my system, it seemed like the most ridiculous idea I'd ever had. I took a deep breath and sought clarification of my employment status. "I figured you wouldn't want me working with you anymore. Or maybe not even in your company."

Tristan looked incredulous. "Really? For that? Not a chance." He winked. "It was probably my fault for plying you with drink. Now can we please go and have breakfast before I collapse from starvation?"

I could hardly say no, under the circumstances. "Sure."

Closing the hotel room door, I followed my boss down the corridor.

"Thanks for being so understanding, Mr. Maxwell. It's—"

He halted suddenly. "Whoa! I can forgive you trying to kiss me, but no way are we going back to you calling me Mr. Maxwell. Now, that should be a firing offense."

"You can't fire me for calling you by your surname."

He smiled mischievously. "I can fire you for trying to drunkenly kiss me, and only you and I would ever know the real reason."

"You wouldn't."

He paused. "Probably not. But if you call me Tristan, we won't need to find out."

An eye roll was the only legitimate response I could give.

IT WAS AN ABSOLUTE revelation watching Tristan demolish a full English breakfast in record time. Just watching caused my stomach to lurch in an alarming fashion. I settled for cautiously nibbling a piece of toast, hoping it would help to settle my stomach. Worst-case scenario, at least it would give me something to throw up. Tristan still managed to keep up a full-scale conversation while he shoveled food into his mouth. If it could really be called a conversation. My contribution mainly consisted of monosyllabic answers. I was still struggling to make sense out of his lack of reaction to my stupidity the previous night.

Tristan was in the middle of extolling the virtues of free-range eggs in comparison to battery hens while I nodded occasionally when a persistent ring tone interrupted his flow mid-sentence. He pulled his phone out of his pocket and frowned slightly.

"I've got to take this. Sorry. It's Maria, my fiancée."

It was all I could do not to rock back physically in my seat. So not only had I tried to kiss my boss, a guy who was straight, but that same guy was also engaged to be married. I'd really exceeded myself this time. Tristan excused himself to the other side of the room to take the phone call in privacy, or as much privacy as you could get in a fairly crowded breakfast room. I watched him across the room. It wasn't like there was anything else to do. There was a slight smile on his face, but his earlier animation had disappeared. I wondered what they were talking about. Maybe they'd had an argument? I hoped to God he wasn't telling her what I'd done. I didn't need an irate fiancée turning up at the office warning me to keep my hands off her man. The conversation continued for a few more minutes before he hung up and returned to the table.

Tristan eased himself back into the seat. "Sorry about that. I would never have heard the end of it if I hadn't answered. You know what women are like."

I grimaced. "Not really." I could sense the questions waiting on the tip of the other man's tongue. Not wanting the conversation to return to the previous night, I got in there first. "How long have you been engaged?"

"About a year?"

"Have you set a date?"

Tristan rubbed his chin thoughtfully. "I kind of just go along with things. It's easier. Maria's quite... She's quite a strong woman. I let her plan stuff."

I stared at my boss incredulously. Had he really just admitted he didn't know when he was getting married? He was getting less perfect by the second: scared of spiders and being railroaded by his fiancée.

"But you do want to marry her?"

Tristan nodded. "Yes, of course. She's beautiful. She's successful. She's..." Tristan trailed off. "Anyway, enough about me. What about you? I know hardly anything about you. I didn't even know you were gay. Or are you gay? Do you like both? I've never met anyone bisexual. Are you bisexual? I always think there must be one you prefer. But I guess it must be nice to have the choice of both."

He finally stopped talking to shovel more food in.

I exhaled slowly. "Does alcohol have any effect on you at all?"

Tristan grinned. "Stop avoiding the question."

I sighed. "I'm gay."

To my relief, the sound of Tristan's phone stalled the conversation again.

BY THE TIME WE BOARDED the train for our journey back to London, my headache had subsided to a dull throb, and my stomach had ceased doing somersaults. The toast had obviously done the trick. I glanced over to the man next to me. He was still talking, still seemingly unconcerned about it being mostly one-sided. I offered a noncommittal grunt in response to his latest question: something about the speed of different trains around the country. I hadn't really been listening.

To my surprise, Tristan grabbed my suitcase and hoisted it up into the overhead lockers before doing the same to his own. "I can tell you're feeling delicate. You hardly ate anything at breakfast, and I haven't had a single sarcastic comment from you all morning."

It wasn't worth expending the energy it would take to deny it, so I simply eased myself into the seat by the window, leaving Tristan the next one.

The seat creaked as he sat down. "You shouldn't drink so much."

I swiveled my head toward him, regarding him through narrowed eyes. "I wasn't intending to drink anything at all, but I felt guilty leaving you in case another spider appeared and you had a coronary."

Tristan's shudder of revulsion was completely unstaged. "Don't even say that word!"

I fought the urge for all of ten seconds. "Spider...spi-der...SPIDER!" I couldn't resist turning just to see his reaction.

Tristan's eyes were screwed shut. "Not listening to you. I'm going to sleep."

Smirking, I turned back to the now-moving scenery as we pulled out of the station. At least I could count down the amount of time in hours now until I could be home, safely away from the confusion of Tristan's company. I still wasn't managing to reconcile what I'd thought I'd known about the man with the evidence of what I was seeing in front of me.

"Oh, and Dominic?"

Reluctantly, I turned back to face my boss. His eyes were open again and locked onto mine. "What?"

"If you feel the overwhelming urge to grope me while I'm asleep, can you do it gently so you don't wake me up?"

My splutter of indignation was drowned out by Tristan's throaty laugh. "In your dreams! I'd rather..." I glanced around the interior of the train for inspiration, spying a frail old man, the wrong side of eighty, a few rows back. "I'd rather grope him than you."

Tristan followed my gaze. "Kinky. But you didn't seem to think that last night. You know, when you lunged at me."

I could hardly believe I was being teased about my misdemeanor already. Maybe, if it was weeks later, or months later, but hours later? "Hardly *lunged*. In a drunken stupor, I may have gotten confused, and for *five minutes*, when I was probably seeing double, I found you slightly attractive. But don't wor-ry—stone—cold—sober—now! Now you just look..." I took a moment to pretend to study Tristan's face, taking the opportunity to actually study the tanned, smooth skin and the perfect bone structure. He hadn't shaved this morning, and the stubble covering his jaw really suited him. "Old!"

Now it was Tristan's turn to splutter. "Old! Ouch, that's really mean."

Remembering that no matter what my personal feelings were, he was still my boss and I couldn't go too far, I turned back to the window. After a short silence, I dared to glance back. Tristan's eyes were firmly closed again. He obviously hadn't taken the last comment too much to heart.

For the first half of the journey, it was hard to tell whether Tristan was fully asleep or just dozing. When he slowly slid sideways, and his head dropped onto my shoulder, it became apparent he was actually asleep. He didn't wake up when I maneuvered him, none too gently, back into an upright position in his own seat. Ten minutes later, the same thing happened, and I repeated the whole process. The third time, I uttered a curse and just left him there.

I spent the rest of the journey staring sightlessly out the window, doing my best to ignore the distracting sensation of the other man's steady breaths tickling my right ear. When his hand dropped and curled around my right thigh, my first instinct was to remove it. I stopped myself. No! Let the straight man wake up and find himself snuggled up to the gay guy. It would serve him right for teasing me earlier. I should take a photo and send it to his fiancée.

Five minutes from Victoria station, Tristan began to stir. The hand around my thigh tightened, moving uncomfortably close to my groin. I willed myself not to get aroused. The head on my shoulder lifted slightly while Tristan tried to orient himself. "Why am I sleeping on you?"

"I don't know. I've been asking myself the same question for the last forty-five minutes."

"You should have moved me."

"I did—several times. But you just kept sliding back over here. In the end I gave up."

Tristan yawned loudly but still didn't move away. "I always sleep well on trains. I think it's something to do with the noise, or maybe the motion. I'm not sure. Maybe it's both. It's very relaxing. Don't you find it relaxing?"

"Erm...Tristan, seeing as you're now awake. Can I have my shoulder back, and do you think you could possibly move your hand?"

I watched with a mixture of irritation and amusement as, realizing where his hand was, Tristan quickly snatched it back before levering himself back upright. "Sorry."

The train slowed to a stop. "It's fine. I'm sure if I check my job description. I'll find getting snored at and dribbled on in the small print."

Tristan looked affronted. "I don't snore!"

"So you're not denying the dribbling then?"

Tristan shrugged and grinned. "It's a possibility." He paused and looked away. "Apologies for...you know..." He waggled his fingers in the air.

I couldn't resist it. He fully deserved it for teasing me earlier. "You should have seen where you had it before. Then you'd be apologizing."

A dull flush spread across the perfect cheekbones. "I did not."

I stood to reach the suitcases, suddenly feeling completely recovered from the hangover. "I guess you'll never know."

Chapter Five

I arrived at work unusually early on Tuesday. I blamed the strangeness of having had Monday off. Even more unusually, Tristan was already there, the door to his office resolutely shut. That meant no coffee. Funny how quickly you could get used to being brought coffee. I wondered if he was avoiding me. Maybe, once he'd had a chance to reflect on the weekend, he'd realized just how out of order my actions had been. The nagging paranoia stayed with me all through the morning, as the closed door continued to mock me, with only the occasional noise from within providing evidence Tristan was actually in there.

It was gone midday before the door finally burst open and Tristan erupted from the other office. Striding over to my desk, he uttered a terse instruction to "Come on!" Halfway through typing an e-mail, I stopped mid-sentence, quickly saving it as a draft, grabbed the notebook and tape recorder, and hurried after Tristan, catching him just as the elevator doors opened. Expecting to travel down a few floors, I was bemused when we exited at the lobby. I grabbed Tristan's arm to slow him down. "Hang on. Where's the meeting?"

Tristan frowned. "What meeting?"

"The meeting that— Where are we going exactly?"

Tristan checked his watch. "To lunch. It's nearly one o'clock. Didn't I say that?"

"No. You definitely did not say that." I waved the notebook and tape recorder in front of his face. "Why do you think I brought these?"

He shrugged. "I thought it was some sort of weird thing. Like you didn't want to be parted from them. Or you worry someone's going to steal them when you're out of the office." He grinned. "Who am I to judge? We all have our strange idiosyncrasies." His brow furrowed as he subjected me to an intense scrutiny. "You didn't bring a coat, either. You're going to be cold."

I decided to ignore the majority of what he'd just said and focus on the most important part. "I brought lunch. I can't go *out* to lunch. I've got work to do."

"Nothing that can't wait."

I opened my mouth to protest, but Tristan got in there first. "I'm the boss. I know exactly what work you've got to do, so you can't use that argument. Now can we go? I'm starving." He set off toward the door to the street, pausing momentarily when he realized I wasn't following. He turned back. "Now what?"

"I don't have my wallet."

"You don't need it. I'm paying."

"Bosses don't take their—" I so wanted to drop the word "minions" casually into the conversation and watch for his reaction. "—personal assistants out to lunch."

"Says who?"

"Says—" I paused mid-argument. Tristan had an honest-to-God pout on his face. I stared at him with a mixture of horror and fascination.

He took a few steps back toward me. "Please come to lunch. Please come and keep me company. Please."

I shook my head in disbelief, glancing over to where the nearby security desk's occupants were watching both of us with great interest. "Fine. If it stops you sulking like a bloody child. I'll come to lunch without a coat and freeze to death, just so you don't have to sit on your own."

"Great." Tristan stalked off, and I dutifully followed, somehow managing to resist pulling a face at his departing back.

I WATCHED IN AMAZEMENT. Tristan had virtually inhaled a foot-long sandwich and fries. It was like the full English breakfast all over again. At the time, I'd put that down to post-alcohol munchies. Now I wasn't so sure. Tristan gestured over at my half-eaten sandwich. "Are you going to eat that?"

I shook my head. "I'm full." It wasn't hard to interpret the hopeful expression on his face. "Seriously, you want this as well? After everything you've already eaten, you're still hungry?"

Tristan nodded, and I pushed my plate over the table toward him, expecting him to laugh and claim he was joking. Without any hesitation, he scooped it off the plate and wolfed it down. I surveyed the lean, athletic figure in front of me, doing my best to block out the sudden unwanted flashback of the sculpted chest I'd glimpsed during our whisky binge. "Where the hell do you put it all?"

Tristan paused, the remnants of the sandwich halfway to his mouth. "Is that a compliment? Thank you. That's very sweet of you. I've never had a compliment from you."

I bristled immediately. "No! That's not what I meant at all. You should be a lot...fatter, that's all. That's what I meant. I'm not complimenting you."

"I go to the gym—a lot." He paused, as if considering something, before adding, "For a long time."

Nodding, I took the opportunity to survey the sandwich shop. There were a few familiar faces who worked for the same company as Tristan and I. Hardly surprising, considering it was just around the corner. I nodded politely at a couple of people I'd previously exchanged pleasantries with, wondering what they were making of me lunching with the boss.

"Do you know Adam?"

Tristan's question forced my attention back to him. He now had two empty plates in front of him. "Who?"

Tristan gestured across the room, and my gaze followed to where he was pointing at a man in his early thirties. "To look at, but I've never spoken to him."

"He works in the IT department. He's good-looking, right?"

I studied him. He was fairly tall, probably a few inches taller than both Tristan and me. Sandy-blond hair curled around his ears, and he seemed to fill his suit in all the right places. "Yeah. I guess. Why?"

Tristan cocked his head to one side, eyeing me speculatively. "I thought so. But you know, I'm not really used to looking for these things, so I thought I better check before..." He lifted his head, trying to catch Adam's eye. When he succeeded, he gestured for him to come across.

"Before what?"

"He's gay. You're gay, so..."

I suddenly grasped his intent. "Oh, hell, no! Don't you dare!" But it was already too late as the man in question sauntered over to our table.

"Tristan. It's good to see you. I haven't seen you eating lunch here for a while."

Up close, I had to admit the guy was indeed good looking. Not in Tristan's league of course, but then so few mere mortals could match that level of perfection. However, that didn't mean I was remotely interested in being paired off with him just because we both happened to be gay.

"I needed to get Dominic out of the office for a while. He's my new personal assistant—"

I swiftly interjected, "It's just temporary. I'm covering for Kevin until he's well enough to return."

Tristan scowled at my deliberate attempt to block his matchmaking attempt. I took the opportunity to make a big show out of checking my watch. "Speaking of work, we should probably get back."

Leaning back in his seat, Tristan crossed his arms and made it clear he had no intention of moving. "There's no rush. Now, where was I? Oh, yes, I was just explaining to Adam how I hate to see you working so hard."

"That's what I'm hired for...*sir*."

Tristan narrowed his eyes at the "sir," and I realized I'd just made my boss even more determined to get his own way. I waited for the comeback, a strange buzz of adrenaline rushing through me at the opportunity to banter with someone who could give as good as they got. He didn't disappoint.

"Isn't he adorable? He insists on calling me sir. I think he likes to imagine we're in some sort of bygone age. Either that or he's into roleplay."

I raised an eyebrow at that one, contemplating how far I could push it with my response. If it had been anyone other than my engaged, straight boss I would have insinuated they were a willing participant in the roleplay, but I decided that would push the boundaries rather too much, at least in front of witnesses. "I'm just very respectful, sir."

Adam was looking more and more perplexed by the minute, his head swinging back and forth between the two of us. With any luck, he'd get so confused it wouldn't be long before he made his excuses and left. Adam opened his mouth to speak, probably with the intention of doing exactly that, but Tristan got in there first.

"Damn it! I've just remembered. I'm expecting an important phone call. I'm going to have to go. Adam, can you keep Dominic company for me?" Tristan eased himself out from the booth and stood.

Adam nodded, looking even more confused. "Yeah, sure."

I started to rise. "There's no need. I'll come back with you now."

Tristan smiled a self-satisfied, smug smile. I wanted to throw something at him. "Take another ten minutes. I insist. You've worked so hard this morning." I was tempted to ask how he could possibly know when he hadn't left his office once, but decided to concentrate on the fact he was leaving. It had been a pretty poor attempt at match-making, as attempts go.

Adam took the place my boss had recently vacated. I waited patiently for Tristan to walk away. As soon as he was out of earshot, I could make my excuses and leave, leaving Adam none the wiser about what Tristan had been up to.

Tristan took a few steps toward the door before turning back and addressing Adam, a glint in his eye. "I'll leave you two to get better acquainted. He's single, by the way, so maybe you two could go out somewhere, get to know each other, see if you hit it off."

Smirking, he turned on his heel and left, and I found myself alone with Adam. Risking a glance at him, it wasn't a surprise to find him looking distinctly bemused. He hesitated before speaking. "You two have an...unusual boss-employee relationship."

Chapter Six

"**S**o then what happened?"

I eyed my friend Paul over the rim of the coffee cup. He'd worked in the mail room for years and was one of the reasons I'd applied to work for the company in the first place. We'd met in a bar just over three years ago, hit it off straight away, and been firm friends ever since. Given we were both gay, single, and got on so well, the inevitable had happened about six months into our friendship. Horribly drunk one night, we'd ending up kissing. It had lasted all of three seconds. Then we'd broken apart laughing, agreeing it was like kissing a brother.

The mail room worked later, so I often stopped by after I'd finished work for the day. It gave us both a chance to moan or get things off our chest. I'd lost count of the number of times I'd sat here commiserating while Paul talked about his bastard of an ex or complained about his father's latest criticism of him. Today, it was my turn to complain. I could normally rely on Paul to say all the right things. Either he was in an awkward mood today, or he just wasn't getting it.

"What do you mean, what happened? Haven't you been listening? My boss tried to set me up with another employee. A guy I've never even spoken to. Who does that? It's weird, right?"

Paul shuffled a letter into the correct pile, his face failing to show the reaction I'd been counting on. He raised his head, a small smile playing on his lips. "You don't think it's sweet?" He frowned as if something had just occurred to him. "Hang on! How did he know you were gay? Did you tell him?"

I paused, playing for time. *Shit!* If I said yes, Paul would want to know why I'd felt the need to share personal information with someone I barely knew, someone I'd vociferously claimed to dislike several times. If I said no, then he'd want to know how he could possibly have found out.

Paul stared at me, not even pretending to work anymore, patiently waiting for my response. Sighing, I prepared to tell the truth. He'd wheedle it out of me eventually anyway. "Okay, so you remember the conference I had to accompany him to? The one in Brighton?"

Paul nodded. "What? Did you hook up with some guy there? You never mentioned it. Tristan didn't catch you at it, did he? Oh, my God! It wasn't on work time, was it?"

It was incredibly tempting to take that idea and run with it. But then Paul would expect a full physical description of the imaginary guy. Not to mention a complete breakdown of everything that happened. It wasn't worth the effort it would take to think up all the missing details. Plus, I wasn't that great a liar. I steeled myself. "Tristan had a bottle of whisky. I might have got a bit drunk...and tried to...kiss him."

It was hard to tell whether Paul's response erred more toward shock or delight. "Oh, my God! You did not? Dom, you little devil! I can't believe you did that. What did he do?"

I screwed my face up at the memory of the embarrassing moment. "Pushed me off. Told me he wasn't gay."

Paul shook his head in disbelief. "What were you thinking? He's engaged."

The look I gave my friend left little doubt of my true feelings. "I know that now! You don't think you could have possibly mentioned it before? Like when you knew I was going to work for him."

Paul laughed. "It's common knowledge. Sorry, I didn't think there was any chance of you throwing yourself at the man you've always professed to hate. I wish I could have seen it. His face must have been a picture."

"He was surprisingly good about it, actually. Better than he should have been under the circumstances, and I never said I *hated* him."

Paul raised a questioning eyebrow. "You never have a single good word to say about him either."

"You read the interview." I'd made sure of it, waving it under his face until he'd grudgingly taken it from me and given it a cursory scan. I'd been really disappointed by his lack of reaction to it, expecting more than a shrug and a comment about not believing everything you read in the media. "How am I meant to have respect for someone who doesn't respect the people who work for him? We're just *easily replaceable minions*, remember? Anyway, stop changing the subject. What kind of boss tries to set up two of their employees?"

Paul smirked. "*I'm* changing the subject? You still haven't told me what happened after Tristan left. I've seen Adam. He's pretty hot for an IT guy. Wasn't he interested?"

I fiddled with the corner of an envelope, reluctant to admit the next part. Paul leaned in. "Maybe I'll go and ask Tristan. I'm sure he will be only too happy to tell me, if I can't get you to answer. I'm sure he was curious enough to ask. And I doubt you fobbed him off, like you're trying to do to me."

I shot Paul a poisonous look. "You're supposed to be on my side."

His only response was a shrug, coupled with another smirk for good measure.

"He said it sounded like a good idea to him, asked if I wanted to get dinner some time, and I said yes."

Paul sat back, amusement written all over his face. "So let me get this straight. You're down here complaining that Tristan set you up on a hot date. A hot date that you've agreed to go on. Dominic, my friend, you have finally taken leave of your senses."

I could see his point. But in an effort to avoid admitting it, I changed the subject, turning the line of questioning round to Paul's love life. Unfortunately, seeing as it was sadly lacking, with only one disastrous date in the last month to talk about, the conversation quickly returned to Tristan.

Paul stared dreamily into space. "He is gorgeous though. It must be nice to look at that every day."

I sniffed. "Not particularly."

"Yeah, right! That's why you tried to stick your tongue down the poor man's throat."

"It wasn't like that. I barely touched him. And I was drunk. I regret telling you now. You *cannot* tell anyone else. If it gets out—"

Paul looked momentarily hurt. "Oh, c'mon. You know me better than that. You know your secret is safe with me. Is it awkward though, having to see him every day after what happened?"

I thought back over the last few days. I'd hardly thought about it. Tristan's teasing acceptance of it on the train seemed to have turned it into a non-issue. "No. Not really. Anyway, I've only got a few more days before Kevin comes back, and then I can get back to normality. I can't wait. It—"

I halted mid-sentence, thrown by the expression on Paul's face. "What? Why are you looking at me like that?"

Paul winced. "You need to work less and hang out at the water coolers with the rest of us. Then you might actually know stuff. Like Tristan being engaged and, although I'm surprised Tristan hasn't mentioned it, considering—"

I banged my coffee cup down on the table. Luckily, the coffee that sloshed out of it missed the pile of envelopes. "Hasn't mentioned what? Spit it out."

Paul grabbed a tissue, mopping up the spilled coffee. "That Kevin's not coming back. Apparently, his—" Paul held up both hands in the universal sign for finger quotes. "—near-death experience made him decide to move to Australia with his girlfriend. So I don't think you're going to be escaping back to your old job and good old John Stone quite as soon as you think."

I sat back, taking in Paul's words. I didn't for one minute think the information wasn't correct. Gossip in this building was always surprisingly accurate. "I wouldn't bet on it."

TRISTAN DEPOSITED THE usual morning offering of coffee on my desk with a cheery greeting and an equally warm smile. I leaned back in my chair and regarded him with a steely stare. Tristan tilted his head to one side and smiled even wider. "What did I do now? Is this about your date? Didn't it go very well? I'm sure there are other people in the company I can set you up with."

I took a sip of the cinnamon latte. It seemed a shame to let it go to waste, no matter how annoyed I was. "The date's tonight. I haven't been on it yet. And if it's a disaster, I DO NOT need you to set me up with anyone else. I'm quite capable of finding my own dates."

"Of course you are. I'm just trying to help. So if it's not that, what's the problem?"

I inclined my head toward Tristan's adjoining office. "Can we talk in there?"

Tristan nodded, the smile finally giving way to a look of slight concern. He led the way into his office, taking his usual seat and gesturing for me to take the other one.

I made myself comfortable and then got straight to the point. "Kevin's back next week, right?"

Tristan opened his mouth to speak and then just as quickly closed it again without so much as a sound coming out.

I leaned forward and made eye contact. "Because if he wasn't coming back... Let's say for example—and I'm just picking this out of thin air—let's say he was moving to Australia because his girlfriend's been offered a job there. You'd have told me, right? Because that would be a ridiculous thing not to mention." I sat back and waited to see how Tristan would wriggle out of this one.

Tristan wrinkled his nose. "I may have forgotten to mention it. But it's not a problem, is it?"

"Not for me." I crossed my arms and aimed for a look of relaxed boredom. "You're the one without a personal assistant after this week."

The sad thing was, his confusion was absolutely and completely genuine. "What do you mean? I've got *you*. *You're* my personal assistant."

I shot him a look that I hoped effectively conveyed, "Are you for real?" As usual, it went straight over his head. "I'm on loan." Now even I was talking about myself like a bloody library book. "I can't just leave Mr. Stone in the lurch. He can barely manage without me." *And he doesn't think I'm just a minion.* "The annoying thing is, if you'd told me, we could have got the advert sorted this week."

"What advert?"

I bit back an irritated sigh. "The advert to find you a new personal assistant. Or have you got someone in mind to move from another department?"

Tristan shook his head, so I carried on. "So we need an advert. I'll write it today and give you a chance to look it over, so you can check I haven't missed anything." I glanced over at Tristan to gauge his reaction. Oh, God! The pout was back. He looked like some sort of male model posing for the front of a magazine. No man had a right to look that attractive while looking like someone had taken all his toys away. "What? And don't look at me like that. It doesn't work on me. I'm immune."

"Or you could just stay and be *my* personal assistant, and we'll find another one for John." Tristan sat back with a smug look of satisfaction on his face, as if everything was completely sorted.

It was my turn to shake my head. "No. Not a chance."

Tristan seemed to know when he was beaten. "Okay. You can write an advert, but I have a few stipulations."

I gave him a dirty look. "Go on."

"I interview any suitable candidates you find, not you. I get the final say on who's hired. And you stay as my personal assistant until we find someone suitable."

I nodded. It sounded reasonable. There was no way it could take that long to find someone suitable—one week at most, if I got the advert out today. I stood up. "I'll get the advert written now." I walked toward the door, disappearing through it only to have to go back when Tristan called my name.

"Make sure it's done by lunchtime."

I frowned. "Why?" Had he become so enthusiastic about the idea that he was suddenly in a rush to get the wheels moving?

"We're going out for lunch. I need a break. And so do you. You're getting that slightly irritable thing that you sometimes do."

I slammed the door on the way out, ignoring the chuckle my action elicited.

Chapter Seven

"So, you never noticed me at all?" I tried to mask how much that information peeved me but failed miserably. We were in a Mexican restaurant near Leicester Square for our first date. Given the area, it was predictably busy but could have been far worse. At least it was a weeknight. On a weekend, it would have been heaving.

Adam grinned. "No. Would it help if I said that, if I had ever seen you, I'd definitely have remembered." He finished the statement with a lingering once-over that apparently showed appreciation of the fairly tight-fitting shirt I'd squeezed myself into.

"A little." I reached over to take a sip of my wine. "As long as you're not just saying that." I was surprised how flirtatious Adam was being. I'd put him down as being fairly conservative at work, but he was wasting no time in making his interest clear.

"Oh, I'm definitely not just saying that." He ate a forkful of food, making sure to curl his tongue around the prongs suggestively. "So, how come you're single?"

I shrugged. I hated that question. There was never a perfect answer to it. *"I work a lot"* sounded too lame. *"I'm pretty fussy,"* while probably being closest to the truth, wasn't the best thing to say to a first date. I'd unfortunately discovered that the hard way. The poor guy had jumped through hoops for the rest of the night, trying to prove he was good enough. I hadn't even learned from that experience. The next guy I'd been 100 percent honest with had immediately stopped making any effort whatsoever, apparently having decided that he'd never live up to my high standards, so there was no point in trying. I didn't have the greatest track record with dates. "I don't know. Just one of those things, I guess. How about you?"

Adam considered the question for a moment. "I used to think I was too young to get tied down. But you know...older and wiser now. I guess I'm just waiting for the right guy to come along." His eyebrow raise clearly asked the question as to whether I thought that could be me. I was tempted to point out it would take longer than fifteen minutes—the amount of time our date had lasted so far—to decide whether I even wanted to put myself in the running. I refrained, simply smiling and raising my glass in a silent toast.

Adam fixed me with an intense stare. "You must be feeling the same. You're what, twenty-seven, twenty-eight? You must be getting to the point where you're thinking about settling down." His foot nudged mine under the table. I wasn't sure whether the movement was an accident or another flirtatious weapon in his arsenal.

"Must I? And I'm twenty-six. Maybe in a couple of years, going by your timeline."

Adam shrugged. "Duly noted." He winked. "Up for fun but not settling down."

I opened my mouth to argue but realized that was pretty much what I'd intimated. Adam took a bite of his chicken fajita, stopping to mop up the bits that spilled out. "So, you could have just asked me out yourself. I would have said yes. You didn't need to get Tristan to play Cupid." His foot nudged mine again. This time definitely on purpose.

I moved my foot back out of reach. "That's not quite what happened."

"Oh?" He leaned forward, a genuine look of interest on his face.

I quickly relayed the true story.

Adam laughed. "What is it with these madly in-love, engaged people who want everyone else to be the same way? Sweet though, isn't it?"

My lip curled. It was the same way Paul had described the action. I was the only one who didn't seem to think the same way.

Adam obviously read my face. "You don't agree?"

I shrugged. "Let's not spoil dinner by talking about Tristan. Tell me all about you."

AFTER DINNER, WE MOVED on to a bar. Adam was proving to be a very charming and amusing companion, with ready jokes to cover every situation. However, he was really ramping up the whole touchy-feeliness. I wasn't entirely comfortable with the fact his hand currently rested on my thigh. It wasn't particularly high up, which just made me feel churlish that it bothered me. I shifted away slightly, hoping he'd take the hint. His hand remained in place, moving a few inches higher. Short of pointing it out or lifting the offending hand and removing it myself, there wasn't a lot I could do. I concentrated on listening carefully to the amusing story he was telling about gatecrashers at his brother's wedding. When he'd finished, I took the opportunity to excuse myself to the bathroom. Once in there, I rang Paul. He answered after the first ring.

"Dominic, this can't be a good sign that you're ringing me while you're on a date. Is it not going well? Is he a dick? Or is it over already?"

"No. I'm still on it. He's definitely not a dick. He's great...very amusing! Very different from what I thought he was like from seeing him at work. I'm having a good time."

"But?" Paul knew me far too well.

"He's...just a bit...touchy-feely." I could have done without the loud laugh on the other side of the phone. "Great. Thanks, Paul. Thanks for your support. I knew I could rely on you."

"You're complaining that your date is too interested in you. Would you rather he wasn't? I'm not sure what the problem is. You're not a virgin, Dom. I've seen you pick guys up in a club."

"That's different. I know I'm never going to see them again. We work for the same company. I don't want to sleep with someone on a first date who I know I'm definitely going to see again."

"Then don't. Tell him you're very flattered, but you want to get to know him better. Just be honest, and if he's not interested in another date, then no great loss, right?"

I mumbled my agreement, hung up, and left the bathroom. I didn't want Adam wondering where the hell I'd got to.

HE HADN'T GOT ANY LESS handsy as the evening had worn on. Now, he had me backed against a wall, one hand on my waist, the other on my neck. To his credit, he had asked if he could kiss me, and I'd said yes, so I could hardly complain. I relaxed and went with it, returning the kiss with slightly forced enthusiasm. He tasted of beer and the Mexican food we'd had earlier. He was a good kisser, not too sloppy, but with enough imagination to make it interesting. It was nice, but only nice. As our tongues explored, I waited for some spark to ignite. He moaned, his hand moving down to grab my ass and pull me tighter against him, his arousal pressing against my thigh. My own dick wasn't quite so interested. I blamed the alcohol. I pulled away, placing a hand against his chest to push him back slightly. He stepped back obligingly, a smile on his face.

"You're really cute, Dominic. Why don't we go back to mine? We can get a cab. It's a ten-minute journey, tops. What do you say?"

I didn't want to hurt his feelings. I wanted to see him again. I'd really had a good time. I remembered Paul's words of wisdom. "Not tonight. I'm really flattered, honestly. But this is only our first date." I smiled. "I'm hoping we'll have a second one. So I can get to know you better." There was a flash of something undecipherable on Adam's face. Maybe it was frustration. Maybe it was annoyance, or maybe I'd simply imagined it.

"Sure." He grinned. "I don't mind you playing hard to get. Gives me something to chase." He stepped forward again, pressing himself back against me. "I assume I get a goodnight kiss, though?"

Chapter Eight

"Taste that."

I recoiled automatically as a sandwich was inelegantly shoved into my mouth. Focused on the report I was writing, I hadn't even registered Tristan's entrance into the office. Even if I had been aware, it was unlikely I could have adequately prepared for the eventuality of being attacked with a sandwich. My instinctive reaction to move away wasn't quick enough to avoid biting off a mouthful. Leaning over, I spat it straight into the wastepaper bin next to my desk. "What the hell, Tristan!"

My boss stood over me, frowning at the remains of the sandwich. "It's off, right? The date says it should be okay till tomorrow." He held the packaging toward me, as if he were presenting evidence in court. "But it doesn't taste right, does it? That's why you spat it out. You agree, right?"

"No. I spat it out because...never mind." Snatching the packaging out of Tristan's hand, I scoured the ingredients carefully, searching for any signs of fish or fish extracts present in the sandwich. The fact I'd had a severe allergy to fish since I was a child meant I was used to having to be careful about what I ate. Since it was apparently a cheese sandwich, it didn't contain any. Breathing a sigh of relief, I still took comfort in sliding the desk drawer open to catch a reassuring glimpse of the epi-pen inside.

"See the date?"

I hadn't even looked at it. I spared it a quick glance, my heart rate slowly returning to normal. "That's yesterday's date, Tristan."

"Is it?" Tristan took the packet back and squinted down at it. "No wonder it tasted disgusting."

"And how kind of you to share it with me."

Tristan nodded, taking the statement as sincere. "I needed a second opinion. And, as usual, you were invaluable in providing one."

I stared steadfastly at my boss. To think I used to believe this man was perfect. He seemed to have absolutely no concept of sarcasm. I could be as facetious as I liked, and the comments just flew straight over his head. No wonder I'd failed miserably in my previous attempts to annoy him.

Tristan eased himself into the empty seat on the other side of my desk. "What have you got for lunch?"

I passed over my packaged salad without comment, watching as he immediately ripped off the cellophane and dug in. He paused in the middle of a mouthful. "What will you eat?"

"I'll go out and get something. Don't worry."

Tristan turned the fork around, offering the forkful of salad to me. "We could share?"

I batted his hand away. "It's all yours. Go for it. I'm not hungry anyway." I quashed the strange feeling of discomfort at the thought of eating from the same fork as Tristan. It seemed a strangely intimate gesture from someone I barely knew. But I was obviously reading far too much into it. Some people just weren't bothered by things like that, and Tristan was clearly one of them. "You can take it back to your office, you know? You don't have to eat it here."

Tristan raised his head. "I know, but I wanted to ask about your big date." He winked. "How did it go?"

"It wasn't a *big* date, and it went...fine." I was hardly going to share details with Tristan about Adam being a little over-amorous for a first date.

"C'mon, more details. Spill. I'm not moving from here until you tell me where you went, how you got on together, when you're seeing each other again, and any other relevant details."

"Why are you so interested?"

"I put you two together. This is my first attempt at matchmaking two guys, so I need to know for future reference whether I'm any good at it."

I was sorely tempted to make up a nightmare scenario. Perhaps I could even make Tristan feel guilty. However, if I had any chance of getting rid of him and actually getting the report finished, then the quickest way of doing that was to tell the truth. "We went out for dinner. Then we went on to a bar and had a few drinks. We got on pretty well, and yes we're going out on a second date."

Tristan beamed across the desk at me, "I knew it! So when do I get my thank you for finding you a boyfriend?"

"Thank you, Tristan, for sticking your nose in where it wasn't needed and finding me a date. Without your timely intervention, I would no doubt have never had another date for as long as I lived, and I would have died alone surrounded by cats. They would have had to break into my apartment to find my decomposing body, which had lain there undisturbed for months, possibly years. But you finding me *one* date has changed all of that. As a tribute, I shall name every one of my future pets after you."

For once, the sarcasm seemed to get through to him, and he laughed. He handed the now empty salad container back to me. "Get a tuna salad next time. It's got more taste."

"Sure thing, boss!" I muttered the next comment after Tristan's departing back: "And then I'll drop dead." I let my eyes linger on the man's perfectly formed ass as he walked away. After all, straight or not, it never hurt to look.

PAUL DEPOSITED THE day's mail on the corner of my desk. "Nothing looks too urgent." He inclined his head toward Tristan's currently closed office door. "How's your day been with super boss?"

I let my gaze follow Paul's to the door, extremely happy in the knowledge Tristan was currently interviewing a prime candidate for the role of personal assistant. He'd whittled the candidates down to the six he'd deemed the most suitable. Hopefully, the candidate currently in there—a middle-aged woman who'd seemed both professional and friendly—would be so ideal, I'd be able to call the rest and tell them the position had already been filled.

"Oh, you know, ordinary run-of-the-mill day. He tried to kill me with a sandwich, ate my lunch, and then interrogated me about the date he set me up on."

Paul made himself comfortable leaning against the edge of the desk. "While I'm sure you're exaggerating, the sandwich bit I've got to hear."

I quickly relayed the incident from that morning. Paul laughed all the way through. "Okay, for once I'll agree with you. That is a pretty weird thing to do."

The adjoining office door suddenly swung open, causing Paul to look guilty and leap to his feet. We both watched in astonishment as a clearly disgruntled woman charged out of the room. She stormed past my desk without saying a word and kept on walking right out the door. Frowning, I left my desk, meeting Tristan halfway out of his office. "What did you do to her? She was perfect. Did you read her resume? She's basically been doing this exact job for the last five years."

Tristan leaned nonchalantly against the doorjamb, hands in pockets, and paused for an irritatingly long time before answering. "I agree on paper, she looked great. But you know, there's other considerations."

I waited for elaboration, but none was forthcoming. "Other considerations?"

"Maria wouldn't approve."

"Maria! What's she got to do with... Oh, you mean because it's a woman?"

Tristan nodded as if we were sharing some great mystery of the universe. "Exactly!"

I spent a moment recalling what little I knew and had seen of the candidate. "But she was in her late forties. I know I haven't met Maria, but I sincerely doubt she'd feel threatened by her."

"I have to feel comfortable though. I can't spend my whole day trapped in here with a woman undressing me with her eyes every two minutes."

I took a step back, unable to hide my surprise. "Really? She did? She had a wedding ring on, and she didn't look the type."

The emphatic nodding was back. "I've heard about cougars. She was probably one of them. No doubt her behavior would have escalated, and before you know it, I'd be cornered by the filing cabinet, trying to fend her off. You wouldn't wish that on me, would you, Dominic?"

I suppressed a smirk at the mental image. I also managed to resist saying that it would probably make my day. "Of course not. I'm just surprised. So what exactly did you say to her to make her run out of here so quickly? She seemed quite upset."

Tristan took his hands out of his pockets and straightened his tie. "Well, obviously I couldn't tell her I was concerned about her sexually harassing me. So I told her she had too much experience, that she'd be wasted here. She seemed to misinterpret that as me saying she was too old, that I didn't think she'd be able to keep up with the demands of the job. She—"

He suddenly paused, staring at something over my left shoulder.

"Sorry. I didn't realize anyone else was here. Who are you?"

I'd completely forgotten Paul's presence. I turned to see an extremely un-comfortable looking Paul shifting guiltily from one foot to the other. "I'm Paul. I...erm...deliver the mail." He held up the pile of envelopes he'd placed on the desk earlier, as if to accentuate his point. "I was just having a quick word with Dominic when—" He trailed off. "I should probably get back to work."

Tristan held up a hand to halt Paul's quick exit. "No worries. You can fin-ish your conversation with Dominic. He needs people to make him take a break. I'm heading back that way anyway." He took a step back into his own office before addressing me again. "So we're agreed then, no female personal assistants. It wouldn't work. You know, what with Maria to think about, and other...stuff." He didn't wait for my response before closing the door.

I sighed, mentally running through the remaining short list. Crossing off the women only left two possible candidates. I prayed one of them would prove to be perfect. If not, I was back to square one. Shifting my attention back to Paul, I found him with the strangest expression on his face. "What?"

Paul gestured at the now closed office door. "What was that?"

"What was what? Oh, you mean Tristan? I keep telling you he's weird."

My friend cocked his head to one side. "No. Not Tristan. The two of you together. The way you speak to each other."

I stared at Paul, bemused. "I have absolutely no idea what you mean."

Paul frowned. "Interesting. Very interesting."

I'D SPENT THE LAST twenty minutes back in my old office chatting to the pretty young temp still covering my job. The job I was still intent on get-ting back once I'd managed to find a suitable replacement for Tristan. That was my whole reason for being here. It turned out she had quite a few con-tacts. And maybe I had flirted a little to get them from her. Unfortunately, not many of them were male. Head down, recording the names she'd suggest-ed, I didn't see Tristan until I looked up to find him glowering at me.

I couldn't hold back a smirk. All that time I'd spent trying to antagonize him, and all I'd needed to do was return to my own office and sit in it. I gave my boss a sunny smile. "Hi, Tristan."

The glower became more pronounced. "What are you doing here, Dominic?"

"Talking to Lydia." I gestured across the desk at the young blonde. "She's been helping me out with a problem. Haven't you, sweetheart?" I accompanied the words with a wink, eliciting a smile from the pretty temp.

Tristan drummed his fingers on the surface of the desk. "He's gay. He has a boyfriend. You're wasting your time."

Lydia immediately looked extremely uncomfortable. "I'm sorry. I was just—"

I cut her off. "Ignore him. For some reason, he's in a mood. He probably hasn't eaten for a whole hour: failure to eat a five-course meal, five times a day, makes him incredibly grumpy. And I don't have a boyfriend. I've been on *one* date with Adam." I aimed the last comment at Tristan. He shrugged, but made no move to leave. "I presume you want me to go back to your office?" Another shrug. Sighing, I got up, shaking my head in exasperation as I left. I couldn't wait to tell Paul about this one.

I'd managed to make two phone calls in the time it took for Tristan to return to the office. He was back to looking his usual cheery self.

I barely let him get a foot in the door. "Did you bring the chains?"

Tristan plonked himself in the chair opposite before responding. "What chains?"

"The ones to tether me to this desk, so I can't wander off around the building without your permission."

"I don't think that's necessary. I just didn't expect you to creep back to your old office."

"I didn't *creep* anywhere. And it's not my *old* office, it's my *current* office that I'll hopefully be returning to very soon. You're acting like I cheated on you with another desk."

Tristan grinned. "It felt a bit like that. Anyway, you can make it up to me."

I quirked an eyebrow. "Go on then."

"What are you doing Thursday evening? Are you seeing Adam?"

I shook my head. "I'm seeing him on Wednesday. We're nowhere near the two-nights-in-a-row stage yet."

"I've got a work thing. Can you come with me?"

I did a quick mental inventory of his schedule. "You mean the Swanson party. That's a social thing. Why would you need me there?"

"I don't *need* you there. I have to go, and I don't want to go on my own."

"Take Maria. Isn't that what you're meant to do? Take your significant other. You know, rather than your PA?"

Tristan pulled a face. "She hates things like that. She won't come."

"Yeah, well, I don't blame her. She's obviously got good taste. I'm not going to go with you either. Why you'd think I'd willingly subject myself to hanging out at a posh party when I could be at home relaxing, I have no idea."

Chapter Nine

I took a moment to take stock of the expensive décor at the busy party, admiring the centerpiece: a huge ice sculpture of a swan.

Tristan was evidently contemplating the same thing judging by his next words. "Do you think you can order an ice sculpture of absolutely anything you want? Or do you think they'd refuse to make certain things?"

"Like what?"

"Like...if you asked them for a...penis. They wouldn't make that, surely?"

I turned to stare at him. "Why would *you* want a penis sculpture?"

"I don't. Obviously. I'm just thinking hypothetically. Do you think they'd make one?"

I gave the question much more contemplation than it deserved. "Probably, if you paid them enough money."

"Yeah, you're probably right."

I shook my head in bewilderment. I was beginning to realize I'd never fathom exactly how Tristan's brain worked. It was best not to try, and just go along with it. I attempted to shuffle my chair back in an effort to create a bit more more space between us. Unfortunately, as it wasn't the first time; my chair was already wedged up against the wall. Another thing I'd learned about Tristan was he had little or no regard for personal space. He was so close, leaning toward me, I could have kissed him in less than a second. Not that I was going to, of course, but if he wasn't sitting virtually on top of me, it wouldn't even have crossed my mind.

Actually, maybe it was me. Adam hadn't been too keen on giving me much space either. Maybe I exuded some sort of aura that I liked to be crowded. "Shouldn't you mingle or something? They're going to find it very odd if you stay over here with me all evening."

Tristan smiled and moved closer still. I gave serious consideration to climbing over him to move my chair to the other side. "I told them you were a business colleague visiting from France and you don't speak a word of English. So they'll just assume I feel I have to stick close to you because you can't talk to anyone else." He gave a smug look that said *"problem solved."*

I frowned. "Why?"

"Why what?"

"Why would you—never mind." I stopped short of questioning why he would avoid talking to anyone else. This was Tristan. The chance of his answer making any sense was pretty slim. To distract myself from the rather pleasant smell of Tristan's cologne, I watched Mrs. Swanson flitting expertly among her guests. The woman ticked all the boxes for perfect hostess.

Turning my attention back to Tristan, I was surprised to find him staring at me, head cocked to one side, brow furrowed, obviously deep in thought about something. I steeled myself to ignore him, but the strange scrutiny continued.

Finally, I could take no more. "What? Do I have something on my face?"

"I was thinking about your hair."

"My hair?" Self-consciously, I reached up and ran a hand through it. "What about my hair? Is it a mess or something?"

"No, it looks fine. I was contemplating the color of it."

I sighed. "Go on. Ask me if I dye it." I was used to the question. I got it all the time.

"Do you dye it?"

I was also used to people's disbelief when I denied it. "No. It's natural. If you don't believe me, I can prove it." I gave a quick glance down to my crotch, in case he was in any doubt what I was referring to. "But this isn't really the right place." Remembering too late this was also my boss, I hastened to change the subject from the color of my pubic hair and the fact I'd pretty much just offered to show it to him. "So when's the wedding?"

Tristan looked thoughtful. For a moment, I thought he was going to say he didn't know.

"The end of February. Maria thought it would be nice to get married on the twenty-ninth, with it being a leap year. I don't know why. It's going to make celebrating our wedding anniversary really tricky."

I did a quick mental inventory from the current date. "Wow! Three months. That's not very long." Realizing I knew next to nothing about their relationship, I decided to delve a bit deeper. "Do you live together?"

Tristan shook his head. "We wanted to wait until after we were married."
"What does Maria do?"

"She's a model. Not an underwear model. You know, classy stuff. She did a perfume campaign recently that you might have seen."

Tristan pulled up a picture on his phone. It showed a very glamorous woman in a red evening dress posed provocatively on a sheepskin rug next to the tagline of a well known perfume. I took the phone to study the photo more closely. "Wow! She's gorgeous." I took a moment to imagine the two of them together. They would make a stunning picture. "So if she's famous, are you going to have press at your wedding?"

Tristan ran his hand through his hair in a self-conscious gesture. "Probably. I don't know. Maria's organizing it. I think she's got some sort of wedding planner."

"You're not involved at all?"

"She asked me if I wanted to be. It's not really my thing, so I left it all up to her."

I nodded as if I had the remotest understanding of somebody leaving the details of the most important day of their lives to someone else. "It's perhaps as well."

Tristan frowned. "Why?"

"I can picture the photographs now: the beautiful bride in her designer wedding dress. You, standing next to her looking—" I gave him a deliberate once-over, not giving myself the luxury of letting my gaze linger for too long on any part of that gorgeous body covered by the fitted suit. "Passable." I left a deliberate pause. "And in the background, surrounded by your celebrity guests, the towering penis ice sculpture."

When Tristan cracked up, a warm glow spread through my body. I joined in with the laughter. We were both still laughing when a middle-aged, bespectacled man paused by our table. He smiled and held out his hand in my direction. "*Bonjour, il est tres bon de vous recontrer. J'espere que vous avez une bonne soiree. Je m'appelle* James." I stared at him blankly, making no move to shake his hand. I turned expectantly to Tristan. He'd made up the lie. He could bloody well deal with the consequences.

Tristan barely paused for breath. "Did I say he was French? What was I thinking? He's German."

I scraped together my knowledge of high school German, which admittedly didn't amount to much. "*Guten tag,* James. *Ich bin* Dominic." I finally took the proffered hand, giving it an enthusiastic shake. I half expected the man to launch into fluent German, which I had no hope of being able to understand. Instead, a look of panic crossed his face. "I don't speak German. Sorry." He virtually ran off, leaving Tristan and me to crack up again.

Chapter Ten

I ushered the potential candidate into the seat opposite mine to wait for Tristan. There was something very likeable about him, and I'd immediately warmed to him. "He's just taking a conference call, but he'll be ready to see you soon. Can I get you anything while you wait? Some water, maybe?"

He shook his head. "No, I'm fine, thanks. This must be a little weird for you. Having to talk to the person who's trying to take your job. I mean, you've probably got good reasons for leaving, but, you know, it's still..."

"Not at all." I took a moment to recall the candidate's name. "I was only ever working here temporarily, Matthew. I usually work in a different department but agreed"—it was amazing I could say that without so much as an eye twitch—"to fill in until we could find a replacement. As soon as we do, I'll be returning to my original position on another floor."

"I see." He leaned forward in a conspiratorial fashion. "So would it be absolutely out of line to pick your brains about the boss?" He inclined his head toward the closed office door. "I could really do with this job. It pays a lot more than my current one, and I've heard great things about this company."

"What do you want to know?"

"I mean, what's he like, for a start? Is he easy to work for, or is he an absolute nightmare? Is there anything I should avoid saying or doing? Any tips you can give me to land this job?"

I pasted on a smile. "Oh, Mr. Maxwell is a great boss. He's very fair—"*And weird. Sandwich-tasting against your will may be part of your job description.* "He's always polite—"*Far too pretty for his own good, and he knows it.* "He's not like some bosses. He's happy to have lunch with you." *Feed him regularly, or he turns into a gremlin. You'll need to regularly sacrifice some of your own food to keep him going.* "As long as you show dedication to your job—"*Never leave the office, or he'll hunt you down and pout at you.* "—then he's great. If you get the job, you'll have a great time working for him." I wondered if I should try and shoehorn one more use of the word *great* into the conversation.

Matthew sat back, a look of contemplation on his face. "Well, he sounds...great. I can't wait to meet him."

As if on cue, the intercom blared to life. "Dominic, are you there?"

I jammed my finger on the button. "Where else would I be, *mein fuhrer*?" Tristan laughed. I was getting used to hearing that throaty sound. "I see you're practicing your German?"

"Well, you never know when you might need it. Sometimes at completely unexpected times."

"If you need help with your French, I can give James a ring. But you'll have to find someone else for German lessons. Apparently, it's not his strong point."

"I think—" I stopped short, suddenly remembering Matthew's presence and the whole reason for starting this conversation. He was still sitting there, thankfully, with a polite, expectant expression on his face. "Oh, are you ready for me to send Matthew in? I left a copy of his resume on your desk earlier, in case you haven't had a chance to look at it yet."

Tristan's voice came over the intercom again. "Who?"

I smiled apologetically at Matthew, lifting my finger from the intercom button so my comment could only be heard by the two of us. "He's very busy."

I pressed my finger back onto the intercom. "Remember, your interview with Matthew Clarkson for the post of personal assistant was scheduled at eleven o'clock. It's now nearly a quarter past, so you're running late. I knew you were in the middle of an important conference call, so I didn't interrupt you."

While I waited for Tristan's response, I offered Matthew another apologetic smile. "He's very, very busy. Sometimes he forgets what he's doing."

Matthew smiled and nodded, seeming to accept my explanation for Tristan's bad manners. "I guess that's why he needs a personal assistant."

"Do I have to see him now?" Tristan's voice held a plaintive note. I could imagine the expression on his face through the wall.

Another apologetic smile in Matthew's direction. My face was going to be stuck that way soon. "He's a bit of a joker. Sorry. Don't let that put you off, though. You'll soon get used to it."

I refused to give Tristan a response. I tapped my fingers impatiently on the desk, calling him all the names under the sun in my head, while I waited for him to crack. It didn't take long. "Are we going for lunch afterward?"

"Yes, Tristan. We can go for lunch after the interview."

A long pause before another crackle of the intercom. "Okay, then. Send him in."

I directed Matthew into the adjoining office, crossing my fingers beneath the desk and being 100 percent sincere when I wished him luck.

Less than ten minutes later, he was back. The short interview time was a surprise. But maybe Tristan had been so impressed, he'd hired him on the spot. The look on his face quickly dashed my hopes.

"What's wrong? What happened?"

He glanced back toward the office, probably checking the door had closed behind him before he spoke. Tristan hadn't even bothered to escort him out. "I'm not sure. It wasn't really an interview."

"What do you mean?"

"He didn't ask about any of my previous jobs."

"Well, they were on your resume. So he probably wanted to find out other things. What did he ask you about?"

"He asked me whether I'd ever had any pets. When I said I used to have a lizard, he...er...asked me a few questions about that. How you look after it. What they eat. How they breed. I mean, I've got to admit to being extremely confused." He cast a quick look around the office. I followed his gaze, wondering what he was looking for. "I mean, do you... have to look after...animals for him?"

"Erm...I haven't so far." *But I wouldn't put it beyond the realms of possibility.* Not knowing what else to say, and unable to offer any useful explanation for the strangeness of the interview, I bid Matthew farewell, promising that either Tristan or myself would call him as soon as possible.

It took less than a second after returning to my desk for the intercom to buzz. "Are we going for lunch soon?"

Ignoring his question, I countered with my own. "How did the interview go?"

The adjoining office door swung open within seconds, and Tristan strolled in. "He was no good."

I bit down on the urge to ask whether the problem lay in the candidate not knowing enough about lizards. "What was wrong with him? He seemed absolutely perfect to me."

"Too young. Not enough experience."

"He's..." I checked the piece of paper on my desk that listed his details. "Twenty-four. He's only two years younger than me."

"Kevin's thirty." Tristan nodded sagely, as if that fact alone explained everything.

I waited for further elaboration or explanation, but it never came. Sighing, I agreed to an early lunch.

Chapter Eleven

I was surprised when lunch involved a cab journey to a Lebanese restaurant in South London. Normally, we walked to somewhere within a couple of blocks. No wonder Tristan had wanted to leave early. I knew it was pointless voicing any objections, so I got into the cab without argument. I congratulated myself on managing not to ask what time we were going to get back to the office, already calculating how late I'd have to stay to wade through all the e-mails I needed to respond to on Tristan's behalf. I decided that if there was ever going to be an award given out for self-restraint, I deserved to be the first recipient.

On our arrival, Tristan was greeted like an old friend by the owner. It was obviously a frequent haunt of his. I wondered if this was somewhere he brought his fiancée. If so, it seemed slightly odd to bring his personal assistant to the same place.

After being seated, I wasted no time in starting my necessary scrutiny of the menu. It usually took a while to work out what it was safe for me to eat. I'd barely looked at the first two starters, unfortunately both consisting of fish, when it was whisked away from me.

Tristan scowled, holding the menu out of reach. "Don't order yet."

"Why?"

Tristan's response was to point across the restaurant. "That's why."

I frowned. Martin, the head of the IT department, was making his way toward us. Tristan waited until Martin got within a few steps of the table before making a big show of checking his watch. "You took your time!"

Martin removed his jacket, slinging it across a chair before responding. "Well, maybe if someone had waited five minutes and shared their cab, I wouldn't have had to wait ages for one."

Tristan grinned. "I've learned from experience that your five minutes is more like thirty. We haven't ordered yet. We were waiting for you, so you can stop complaining."

Martin smiled. "Stop complaining! Since when did your demand for me to do that make the slightest bit of difference? Keep dreaming, old man. Keep dreaming."

Watching the two banter, I suddenly felt like the world's biggest spare part. It was clear this was a pre-arranged lunch date between two men who knew each other really, really well. And for some reason, I was here too. I stood up quickly. "Listen, I'm going to leave you two to it. Go back to the office."

Martin shot up from his chair like a jack-in-the-box, less than two seconds after sitting down. "Good God, no! Don't leave. Don't make me have to suffer his company all on my own. You have to stay so I've got someone interesting to talk to. I only agreed to come because he said he was going to bring his new super-efficient PA." He put his hand to his mouth, speaking in an exaggerated stage whisper. "Between you and me, I've got a secret plan to poach you, but don't let Tristan know. My PA's great, but it'll piss Tristan off no end, so it'll be worth it." He held his hand out. "I'm Martin, by the way. It's always good to know the name of your future boss."

I laughed, liking the man immediately, and shook his hand. "Dominic."

I glanced at Tristan, wondering what reaction he'd have to being deliberately wound up. The answer was none, apart from a slight weary head shake. He waved me back into my seat, and I acquiesced without argument. Martin followed suit, donning a pair of glasses and grabbing a menu.

I reached for the menu Tristan had taken off me earlier. "So, how long have you two known each other?"

Martin pulled a face. "Too long," he said, getting his answer in just before Tristan chimed in with, "Since eternity began."

They both laughed at each other's similar answers.

I didn't get a proper answer to my question until after the waiter had taken our orders. I'd finally managed to find a main course that couldn't possibly contain any fish. I'd left my epi-pen back in the office, so I couldn't afford to take any risks. Tristan handed his menu to the waiter before sitting back in his chair. "Martin was in the same year as me at university."

Martin interrupted. "I know what you're thinking. That I seem so much more sophisticated and distinguished than this one." He inclined his head toward Tristan while stroking a hand through his graying hair. "But some of us wanted a bit of life experience first. I'd traveled for a few years."

Tristan coughed. "Ten years."

Martin shot him a dirty look. "Okay, ten years. There was a lot to see."

Tristan continued with a slight smile on his face. "Then he decided that he might actually need to get some qualifications, so he turned up at university with a long beard, still looking like a scruffy back-packer. I felt sorry for him, because everybody else gave him a wide berth."

"Felt sorry for me! Remind me who was standing like an idiot in the canteen, unable to pay for their lunch because they'd left their wallet in their room? And who swooped in and lent you the money?"

Tristan laughed. "Swooped! Martin, I don't think you've ever swooped anywhere. But yes..." He directed the next comment at me. "He was kind enough to lend me money—a very small amount of money, may I add—to pay for my meal. A fact that he has never let me forget for the past twelve years. Even though in that time I've bought him numerous meals that repay the debt more than a hundred times over. I've also given him a job. Oh, and a wife!"

"You didn't *give* me a wife." Martin turned to me with a look that said, *"Who is this guy?"*

I had to admit I was beginning to find this lunch thoroughly entertaining. "How did you give him a wife?" I studiously ignored Martin's frustrated mumbles next to me while I waited for a reply from Tristan.

Tristan smiled. "I set them up. I knew they'd be perfect together."

Martin's snort was so loud, a woman three tables down turned to see where the noise was coming from. "You didn't set us up. You introduced her to me. End of story. I did all the hard work. All the wooing and such. Did you help with any of that? No! Didn't think so."

Tristan suddenly slammed his hand down on the table in front of me. I jumped. "See how good I am at matchmaking!"

Martin suddenly gave me a look of pity. "Please tell me you're not letting this idiot run your love life. I married Rebecca in spite of him, whatever he might say to the contrary."

Tristan crossed his arms and looked absurdly proud for a moment. "I set him up with Adam."

Martin looked momentarily confused before comprehension dawned. "Adam. As in Adam, in my department." A look of concern crossed his face. "Is that a good idea?"

It was Tristan's turn to look unsure. "Why? He's a nice guy, right? I wouldn't have introduced them if not."

I suddenly became very interested in what Martin had to say, leaning forward slightly, to make sure I didn't miss anything important.

He took his glasses off, using the napkin to clean them. "Yeah, he's a nice guy. But, I've heard, he can be a bit of a...player. I don't know anything for sure. It's probably not true. Just be careful."

I was touched by Martin's seeming concern. If I wasn't so hell-bent on returning to being John Stone's PA, I might have sounded him out on whether he was serious about the job offer. "Don't worry. I'm a big boy. I can look after myself."

The rest of the meal passed in a similar vein, the banter flowing freely, with each man doing their best to wind the other up. I was beginning to see why my attempts to annoy Tristan had been met with such a lack of reaction. It was nothing he didn't hear on a daily basis from his friend. Even Paul and I weren't quite so savage in our attacks on each other. It was impossible to pick out which bits were true, which bits were exaggerated, and which bits were complete fantasy, so I stopped trying and just sat back and enjoyed the show.

At one point, Martin whipped out his phone to show pictures of his three children. It turned out that Tristan was a godparent to all three. Martin claimed it was because he needed someone with enough money to look after them if anything happened to him and his wife, and Tristan had the most money out of anyone he knew. But it was easy to see how fond Tristan was, from his reaction to the photos.

Two hours passed in a blur. I'd had such a good time, it was hard to be annoyed, even when I found myself having to stay at the office long after Tristan had swanned off home.

Chapter Twelve

Adam moved in closer on the sofa. We were at his friend's house. It was apparently a housewarming party, but so far I hadn't met the owners of the house. Despite spending time, trying to work it out, I remained clueless. That was probably largely due to the fact, that soon after arriving, Adam had quickly maneuvered us onto an empty sofa and proceeded to initiate a heavy petting session. Twice, I'd suggested finding the hosts, reminding Adam he'd brought a housewarming present. Twice, he'd shrugged it off. The kissing I was fine with, but the octopus hands were fully in force again, and there were only so many times you could pluck a searching hand from under your shirt and move it somewhere else. Despite my growing arousal, when his hand strayed to the zipper on my jeans, I pulled away, shifting farther down the sofa. "Let's talk."

Adam picked up his beer bottle from the floor and took a long drink before relaxing back against the sofa. "About what?"

I shrugged. "I don't know. Anything. How was work?"

He rolled his head sideways, making eye contact and staring for the longest time. "You want to talk about work?" He sat up. "I've got a better idea. Why don't we go upstairs? This place has got three bedrooms. There's sure to be at least one of them spare. Gary won't mind. As long as Alison doesn't find out, we'll be fine." He rooted around in his pocket, pulling out a strip of condoms. "Look what I've got!"

I had no idea who Gary or Alison were supposed to be. I assumed they were the couple throwing the housewarming party. "We've just arrived."

He pulled a face. "So! We'll only be gone ten minutes."

It was all I could do not to laugh. If he really thought ten minutes was an attractive proposition, then I was really glad I was about to turn him down. I liked to think I was worth more than a quickie in a stranger's house. "Sorry. I'm not really comfortable. You know, in someone else's house. People I haven't even met. Let's just talk instead."

"Fine. Sure. Whatever you want." He didn't seem overly annoyed, but then he didn't seem altogether happy either. I watched as he stuffed the condoms back in his pocket, trying to think of something to say to break the tension which had built up between us.

I was saved from trying when he pointed across the room. "Listen, Gary's over there. I'm just going to go and have a quick word. I'll be back in five minutes. You'll be all right on your own, won't you?"

I nodded, about to suggest I could accompany him, give him a chance to introduce me to the others. It would be nice to know more than one person at the party. But he'd already leaped to his feet and was halfway across the room. The empty seat next to me was quickly taken by a blonde girl and her boyfriend. At least I assumed he was her boyfriend when they immediately started making out. I concentrated on my beer bottle, studiously ignoring them. After all, it wouldn't be for long. As soon as Adam came back, I'd insist on him introducing me to some people. I looked over at him. He was chatting enthusiastically with a man I assumed was Gary. Three other men had joined them.

Ten minutes later, there was still no sign of Adam bringing his conversation to an end. The couple still sharing the sofa didn't seem to mind that they weren't the sole occupants of it. I glanced across at them, immediately wishing I hadn't as I witnessed the girl unzipping her boyfriend's trousers and sliding her hand inside. I coughed loudly, hoping it would serve to remind them of my presence. They either didn't hear, or more likely didn't care, and carried on regardless. I settled for looking away, figuring what I couldn't see, I didn't know.

I considered walking across and joining Adam, but if he'd wanted me in the conversation, then wouldn't he have invited me over there in the first place? I didn't want to go where I wasn't wanted. If I went over there, I could just end up standing like a lemon, unable to join in, because I didn't have a clue who or what they were talking about. Though even that might be a better alternative to the live sex show gradually progressing next to me. It was a big sofa, at least a four-seater, but I could have sworn the couple were gradually moving closer. Before I could make my mind up one way or another, I felt my phone vibrate. Pulling it out of my pocket, I read the message.

Tristan: *What are you doing?*

Dominic: *How did you get my number?*

Tristan: *I already rang it once, remember? At the hotel.*

Tristan: *So same answer—employee file. I programmed it into my phone.*

Tristan: *And you must have programmed my number into your phone to know who it was.*

Dominic: *I don't think you're meant to use it to hassle me outside work.*

Tristan: *Hassle you. :(I only asked what you were doing.*

Dominic: *I'm at a party.*

Tristan: *On your own?*

Dominic: *Who goes to a party on their own? What kind of saddo do you think I am? Don't answer that.*

The irony of writing the last message while I sat alone on a sofa, talking to no one, wasn't completely lost on me. But Tristan didn't have to know that.

Tristan: *With a friend or with Adam?*

Dominic: *With Adam.*

Tristan: *I'll leave you alone then. Enjoy the party X*

I stared at the kiss at the end of the message. I was sure that was way outside the boundaries of a boss/personal assistant relationship. Another message came through almost straightaway.

Tristan: *Sorry. Didn't mean to put that at the end. Force of habit. Forgot who I was messaging.*

My fingers hovered over the keypad, trying to think of a suitably breezy message. I typed one out.

Dominic: *I'll forgive you. You should be careful sending kisses to gay guys. They'll get the wrong idea.*

I deleted the message without sending it. Too accusatory. It made it sound far sleazier than it was.

Dominic: *I won't tell Maria.*

No good either. It sounded like I was making veiled threats.

Dominic: *That's okay darling XXXX*

That went way beyond breezy and into some sort of flirtatious response, I didn't even want to contemplate. I deleted that too.

Sighing, I slipped my phone back into my pocket without replying. It vibrated again almost immediately.

Tristan: *Ask me what I'm doing.*

Dominic: *I can't. I 'm busy partying.*

Tristan: *:(*

It was a shame there was no pouting emoticon for Tristan to use. I was tempted to switch my phone off and simply ignore him. A particularly loud moan from the couple next to me served as a useful reminder that a distraction would be more than welcome.

Dominic: *What are you doing?*

Tristan: *I'm at a diner.*

Tristan: *On my own :(*

Dominic: *Where's Maria?*

Tristan: *Working.*

Tristan: *If you get bored at the party, come and join me.*

Tristan: *I could really use the company.*

Tristan: *I'll buy you food.*

Dominic: *Why don't you ask Martin?*

Tristan: *Tried. His wife won't let him come out.*

Dominic: *Guess you'll have to stay on your own then. I'm having fun. I'm going to go and dance now. So if you send any more messages, I'm not going to be able to reply.*

Of course I wasn't going to dance. There were only two people dancing, and they were so drunk it was more a case of swaying and stumbling around in a vague approximation of something rhythmic. I stared at Adam, hoping he'd look over. He'd been over there at least fifteen minutes now. So much for five minutes and then he was coming back. He remained oblivious to my attempts to get his attention. A glance at my phone revealed another string of messages.

Tristan: *Okay. I'll just talk to myself.*

Tristan: *I can't imagine you dancing. Trying to decide whether you're a good dancer or not.*

Tristan: *The waitress won't leave me alone.*

Tristan: *I'm being cougared (is that even a word) AGAIN!*

Tristan: *If she kidnaps me and I don't show up for work tomorrow, ring the police.*

Tristan: *It'll probably be too late and she'll already have had her wicked way with me.*

Tristan: *But at least I'll know you cared.*

Tristan: *Dominic?*

Tristan: *Right! Busy dancing. I thought you were making it up.*

Tristan: *The food here is pretty good. If the dancing makes you hungry, you should come and eat. Did I tell you I'm buying?*

Tristan: *I had a burger.*

Tristan: *There's a crazy dog outside. I think it's got rabies. Either that, or it just wants my burger. Probably the burger. We don't have rabies here, right?*

Tristan: *The waitress is back. Help!*

Tristan: *I'll ring Martin. He'll know what to do. He won't be busy dancing. I don't think he's ever danced. If I'm lucky, his wife will let him answer the phone.*

I shook my head at the deluge of messages, sliding the phone back into my pocket without answering. Tristan was obviously bored. I risked another glance at my sofa mates. The girl sat astride her boyfriend, her already short skirt pushed up to an indecent level. If I stayed here much longer, I was going to see more female parts than I ever had before or had ever wished to. She moaned as her boyfriend's hand hitched the skirt up farther. Launching myself off the sofa, I headed over to where I'd last seen Adam, stopping short when I realized he'd disappeared. A quick search around the house reaped no results. Had he left without bothering to tell me? I stood in the middle of the room, unsure what to do. I could get another drink, but I didn't particularly want one. I could attempt to make conversation with a stranger I'd probably never see again, but that held even less appeal. No way I was going back to the sofa. They were probably in the middle of full-blown sex by now. I noticed a few strange looks start to come my way. They were probably wondering why I was just standing there looking uncomfortable. I pulled my phone out as it vibrated again.

Tristan: *I'm glad you and Adam are getting on really well. You deserve to be relaxing and having a good time.*

Dominic: *Just tell the waitress you're getting married. Show her a picture of Maria. She'll realize she can't possibly compete.*

Dominic: *If that doesn't work, call the police BEFORE she kidnaps you.*

Dominic: *Eat the burger and then the dog will go away.*

Dominic: *What have you done to upset Martin's wife? Actually, don't answer that. I don't want to know.*

I did another circuit of the house, including the upstairs, looking for Adam. It garnered exactly the same result as last time. He seemed to have vanished into thin air. I couldn't see any of the men he'd been talking to, either, or I would have asked them if they knew where he was.

Tristan: *You must dance very quickly. Your advice as always is excellent.*

Tristan: *I'm also considering offering the dog the burger in exchange for setting him on the waitress.*

Tristan: *Martin's wife thinks I'm a bad influence. I have no idea why. I'm always very charming when I go round for dinner. Plus, I introduced them. You'd think she'd be grateful. Maybe that's it. She bears a grudge because she's stuck with Martin and she thinks it's my fault. I'll apologize next time I see her. Offer to find her a new husband.*

I took another moment to scan the party. Still no Adam. It was hard to believe he would have just left without telling me. Maybe there'd been some sort of emergency and he'd had to leave in a rush. I couldn't think of any other rational explanation.

Dominic: *Where are you? I'm on the way.*

Tristan: *:)*

IT TOOK A WHILE TO spot Tristan in the diner. I'd been looking for a man in a suit, not one casually dressed in jeans and a T-shirt, with his usually slicked-back hair falling rakishly over his forehead. It wasn't till he waved that recognition dawned. I strolled over, trying hard not to stare at the bare, muscular arms revealed by the lack of a jacket. He beamed at me as I reached his table, dimples showing up prominently in his handsome face. "Dominic! You came. I knew you would."

I slid into the booth opposite him, wondering what the hell I was doing here. Okay, so the party had been bad, but I could have just gone home. In fact, I should have gone home. "Did someone steal your suit?"

He looked puzzled. "You think I go home and spend all evening in a suit?"

I peered over the table. "Are those jeans even designer?"

Shrugging, he pushed the menu toward me. "What do you want to eat? My treat. For coming and keeping me company."

I took a moment to peruse it, noting the *three* empty plates in front of Tristan on the table. I gestured at them. "Is there anything left you haven't already eaten?"

He flashed another smile. "I was hungry. I spent an hour and a half at the gym."

"An hour and a half," I echoed his words. The thought of Tristan sweaty and straining in the gym for that length of time left me unable to add anything to the half-finished sentence. I squinted across the diner. "Where's the mad waitress?"

Tristan shot me a confused look. "Mad?"

"Yeah. She was..." He continued to stare blankly at me. "Never mind."

Tristan let it go. "You don't seem particularly drunk for someone who's been to a party."

"I only had one beer. You know...what with the...dancing...and talking to Adam. I didn't really have time to—" Something in Tristan's stare made me think I was being less than convincing. Tempted to confess just how dreadful the party had actually been, I quickly changed the subject. "So, Tristan, the interview tomorrow?"

He acknowledged he knew what I was talking about with a subtle incline of his head. To be honest, meeting him here was giving me the perfect opportunity to discuss something that had been playing on my mind.

"The candidate tomorrow, can you promise me you'll give the guy a chance?"

Tristan looked affronted. "Of course I will. Why wouldn't I?"

"Because I'm sure he'll be great if you give him a chance. He's older so that won't be a problem. He's straight, so he's not going to be cornering you by the filing cabinet. He's got a lot of experience."

Tristan cut me off. "I'm sure he will be perfect. I've got good vibes about this one. You know, third time lucky."

"Really?" I couldn't hide my surprise. "Well, it's great you've got a more positive attitude."

Tristan nodded emphatically. I sat back, feeling far more confident that by the end of the next day, I should know when my temporary stint as Tristan's PA would be coming to an end.

Tristan leaned forward to emphasize the point he was about to make. I absently noted the flex of muscles in his tanned forearms. "But, if he's not suitable... I'm sure he will be! But if he's not, then we should leave any more interviews until after Christmas. It's a busy time of year. There's a lot to do. You know, there's the Christmas party and then...other things...so no more interviews until the new year." He smiled and relaxed back in his chair.

I frowned. "I—" My phone chimed, announcing a new message. If it wasn't for the fact both of Tristan's hands were on the table with his phone nowhere in sight, I would have suspected it was from him. I took a quick look.

Adam: *Where are you?*

I pushed the menu back over the table toward Tristan. "Can you order something for me? Something sweet. You'll probably end up eating half of it anyway." He readily agreed, heading straight to the counter. I took the opportunity to answer the text.

Dominic: *I left. I thought you'd gone. I looked for you everywhere.*

The response came back in a matter of seconds.

Adam: *I told Gary I'd go to the shop for him. They were out of ice. I was only gone like ten minutes. You can't have looked for very long. I can't believe you left without saying anything.*

Shit! Now what was I supposed to say?

Dominic: *Yeah well, you'd already left me on my own for fifteen minutes.*

Okay, that made me sound like a petulant child. I deleted it and tried again.

Dominic: *Didn't think you'd be that bothered.*

That was no better.

Dominic: *Sorry. I really thought you'd left. I couldn't see any of your friends either. I thought maybe there'd been some sort of emergency. I'll make it up to you.*

Much better. I congratulated myself on my ability to use amazing tact and diplomacy.

Adam: *;) Oh yeah! Tell me more.*

Dominic: *I didn't mean like that.*

Adam: *The party's winding down. Do you want to come round to mine? You can start making it up to me.*

Dominic: *Another time. Sorry. I'm really tired. I'm about to go to bed.*

I winced at the lie I'd just told. But I could hardly admit I'd left the party to meet up with another guy. Even if it was just Tristan. Actually, that would probably make it worse. Who the hell left a date to spend time with their boss?

Adam: *I could come round to yours. What's your address?*

Dominic: *I'm already half asleep. Maybe tomorrow night.*

Adam: *Okay. Sweet dreams. Xxxx*

Dominic: *You too. XXX*

I was sending the last text when Tristan eased himself back into the seat. "Food is on the way. Now let me tell you about that dog."

Chapter Thirteen

Yawning loudly, I cursed myself yet again for staying out and chatting with Tristan until the early hours of the morning. It certainly hadn't been intentional. I'd scarcely believed my eyes when I'd glanced at my watch to find it was almost three a.m. Thinking back now, I had no idea what we'd possibly found to talk about, but conversation had flowed freely, with an awful lot of mutual laughter thrown in for good measure.

Unfortunately, one thing I could remember was my growing fascination with Tristan's forearms. At various times during the evening, I'd found myself transfixed by them. Apparently, I'd developed some sort of strange forearm fetish. I'd half expected him to turn up to work today with his sleeves rolled up. Much to my relief, the offending forearms had been safely covered by the usual tailored suit jacket. Conversation had been minimal, a marked contrast with the previous night. I was probably mostly to blame for that though, as the majority of Tristan's comments or questions I met with nothing more substantial than a tired grunt. He'd simply laughed before disappearing into his office.

The candidate we'd discussed last night, the one Tristan had assured me was likely to be perfect, was currently being interviewed in Tristan's office. Unlike the last interview, Tristan had called him through as soon as he'd arrived. So I'd had no opportunity to form any sort of opinion about him beyond him exuding a very professional air. I had one eye on the door, poised and ready to jump up and intercept him to find out how the interview had gone.

He'd already been in there more than half an hour. Surely that was a good sign. Maybe it was taking longer because Tristan was already discussing the finer details of the position. Maybe, he'd already offered him the job and they were negotiating salary? Reassured that an interview could only take this amount of time if the person was going to be hired, I began to devise a theoretical to-do list to transfer offices again.

The adjoining door swung open, and I leapt from my desk, waylaying him before he could leave. "How did it go?"

The candidate looked a little surprised at my sudden appearance in front of him. "Good. Really good, actually."

I considered carefully how to phrase my next question. "And it was a normal interview?"

His brow furrowed. "Normal?"

"There were...no...unusual questions?"

He looked even more perplexed. "Unusual?"

I bit back an impatient sigh. Worried Tristan would leave his office and find me interrogating the candidate, I got straight to the point. "He just asked you questions you'd expect to be asked in an interview?"

"Yes of course." The look on his face had changed. He had the look of someone humoring a person they suspected was slightly mad. I was immediately insulted that someone could spend time with Tristan and then look at *me* like I was insane.

"So did he let you know whether you'd been successful or not?"

The guy straightened his glasses. He glanced at the door over my shoulder, giving the appearance he was considering making a run for it. I offered a smile. His frown deepened. "He said he would call and let me know this afternoon. But between you and me, I'd be extremely surprised if I didn't get the position. We seemed to hit it off, and he really liked my ideas for how I could make his daily schedule run more efficiently."

I stuck out my hand. "Well, congratulations. Thank you for coming in."

He stared at it for a beat too long before reluctantly shaking it. He edged his way around me to get to the door. I called an enthusiastic farewell after him. If he responded, it was drowned out by the sound of the door closing. I had a sneaking suspicion he probably hadn't bothered. Not the friendliest guy, but then as long as he was good at his job, it wasn't crucial. Beneficial, but not crucial. He'd obviously been confident the post was his, so who was I to find issues that weren't there?

During the next hour, I turned my theoretical to-do list into an actual list. Itching to start implementing it, I waited impatiently for confirmation. Tristan's door, however, remained resolutely and frustratingly closed. In the end, unable to wait any longer, I knocked loudly. The instruction to come in came almost immediately.

I found Tristan frowning at something on his computer screen. He acknowledged my presence and then went right back to frowning.

"So the interview went well?"

He lifted his head momentarily. "Yes. Very well."

"Have you called him yet?"

"Yes. About fifteen minutes ago."

Momentarily shocked into silence by Tristan's unusually straightforward answer, it took me a moment to formulate my next question. "When can he start?" I was praying for as short a time as possible. Best-case scenario: he'd already given notice at his current position. That would cut the start time down considerably. Worst-case scenario: he'd still have to hand his resignation in, which meant a longer delay. Unless he could somehow convince his workplace to release him early. Which was always possible. Particularly if Tristan agreed to some sort of payoff. I calculated some timeframes in my head. If I could get him up to speed before Christmas, I could be back in my office before the new year.

Tristan transferred his frowning from the computer screen to me. "Start?"

I spoke slowly like I was talking to a child. "I need to know dates so I can sort out a handover period, make sure he knows everything about the company that he needs to."

"Oh, I didn't give him the job."

I let the offhand words run through my brain a few times. "But...he thought...he said...I thought...you said, yesterday...I assumed..."

Tristan cocked his head to one side and looked greatly amused. "You need to get more sleep, Dominic. You're not making any sense."

I glared at him. He knew full well why I'd had so little sleep. "What was wrong with him?"

Tristan sat back in his chair, steepling his hands in front of him, a thoughtful expression on his face. "I could never work with him. He was far too much of a yes man. I need someone with a bit more backbone." He smiled breezily. "Never mind. I'm sure we'll have more luck *after* Christmas."

PAUL LEANED AGAINST the wall of the office with his arms crossed. I'd just finished relaying the latest details of the interviews. He was shaking his head even before I'd finished the full story. I stopped, irritated. "What?"

"I'm just really amazed you're buying this."

"Buying what?"

Paul lowered his voice, obviously concerned it would carry through the closed door to Tristan's ears. "So let me check I've got this right. The first candidate, a middle-aged married lady, was after his body, and a fully-grown man was concerned he wouldn't be able to fight her off. The second candidate was too young, even though he was fully qualified and had a great deal of experience. The next candidate agreed with him too much. Have I got it right?"

I shrugged. "Pretty much. I don't get what your point is."

He peered at me closely. "And you completely believe these explanations? From a man you couldn't stand a few weeks ago?"

I shifted uncomfortably in my seat. "Why wouldn't I? What are you trying to say?"

Paul laughed. "Dominic, he's playing you. I mean, what do you think he's going to come up with after Christmas? Too fat, too thin, too hairy, too loud, too quiet, too masculine? I'm sure he's got hundreds of reasons tucked away in his brain that he can produce as an excuse not to hire them."

"He wouldn't do that. He's far too...ditzy."

Paul laughed again, louder this time. "Right! The ditzy CEO of the major international company."

"What would he possibly get out of doing that? It doesn't make any sense."

Paul shook his head ruefully. "Easy. He gets to keep you as his PA. You're forgetting he requested you personally. He didn't let you wriggle out of it when you tried. He put up with you acting like an absolute asshole without saying a word."

I regretted telling Paul about my efforts to get sent straight back to John Stone.

"For some reason, he seems to have decided you're the perfect PA for him. And I really don't get it, Dominic. Because you're normally really clued up. I never have to point out the obvious to you. Your crush must be getting in the way of you seeing reason."

"My what?" My voice came out in a high-pitched squeak. "I DO NOT have a crush on him."

Paul swiveled his head toward the door. "You might want to lower your voice, or you're going to be explaining that to him."

"Seriously—" I lowered my voice to a hiss. "I do not have a crush on him. That's ridiculous. In fact, it's beyond ridiculous. It's—"

"You tried to kiss him."

"That was weeks ago, and I was drunk. I know for a fact that you've done equally stupid things when you're drunk. I was even there for some of them."

Paul didn't bother to deny it. "So you never look at him in that way?"

A sudden picture crept into my head of Tristan's forearms. "No. Never."

Paul crossed his arms and looked smug. "Because I think, Dom, and maybe I'm wrong. I think the reason you're so dead set on getting out of this office, even though the two of you clearly get along well, is that you want him, and you know you can't have him. I think that's the reason you never liked him. You lusted after him from the moment you first saw him."

I made a snort of derision. "You're wrong. You're forgetting again the opinion he has of his employees. I'll give you, he hides it well. But the evidence is there in black and white. And you seem to be conveniently forgetting the fact I have a boyfriend."

Paul quirked an eyebrow. "Oh, Adam's your boyfriend now, is he? Because when we spoke a couple of days ago, you weren't even sure you liked him. You were worried that he's only after your body. Said he seemed more interested in getting you into bed than getting to know you. You've discussed it, have you? Cleared up all misunderstandings and decided that you're an item now?"

I settled for repeating myself. "You're wrong."

Paul sighed. "I'm just worried about you, Dom. I agree you'd be better off working for Mr. Stone again, so you need to be a bit more assertive with Tristan. Stop letting him get away with these bullshit reasons for not hiring people. It would help, for a start, if you could take a step back and be a bit more aware that he's clearly manipulating you. Funny how you can see straight through Adam trying to manipulate you into bed, but you're blind when it comes to Tristan."

A loud crash from the adjoining office followed by a string of epithets interrupted our conversation.

I immediately took a step toward the door. "I need to go and see what he's up to."

Paul shook his head slowly. "No, you don't. You don't at all. You could just ignore him. He's a grown man. He can take care of himself." There was a clear challenge present in his eyes.

I glanced at Paul, then back at the door, torn between proving Paul wrong and checking on Tristan's welfare. Another crash made my mind up. "I'll see you later, Paul."

Barging into the office without knocking, it took me a moment to make sense out of what I could see. Tristan was over against the far wall, hands wrapped loosely around a golf club. His discarded jacket was draped over a nearby chair and his sleeves were rolled up, meaning the forearms were out again. The forearms I had absolutely zero interest in, I reminded myself. A line of golf balls rolled haphazardly around the floor.

He didn't seem at all surprised by my sudden, uninvited entrance into his office. "Hey, Dominic. Do you know anything about golf?" I shook my head, wincing, as he maneuvered one of the runaway golf balls in front of him before taking a mad swing at it. It bounced off the wall less than a foot from my head, leaving a huge dent.

"By the looks of it, neither do you."

Tristan shrugged. "I'm trying to learn. Martin suggested it's a good way to unwind."

"Did he suggest that you try it in the office? Because I'm not too sure it's the best place." Having seen the relationship they had, I wouldn't have put it past the older man to have suggested exactly that.

I ducked as another golf ball flew over my head, hitting the floor with a crash. I wondered if wrestling a golf club from a boss was classed as acceptable behavior. "Haven't you got work you should be doing?"

He hooked another ball with the end of the club, stopping it with his foot when it tried to roll back the other way. "Nope. Finished it all. I was bored."

I panicked as he lined up another shot. "Why don't I book you some golf lessons?"

He paused, and the ball took the opportunity to roll out of reach again. "When?"

I had absolutely no idea where to book golf lessons, whether there was a waiting list, or basically anything about golf. It was just an irritating sport on TV I never watched. "I'm sure I can sort something out for tomorrow afternoon. You haven't got anything on your schedule after the meeting at three."

I held my breath as Tristan took time to contemplate the idea. While I waited, I began to formulate a possible strategy for the golf-club wrestling. It mainly consisted of running at Tristan, tackling him to the ground, and staying well away from the distracting forearms.

"Okay. That sounds good."

I tried not to let too much relief show on my face. Approaching him warily, I held my hand out for the golf club. He shook his head and moved it behind his back. "I should practice more."

"But what if you're doing it wrong? Best to let the experts teach you properly tomorrow."

"I suppose so." He reluctantly handed the club over. "It's Martin's, so be careful with it."

I assumed it was safe to leave the golf balls as long as he had nothing to hit them with. "As for work, I'm about to send you the report I finished typing. You need to look through it. See if it needs any amendments."

Still clutching the golf club, I eyed the wall of miraculously still intact windows. At least I only had to finish typing a report I'd just lied and said was already complete. Then, I needed to find an available golf lesson at short notice. It could have been far worse: I could have had to call someone to replace broken windowpanes. The dents in the wall could wait. Tristan made them, he could bloody well put up with them for a while.

Paul had gone. I'd half expected him to wait. I'd gotten the distinct impression he hadn't finished saying everything he intended. I wondered if he'd stayed and listened to any of the conversation through the door. I hoped he had. At least it should have made him realize I had much better taste than to have a crush on someone who attempted to play golf in their office and then acted like a child when I confiscated the club.

Chapter Fourteen

I'd be lying if I didn't admit that Paul's comments had made me think. Not the ones about Tristan; they were clearly ridiculous and based on nothing. One drunken attempted kiss and a slight interest in a man's forearms didn't mean a thing. But the ones about Adam had hit a nerve. Maybe I wasn't giving him enough of a chance. The fact he had a healthy sex drive and wasn't afraid to show it surely shouldn't be held against him. So, after finishing the report I'd claimed to have already finished, and miraculously finding a place nearby for golf lessons at short notice, I decided to head down to the IT department. After all, I had the perfect excuse of a golf club to return.

A few questioning eyebrows were raised at my appearance in the elevator holding it. At my announcement of "Don't ask," most of them simply shrugged and looked away. Unfortunately, Lydia, the pretty temp I'd befriended the other day, wasn't so easily put off. She sidled over from the other side of the elevator, a questioning smile on her face. "Have you been playing golf?"

"Me? At work? No! *I'm* not that mad."

Her brow furrowed. "Who? Tristan? How exciting!"

"That's one word for it." The elevator stopped at the floor for IT. I stepped off, giving a cursory wave to Lydia. The IT department covered the whole of the floor and, unlike most of the other departments, was all open plan with only cubicles to separate the desks. The only office was Martin's in the center of the floor. I headed for it, banking on him being okay with me turning up unannounced. His PA's desk was empty, but Martin's door was open. Rather than knocking, I hovered outside, waiting for him to lift his head and notice me. It didn't take long. He clutched his stomach and laughed uproariously as he spotted the golf club held in my hand, before gesturing for me to come inside.

I held it up. "This is yours, I believe. I wanted to return it."

Martin sat back, a big grin on his face. "Let me guess. You had to take it off him."

I handed it over. "Did you suggest he should use it in the office?"

The grin had subsided to a more subtle but no less telling smirk. "What do you take me for? I wouldn't suggest a thing like that. But I may know him well enough to have known when I handed over the club and the golf balls *in the office* that he wouldn't be able to wait. He's very predictable, is Tristan, and very impulsive."

I frowned at him. "And you didn't consider the possibility of him smashing the windows?"

"Did he?"

"Well, no...but—"

"There you go, then!" He shrugged. "No harm done, and it made your day a bit more interesting."

I casually scanned the nearby cubicles. I had no idea which one was Adam's.

"Looking for someone?"

My eyes flicked back to Martin. "No. Not really."

"So, you don't want me to tell you where Adam is?"

I affected what I hoped was a look of nonchalance. "Well, maybe while I'm down here. I'd hate for him to hear I was here and I didn't even bother to say hello."

Martin smiled. "Fifth cubicle on the right. Near the back. Tell him he's got my permission to skive for ten minutes."

I turned to walk away, only to have to turn back when Martin addressed me once more. "By the way, Tristan's really enjoying having you as a PA."

I screwed my nose up. "I don't know why."

Martin laughed at the expression on my face. "Don't you? You're good at your job. Actually, better than good from what he's said—" I tried my best not to look too pleased at the unexpected compliment. "—without being boring. He hates boring. You provide a challenge. If there's one thing Tristan loves, it's a challenge. Always has. Have you met his fiancée yet?"

I shook my head. I hadn't seen anything of her in all the time I'd been working for Tristan. "Why?"

He cocked his head to one side. "I just wondered what you made of her. Whether you thought she was right for him or not."

"I hardly know him. And it's really none of my business. They're getting married soon, so I should hope they're right for each other." I couldn't help asking, "You don't think she is?"

"Tristan knows exactly what I think."

Realizing I wasn't going to get any elaboration on the strange, cryptic comment, I left the office and went in search of Adam.

To say he was surprised to see me would be an understatement. He stood, a genuine look of happiness on his face, as I approached his desk. "Hey! What are you doing down here? Don't say you came to see me."

"Sort of. I had to return something to Martin, but it seemed like a good excuse to come and say hello."

"Well, hello." He sneaked a peek over the row of cubicles. "You better not let Martin catch you, though. You'll get me into trouble."

I perched on the edge of his desk, trying my best not to get annoyed by the fact his eyes automatically dropped straight to my ass. "Oh, we're fine. He said you've got permission to skive for ten minutes."

He sat back in his chair, and a broad smile filled his face. "Really? This gets better and better. So, what are you doing tonight? Want to come round to mine? I'll cook dinner and then, we can...hang out."

The way his gaze slid over my body as he said the last two words left no doubt what his version of "hanging out" meant. I gave an internal sigh, trying to make sure it didn't show on the outside. Adam was a good-looking guy, but I really was beginning to feel like he was only interested in one thing. I could go ahead and sleep with him, but then what? Would he rapidly lose interest, or was I just being paranoid?

"How about the cinema?"

His brows knitted together. "The cinema? You'd rather see a film?"

"I haven't seen one for a while. We could have dinner first, or after if you prefer. I'll message you a list of films. I tell you what. I'll let you choose which one."

He looked less than impressed with the choice of activity but grudgingly agreed. We made small talk for a couple of minutes before Adam raised his head, his attention on the office I'd just left. "Do you two go everywhere together?"

Confused, I followed his gaze to find a familiar figure deep in conversation with Martin. The fact that both of their gazes were clearly fixed on Adam and me, and they were making no attempt to hide it, made it clear what the subject of the conversation was. I turned back to Adam, conscious that I still hadn't answered his question. "Hardly. I don't know what he's doing down here." I took a step in that direction, intent on finding out. "I'll see you later." Not waiting for Adam's response, I stalked back toward the office.

Neither of the two men seemed surprised at my approach. I paused by the door, fixing Tristan with my scrutiny. I was relieved to see he was back to being fully dressed. "Are you looking for me?"

Tristan grinned. "No. Just a happy coincidence." He inclined his head toward Adam's cubicle. "How's it going? Is he behaving himself? Because, if not, just say the word and I'll fire him."

I raised an eyebrow. "Sure you would. So, why are you here?" An imp of an idea came to me, and I decided not to hold back. "Are you carrying out a tour of the building to make sure all your *minions* are working hard enough?" I watched his face closely, interested in what his reaction to my comment would be. There wasn't even the slightest flicker of anything, apart from a neutral smile.

"Just catching up with Martin on a couple of things." Martin nodded obediently next to him, a look of amusement on his face. "Good conversation with Adam?"

Disappointed at his lack of guilt or even any reaction, I offered my own nod, simultaneously scanning the office for any sign of the offending golf club. The last thing I needed was to discover it had found its way back into Tristan's possession. There was no sign of it. Relieved that Martin must have put it away, I said my goodbyes and left them to it.

Chapter Fifteen

After Paul's crazy accusations a couple days ago, I'd gone out of my way to avoid him. He hadn't called or texted either, so it was safe to assume he was doing the same. Amazing how easy it is to avoid someone, even if you work in the same building, if you're both doing it.

Things with Adam were...okay. The cinema date had passed without any major issues. I'd regretted letting him pick the film when I'd had to sit through an arty film that made no sense at all. Adam had tried to explain it, but to be honest I still wasn't any clearer. We were still doing the same dance: Adam doing everything in his power to try to accelerate our relationship to the next level, and me still managing to successfully swerve it. Yet neither of us had directly addressed the problem.

As for Tristan, he'd returned from the hastily arranged golf lesson, scowling. After ten minutes ranting about how bored he'd been, he'd demanded to know why I'd made him go and generally been far more grumpy than I'd ever seen him before. I'd nodded and smiled, somehow managing to hide my amusement under a mask of seriousness, and taken the blame without argument. Then I'd promised to cancel the rest of the lessons and agreed to never *make* him do anything like that again. I'd actually added "against his will," knowing I could slip that in without him noticing. Eventually, I'd pacified him enough to deliver him—on time—to a meeting where he'd suddenly transformed into a professional businessman. It never ceased to amaze me how much he changed when he set foot in front of a conference desk. No wonder Paul had struggled with my use of the word "ditzy" to describe Tristan, if this was the only side he'd ever seen of him.

Tristan's schedule for the rest of the week had been unusually hectic, so I'd barely seen him. For the last thirty-six hours, we'd communicated solely through sticky notes, emails, and texts. It was already eleven o'clock, and I hadn't caught so much as a glimpse of him, which meant it'd been a non-coffee-delivery day. I hated those days.

As if on cue, Tristan walked through the door, collapsing into the chair on the other side of my desk in an over-dramatic parody of complete exhaustion.

He waved a languid arm. "Did you bring lunch, Dominic?"

It figured the first thing on his mind would be food. I sighed before reaching over and rummaging in my desk drawer, ready to sacrifice my sandwich.

Tristan held his hands up in a clear command to stop. "I don't want your lunch. I just asked if you'd brought any." He pulled a flyer out of his pocket, passing it across the desk toward me. Picking it up, I began to read. It advertised the opening week for a new steakhouse a few blocks away, complete with first-week special offers. "Can you book us a table here? I haven't seen you properly for days, and we need to catch up. Plus, I'm starving. I need to eat a decent lunch today."

It was on the tip of my tongue to refuse, but the idea of a break from the office for an hour and having a chat, even if it was with Tristan, was appealing, so I grudgingly agreed. Tristan smiled at the lack of argument, muttered something about a conference call from hell to make, and disappeared through the adjoining door.

"WHERE'S KEVIN?"

I looked up sharply, startled both by the words and the tone of voice. Focused on responding to urgent emails, I hadn't registered anyone had entered the office. Strange, really, when the expensive perfume emanating from the woman standing in front of me was strong enough to make its own announcement. I let my gaze travel up from the dangerously high heels and never-ending, nylon-clad legs, along the tight-fitting designer dress to the glossy hair and bright-red lipstick. It took longer than it should have for my brain to sift through the evidence and come up with a conclusion. This was Maria.

I stood with a smile, my hand outstretched. "You must be Maria. I've heard a lot about you." I hadn't really. I knew more about where Tristan's suits came from than I'd managed to shoehorn out of him about his fiancée. But

I suspected she wouldn't exactly appreciate hearing that. "I'm Dominic. It's really good to meet you."

She didn't return my smile or shake my hand. "Well?"

Right! Her question. I let my hand drop back to my side, making sure to hide how much the deliberate snub irked me. "Kevin left. He had a...emergency health thing, and decided not to return. I'm covering for him temporarily until Tristan finds a replacement."

"Tristan!" She arched a perfectly shaped eyebrow. "Do you mean Mr. Maxwell?"

If only this lady had been present when I'd been so insistent on calling him by his surname, I would have had formidable backup.

I offered another smile, this one far less genuine. "*Tristan* insists I call him by his first name. *Tristan's* my boss, so I do what I'm told. You know what *Tristan* can be like."

Hands on hips, she took a long, hard look. It took a considerable effort to remain unaffected by the scrutiny. Finally, she spoke. "I guess that explains the flowers for my birthday. I thought Kevin was having some sort of breakdown."

A couple of weeks previously, Tristan had asked for jewelry and flowers as a gift for his fiancée. I'd followed his instructions to the letter—if you could call "the flowers have to be pink and expensive" instructions.

"I'm very sorry to hear you didn't like the flowers. What was the problem with them? I'll make a note so it won't happen again." I grabbed a piece of paper and a pen.

"I hate pink flowers!" She screwed her face up in a grimace, obviously traumatized by the memory of the horrendous flowers I'd inflicted upon her. "I thought you said you were temporary."

"I am. But I can make sure my replacement has the relevant information, and then we can avoid any further disappointment. How was the jewelry?" She'd received a bespoke ring with a huge diamond. I'd nearly fallen off my chair at the cost. I could have refurbished my whole apartment for a fraction of the price. She was a seriously lucky woman to have a fiancé willing to spend that amount of money on her.

She shrugged. "Acceptable, I suppose."

I bit back the urge to ask what would have made it more acceptable—more diamonds, delivery with a top-of-the-range Ferrari, delivery on the severed finger of the personal assistant responsible for the flower atrocity?

I kept the smile pasted on my face, unwilling to let her know her hostility had me rattled. "I'll call through and tell Tristan you're here. I know he had a conference call to make, but hopefully he's already finished." I wondered whether he'd been expecting Maria, or if she was just in the habit of dropping by unexpectedly.

Pressing the intercom button, I informed Tristan of Maria's presence in the office. In less than a minute, he was there, greeting his fiancée in front of my desk. I looked away politely as they exchanged a brief kiss. Something clawed at my insides, and I absently wondered which part of breakfast was disagreeing with me.

"Darling, you could have mentioned Kevin was no longer here. Then it wouldn't have come as such a surprise when..." She waved her hand in my direction, making it abundantly clear she'd forgotten my name. I supplied it again.

"Didn't I mention it?" Tristan looked slightly uneasy. Maybe he hadn't been expecting her? Maybe it was just the lingering effects of the conference call. Or maybe he was starting to suffer the effects of perfume poisoning, I thought maliciously.

She tucked her arm through his, wrapping a possessive hand around his biceps. "No, you didn't. Or clearly I would have known. Poor Kevin! I always liked Kevin. You should have told me, darling."

I'd been right when I'd envisioned how beautiful they would look together. The towering high heels brought her almost to the same height as Tristan, and their coloring was perfectly complementary. If I'd had a drink, I would have pulled an impromptu toast to the model couple. I didn't think the effect would be quite the same from a water bottle, so I settled for simply taking a drink from it instead.

"So where are you taking me, darling?"

"Taking you?" Tristan's confusion was clear. It didn't take a genius to work out the situation. She *was* expected. However, Tristan had either forgotten or had simply been too busy to process the day or time properly. Un fortunately, he hadn't bothered to let me know, so therefore I hadn't been able to do my usual job of reminding him.

"You didn't forget about me, did you?" She batted her eyelashes at him in an impeccable impression of a hurt damsel in distress. I wanted to vomit.

Tristan looked completely crestfallen. "I...I—"

I interjected, directing my initial comment to Maria. "He's such a tease, isn't he? Tristan, you know full well you asked me to make lunchtime restaurant bookings for the two of you. Don't wind your poor fiancée up when she's arrived looking so gorgeous." Maria visibly preened at my words. That's where I'd gone wrong: I was obviously meant to be in awe of her beauty and fawn over her.

Tristan shot a strange, undecipherable look my way. It didn't look much like the gratitude I would have expected from him.

"Now run along, the two of you. Have a lovely lunch. Don't feel the need to rush back, Tristan. I'll hold the fort." I shooed them away, relieved when they left, and I was finally able to lose the forced smile that felt like it had been plastered on my face for hours. The peculiar feeling still gnawed at my stomach. I made a mental note to pick up indigestion tablets on the way home.

Tristan obviously took me at my word. He not only didn't rush back, he hadn't returned by the time I left the office for the day.

I SPRAWLED ACROSS THE sofa listlessly, trying to concentrate on a documentary about penguins. I picked up my phone as it chimed to announce a message.

Adam: *How was your day?*

I hadn't seen him all day. As neither one of us had made a special effort to seek the other one out, this was the first contact we'd had since the previous day.

Dominic: *Good. Yours?*

Adam: *Pretty boring. Fancy coming round and making it a bit more interesting?*

I rolled my eyes. The message was predictable. If I tallied up the amount of times he'd tried to get me back to his in the short amount of time our relationship had been going on, it would definitely already be into double figures. I could probably suggest going out somewhere. But could I be bothered? It would mean getting changed and either using public transport to get there or wasting money on a cab.

Adam: *Or I can come round to yours. Save you the journey. I still haven't seen your apartment.*

I shook my head as I read the message. No way that was happening. I was funny enough at the best of times about inviting boyfriends into my personal space. No way I was going to spend an evening fighting Adam off in the comfort of my own home. Deciding I really didn't have the energy to go out, I cast around for a suitably convincing excuse. While I was still contemplating it, my phone chimed again. Had Adam changed his mind?

Tristan: *Thank you for attempting to dig me out of a big hole today. It was very sweet.*

Dominic: *I AM NOT sweet! Don't you dare tell anyone that, or even suggest such a thing.*

Dominic: *I just wanted to get rid of you for the afternoon.*

Dominic: *My plan worked.*

Dominic: *What do you mean attempting? Wasn't Maria happy?*

Tristan: *It wasn't her sort of place.*

There was a gap of a couple of minutes before the next message arrived.

Tristan: *I chose it knowing you'd like it.*

Dominic: *Was it that down-market? What...sticky tables, mismatched cutlery? That sort of thing? :D*

Tristan: *Hardly. We'll go some time. You'll like the food. And it's got a nice atmosphere.*

Adam: *Or we could meet somewhere? If you fancy going out?*

Right! Adam! I still hadn't replied to him. I was meant to be thinking of a reason I couldn't see him tonight.

Tristan: *What are you up to this evening? Anything exciting?*

Dominic: *Watching a penguin documentary in sweatpants and eating ice cream.*

Maybe it was meeting his glamorous fiancée, but I was suddenly incredibly unwilling to admit my life was that mundane. I deleted the last message without sending it.

Dominic: *I'm meeting Adam.*

Adam: *Strange way to agree! But I'll take it. Where do you want to go?*

Shit! I'd sent it to the wrong person. Now I had no choice but to meet Adam. I'd have to forever remain in ignorance about the fate of the penguin cruelly shunned by the rest of the group. Careful to get the right person this time, I sent the same message to Tristan.

Tristan: *Have fun. I'll see you tomorrow. I've got meetings scheduled until 14:00 but I'll see you after that.*

Dominic: *Why are you telling the person who sets your schedule, confirms your schedule, and reminds you about your schedule, what your schedule is?*

Tristan: *In case I was wrong. I was hoping you'd say my meetings are over by 12.*

Dominic: *Sorry, it's definitely 14:00. You were right for once. Wonders never cease!*

Tristan: *It had to happen eventually :)*

Dominic: *I have to go. I need to make myself look pretty for Adam.*

There was such a long gap before Tristan's next reply, I'd changed, sorted out a venue with Adam, and assumed Tristan wasn't going to bother.

Tristan: *You always look great. Have a great evening. X*

Tristan: *I meant to put an X that time. Just so you know.*

I hoped he wasn't expecting me to respond in kind. No way was I comfortable sending kisses to my boss, even if it was just a text version.

Dominic: *Thanks. You too.*

Chapter Sixteen

Quarter past two. I had to stop looking at the bloody clock. I wasn't usually so conscious of time passing, or rather not passing in the case of today. I didn't know what the hell was wrong with me. It wasn't as if I didn't have enough work to do, I had plenty. Sighing, I responded to a few more emails before inevitably checking the time again. Half past two. At this rate, it would seem like forever until five o'clock finally rolled around. Funny that I hadn't seen Tristan, when his last meeting should have finished thirty minutes ago. Not that that had anything to do with my seeming obsession with time. Resolving to avoid clock-watching, I concentrated on clearing my workload. I lasted until three before realizing I was watching the second-hand tick around.

At a quarter past three, an unusually stressed-looking Tristan passed my desk with a perfunctory wave and brief greeting before disappearing straight into his office, with the door firmly closed. I toyed with the idea of using the intercom to check if he was okay but decided against it; I was his personal assistant, not his mother.

It was another very slow half hour before his next appearance. He dropped straight into the spare chair and leaned forward, elbows braced on the table. "So...Dominic! How are you?"

I stopped what I was doing, taking a moment to scrutinize him. He looked tired. "How am I? How are you? You seemed stressed before."

Tristan aimed a long, searching look my way. "Is that genuine concern?"

I leaned forward, mirroring his position. "Of course. If you drop dead, I'll probably have to sort out the funeral. I've got enough to do as it is. How were your meetings?"

"Long...and tedious. And all I got to eat was a tiny sandwich." He held his thumb and forefinger up to demonstrate the supposed size of the sandwich. I sincerely doubted it had been quite that microscopic. Opening my desk drawer, I rifled through it, pulling out a chocolate bar and flinging it in his direction. Catching it one-handed, he wasted absolutely no time ripping the wrapper open and devouring it.

I shook my head in mock disgust. "I have no idea how Maria puts up with you. Never mind why the hell she wants to marry you." Tristan paused momentarily in his enthusiastic destruction of the chocolate, and I got the distinct impression I'd said something wrong. "Anyway, you never answered my question. Is everything okay?"

He nodded, but it was less than convincing. He passed the now empty wrapper back for disposal and then simply stared.

I threw the wrapper in the wastepaper bin less than a meter away from where Tristan sat. Why he was incapable of doing that himself, I had no idea. I was beginning to feel like his maid. "Tristan, I have no more food. So, if you're waiting for me to magic something up, you'll be waiting a long time. You may as well go back to your office."

"I'm fine here." He sat back in his chair, watching me with a strange, contemplative look on his face.

"What? You're just going to sit there and watch me work?"

Another nod. Figuring he'd quickly get bored, I carried through on my threat to work.

Five minutes of blatantly ignoring him didn't produce the desired result. He was still there. Neither of us had uttered a word, but he was still there. It briefly crossed my mind that if Paul and I had been talking, this would have made another great piece of evidence to demonstrate Tristan's weirdness. Then again, discussion of the man would probably only have led to more accusations of harboring secret feelings.

I sighed and lifted my gaze from the computer screen. "Seriously, Tristan, what do you want?"

He shrugged. "Not entirely sure." The glance away betrayed that statement as an obvious lie. "I just don't fancy sitting in my office." That wasn't particularly convincing either.

"Why don't you go home, if you've got nothing urgent to do? Take Maria out."

He pulled a face and changed the subject. "Are you seeing Adam tonight?"

I answered honestly. "The only date I've got tonight is with my sofa, a season-three *Game of Thrones* box set, and an extra-large pizza."

He smiled. "Sounds good. I'll bring the pizza."

I stared at him, replaying his words. They came out exactly the same. "Did you just invite yourself round to gate-crash my lazy evening?"

The smile faltered, and he looked suddenly sheepish. "Maybe...well, yes but..."

There was definitely something strange going on with him today. I couldn't quite put my finger on what it was: an air of...sadness? Loneliness? Vulnerability? Whatever it was, was I really going to stick the knife in by turning him down rather than attempting to make him feel better? "Fine. Come around at seven. Bring two extra-large pizzas, neither with anchovies. Oh, and some beer. Bring beer."

Tristan jumped up, looking much happier than he had a few minutes before. "Beer. Pizza. Got it. Anything else?"

I shook my head wearily, wondering just what kind of evening I'd let myself in for.

EVEN THOUGH I WAS EXPECTING him, I still didn't feel mentally prepared for the sight of Tristan outside my door clutching two large pizza boxes, beer, and seasons one and two of *Game of Thrones* on DVD.

I frowned. "I've seen those. I said I was watching season three."

Beaming from ear to ear, he shouldered his way through the door without waiting for an invitation. "I didn't know whether you'd be prepared to run through all the characters and give me all their backstories, so I thought we could start from the beginning."

I gave him a dirty look, but he was far too busy gazing curiously around the living room of my apartment to notice. While he was distracted, I took the opportunity to scrutinize him, letting my gaze travel quickly over the long, jeans-clad legs, which showed off his ass to perfection, and up to the plain white T-shirt covered by an expensive brown leather jacket. He swiveled and shoved the pizza boxes into my arms before shrugging the jacket off. I congratulated myself on barely noticing the now uncovered forearms.

Tristan threw his jacket over a nearby chair. "I love your apartment!"

Turning in a slow circle, I tried to see it from Tristan's point of view. I imagined wherever he lived was a lot bigger, a lot grander, a lot better decorated, yet I knew him well enough to know he wasn't just saying it. "Really. Why?"

Tristan walked over to the sofa, picking up a cushion and examining the large rabbit emblazoned across the front. "It's so homey. Mine's just..." He seemed to be searching for the right description. "I don't know. It's like a show home; it's got no character."

I smiled at his crestfallen expression. "You have to make a place homey, Tristan. You know, add stuff, cushions, curtains, plants, that sort of thing. I'm sure..." I'd been going to say I was sure Maria would take care of that once they were married, but having met the woman, I wasn't too sure domesticity came high up on her list of priorities. I was probably being unfair. After all, I'd only met her once, for five minutes. I was probably judging her harshly just because she was a model. The mention of Maria hadn't elicited a positive response before, so bringing her name up again didn't seem conducive to keeping Tristan out of the strange funk he'd been in earlier. I was assuming they'd had some sort of disagreement. It seemed to be the logical explanation.

Tristan placed the cushion gently back on the sofa. "I don't think I'm very good at that. I need..."

Whatever the end of the sentence was, it was lost as he wandered out of the living room. I assumed he was taking a look at the rest of the apartment. I wasn't sure how I felt about him roaming around my bedroom.

Tempted to follow him to keep an eye on what he was doing, I busied myself with putting the beer in the fridge. I left two bottles out, opening them both before loading up the first season one DVD in the player. There was no way I could cope with Tristan asking question after question, if I did indeed start him at season three. I'd end up killing him.

Checking the pizzas, I was relieved to find they were both anchovy free. Either Tristan had actually listened or, more likely, didn't like anchovies himself. Seating myself on the sofa, I waited patiently. After five minutes, my patience was waning. The apartment was silent. What the hell was he doing? I called his name. The muffled reply came from the bedroom.

"Tristan, what are you doing?"

"Just looking."

"Looking at what?"

"Things?"

"What things?"

He appeared in the doorway. "Did you miss me?"

I rolled my eyes and passed him a beer, gesturing for him to sit on the vacant end of the sofa. He sprawled across it, leaning forward to grab a slice of pizza. I started the DVD, resigned to watch episode after episode I'd already seen.

Halfway through the first episode, I caught Tristan staring. "What?"

"So, this is your favorite show, right?"

I shrugged. "One of them. Why?"

He smirked. "I had no idea you were such a bloodthirsty pervert."

I threw a cushion at him. He ducked it successfully, and it sailed over his head, hitting the bookcase on the far side of the room. Laughing, he went to retrieve it. "I mean...if you weren't gay, I'd think it was just an excuse to look at naked breasts."

"Well, if you don't like it, you know where the door is."

He plonked himself back down, hugging the cushion to his body. "No. It's fine. How many seasons are there?"

At some point, he'd taken his shoes and socks off. Talk about making himself at home. I stared at his bare toes while I answered. "Six."

He flashed a smile. "I better concentrate, then. We've got a lot of episodes to get through."

Was he insinuating we were going to watch them all together? Like it was going to become *our thing*? I wasn't sure how else to interpret the comment. My phone chimed halfway through the second episode.

Paul: *How long are we going to avoid each other for? I miss you. I've got no one to talk to at work. No one that's not incredibly irritating, anyway.*

I smiled at the message, relieved he'd been the first to break the silence. Putting my phone on silent, I typed a quick reply.

Dominic: *I miss you too. We should just forget about it. Agree to disagree?*

Paul: *I'm sorry I said you had a crush on Tristan. I should have just accepted your word you didn't. You two just seem to get on really well. Better than a boss/employee normally would. But I obviously read too much into it.*

At the mention of his name, I cast a surreptitious glance across at my houseguest. He seemed engrossed in the action on the screen. His previously slicked-back hair had lost the battle against whatever hair gel had been keeping it in place. I flexed my fingers, resisting the temptation to lean over and brush it out of his eyes.

Dominic: *We get on okay, I suppose. When he's not being incredibly irritating. Which is most of the time.*

Paul: *Anyway, it was unfair. It's both of you, not just you. Maybe I should accuse Tristan of having a crush on you—lol*

Dominic: *That's*

I didn't finish the message, as my phone was unceremoniously yanked out of my hand by a grinning Tristan. "Let's have a look. You're obviously having a fascinating conversation."

Given the subject matter, I immediately panicked at the possibility of Tristan reading it. If he even glanced at it, he'd be sure to notice his name, and then who could blame him for reading the rest of the message? I lunged across the sofa, attempting to snatch my phone back. Tristan moved away too quickly, holding it in the air, just out of reach. "Give it back!"

Tristan shook his head. "No. I want to see what's so interesting."

"DO NOT read my messages!"

He laughed. "You see, now you're so adamant I can't read it, you've got my imagination going into overdrive. Now, I have to read it."

I put every ounce of conviction I could into my voice. "If you read my messages, I promise you, you will have *no* personal assistant from tomorrow. I don't care if you don't have anyone to replace me. Now give me the phone!"

Tristan simply stared for a minute. Perhaps he was trying to judge how serious my threats were. I met his gaze head-on, ensuring my expression said extremely bloody serious. He tossed the phone over. I caught it.

He shrugged. "I didn't particularly want to read phone sex between you and Adam, anyway."

So, that was the conclusion he'd come to. I checked the phone.

Paul: *What does that mean?*

Paul: *You keep sending me gibberish.*

Paul: *Dominic? What's going on? Are you ok?*

During the brief tussle, Tristan had apparently managed to press a few random keys, as well as the send button—twice.

Dominic: *Sorry. I had a bit of a problem with my phone. It's sorted now.*

I could feel Tristan's gaze on me. I refused to acknowledge it. I wondered how happy he'd be if I took *his* phone and threatened to read his messages.

Paul: *Glad we're talking again. I'll keep my mouth shut from now on. You're going to the Xmas party next week, right?*

Dominic: *Sure. Even though it's stupidly early. Free drinks. Free food. I'll put up with the company for that.*

Paul: *I was going to say we can hang out together. But you'll probably be with Adam ;)*

Dominic: *I'll find five minutes free for you.*

Paul: *Xx*

Dominic: *Xx*

I placed my phone on the table near the sofa. "I wasn't messaging Adam." I had no idea why I felt the need to correct Tristan's assumption. "And it wasn't sex stuff. It was just...personal."

Tristan smiled. "I should hope it wasn't sex stuff, if it wasn't Adam."

I didn't respond and we returned to watching the TV show in companionable silence. There were several moments over the rest of the evening when I could sense Tristan's gaze on me. I put it down to him trying to puzzle out why I'd flipped when he'd taken my phone. As soon as I glanced over, he looked away. When we both started yawning, we called it a night.

Chapter Seventeen

Mid-morning, I was surprised by the arrival of Kevin. He strolled in with a bright smile, looking a million times better than the last time I'd seen him in the hospital. I returned the smile, genuinely pleased to see him. "It's good to see you on your feet. I thought you'd be halfway to Australia by now."

"Not yet." He sighed. "I had to wait for clearance from the doctor. Plus, you know, there's a lot to sort out before we can go." He grimaced. "Packing and stuff. We've got things we need to put in storage. There's not a lot you can take with you when you're moving halfway across the world." He paused by the edge of the desk, fiddling with a pen. "I didn't expect you to still be here. You made it clear you were only going to be temporary."

"I am."

He raised an eyebrow. "How many weeks has it been now? Doesn't seem that temporary to me. If you were adamant you weren't staying, which you seemed to be when we spoke before, you could have easily found a replacement by now."

I studied him, trying to work out whether he knew more than he was letting on. For all I knew, he and Tristan spoke regularly. "You think I haven't tried?"

He shrugged. "So, what's the problem?"

"What's the problem?" I cast a pointed glare toward Tristan's office door. He wasn't even in there, so it really was wasted. "Mr. Picky, that's what the problem is."

Kevin looked perplexed. "Tristan—picky? Really? That doesn't sound like him."

The only response I could give was a shrug. Kevin seized on the opportunity to change the subject. "I've just come to pack up my personal things." He scanned the desk, frowning when he saw no evidence of any of his belongings. I reached behind the desk, bending over to lift a cardboard box from the floor. I passed it over to Kevin. "I already packed for you. I was going to have it posted to Australia if you didn't find time to come in."

He took it off me, placing it on the floor at his feet. "Dominic, you're so organized! Thanks. Is Tristan around? I was hoping to say a proper goodbye to him."

I shook my head. "He's at a meeting in the conference room till eleven."

Kevin checked his watch. "I'll wait around for half an hour, if that's all right with you."

I gestured toward the empty chair. "You might as well. I'm getting used to having someone sitting there watching me. How did you put up with that?"

Kevin leaned forward, a quizzical expression on his face. "What do you mean? Who sits here?"

"Tristan." I waited for the dawn of realization on Kevin's face. It never came. "He must have done it with you?"

"Done what?"

I sighed. It had happened every day for the last week. I'd assumed it was just a Tristan thing. Now, it seemed like it was a new thing. I was suddenly reticent to put it into words, but Kevin's expectant stare as he sat and waited for an explanation left very little choice. "He...you know, when he's finished his work. You know how super-efficient he can be sometimes. He comes and sits here, where you're sitting now   "

Kevin leaned even farther forward. "And does what?"

"Just sits there and watches. Chats sometimes. I have to try and ignore him so I can get work done. He never did that with you?" I was fairly sure of the answer, but I asked the question anyway.

Kevin's expression turned thoughtful, as if he was running back through past events. "No. Never. I would have found that really weird. What's that about? Does he not trust you?"

Shrugging, I made a concerted effort to change the subject. "Are you staying for the super-early Christmas party tonight?"

Kevin relaxed back into the chair, laughing. "I noticed that. Who has a Christmas party on the first of December? It's not normally that early. I wish I could come, but unfortunately it's my mum's birthday today. She's already upset I'm deserting her to go to Australia. No way will she forgive me if I miss it for a works do. It would have made for a great opportunity to say goodbye to everyone." He took a long, lingering look around the office. "I'm really going to miss this place and the people."

Determined to keep the subject firmly away from Tristan, I spent the next twenty minutes asking Kevin questions about Australia.

I WAS AN HOUR LATE arriving to the Christmas party. Tristan had tried everything to get me to accompany him earlier: bribery, blackmail, and of course the obligatory pouting. I'd steadfastly resisted, listing all the things I still needed to do. They could have waited, but arriving *with* the boss just felt all sorts of wrong. Eventually, he'd realized he was fighting a losing battle. He'd given up, extracting a promise I would definitely show, before leaving me to it. The venue, a restaurant a few blocks away, had been specially booked for the occasion. I could only assume, seeing as no one seemed to know, that was the reason for the early date. Knowing it would take less than ten minutes to walk there, I didn't bother rushing.

Paul's amusing texts throughout the day had kept me entertained. They'd mainly speculated on whose behavior this year would provide the major talking point. The previous year hadn't disappointed, when Beth from Accounts had gotten horrifically drunk, stumbled against an artfully arranged pyramid of champagne flutes, and sent the whole lot crashing to the ground. She'd never lived it down.

I'd also spent a lot of the day contemplating what to do about Adam. It was clear our relationship was going nowhere. I liked him, but more as a friend. I wasn't desperate to go to bed with him. He didn't make my heart beat faster or give me butterflies. I was basically stringing him along, which wasn't fair to him. He'd done nothing wrong, apart from being a little too pushy. I'd decided to talk to him at the party, explain my feelings, and we could both go our separate ways with no real harm done.

I'd barely taken two steps into the restaurant when Tristan appeared out of nowhere, effectively blocking my path. I took a step sideways, intending to go around him. He mirrored the move, placing himself back in front. I couldn't even see the damn restaurant, never mind walk farther into it.

I glared at him. "Tristan, can you move? I've only just got here. I want a drink." I tried a step in the opposite direction. Again, he moved, preventing any forward progress, an intense look of concern on his face.

"Don't look over there."

"Over where?"

I craned my neck in an attempt to peer around him.

Tristan hissed at me. "I said don't look!"

"Why?"

"Because."

I stared at him. He stared resolutely back without speaking. "Well, with a good reason like that, how could I possibly argue?"

I waited, but no further explanation came. It was obvious he was trying to prevent me from seeing something. But I had no idea what.

"So we're just going to stand here all night, are we?"

He shrugged.

"Or you could get out of the way, and I could find out what the problem is." I tried an experimental shove of Tristan's shoulder. If I couldn't go around him, through was the only option. He remained firmly in place. "Seriously, Tristan. I don't know what the issue is, but we can't stand in the doorway all night. Move!"

He finally stepped aside. "Don't say I didn't warn you."

Now I could see it, I scanned the restaurant, trying to work out what the hell had caused Tristan's strange behavior this time. Beth stood quietly in a corner, clutching what could only be a soft drink. The poor girl obviously didn't want to run the risk of repeating last year's mistake. I could hardly blame her. It had taken months for the gossip to die down. Talk of this year's Christmas party had predictably re-ignited it all over again. She'd have had to be deaf not to have heard it.

Paul was over by the bar, waiting to be served, chatting to a leggy blonde woman I didn't recognize. Even from this distance, I could spot her flirting. I wondered how long it would take her to work out Paul was gay and she was wasting her time. Knowing Paul, he wouldn't bother to tell her. He liked the attention.

Nothing rang any alarm bells yet. I continued to study the busy room. At the farthest point of the room, some guy had obviously gotten lucky early in the evening and was making out enthusiastically with his conquest against the wall. It wouldn't be a Christmas party without a bit of inter-departmental bonding.

John Stone sat grumpily in a corner. I smiled at the familiar sight of my old boss, immediately reprimanding myself for thinking of him as my old boss rather than my current one. I'd go over and talk to him later. It would be nice to catch up.

I began to consider that perhaps this time, Tristan really was losing it. He stood directly next to me, his shoulder brushing mine. I could feel the tension emanating from his body. I scanned again. I'd obviously missed something. Paul now had his drink but was still deep in conversation with the same woman. A group of people, who I knew vaguely, kept throwing expectant looks between myself and the pair making out against the wall. I let my gaze return to them, suddenly recognizing the familiar back of the head. "Oh, that's...Adam. Who's...who is—"

My comment wasn't directed at anyone in particular, but Tristan responded anyway. "New guy from IT. I think his name is Jim. Or Ben. Or Lon. Something with three letters, anyway."

I nodded, as if the name of the man who currently had his tongue down the throat of the guy everyone knew I'd been seeing was of key importance.

"Do you want me to punch him?"

I swung round to look at Tristan. He looked deadly serious.

"No. I just..." I didn't know what to do with myself. What were people expecting me to do? Was I meant to storm over there, detach Adam from the other man's face, and berate him publicly? Was *I* meant to punch him? Punch the other guy? Was I meant to pretend I hadn't noticed? Get myself a drink and avoid looking in their direction? I simply stood there. No matter what I'd decided about bringing the relationship to an end, in everyone else's eyes, we were an item. "I think I'm just...going to leave."

One good thing about the close proximity to the door was it only took a few steps to be back outside. Taking a deep lungful of fresh air, I tried to work out the best route home. It took a moment to register Tristan had followed. I attempted a smile. "I'm fine. Go back to the party."

Ignoring my assurances, Tristan took my arm and steered me across to a nearby car. "I'll take you home. We'll get beer and pizza on the way. No, something stronger. We'll get some whisky."

I got in the car, absently noting it was a very expensive-looking BMW. The driver's seat creaked as Tristan got in. "I don't need whisky. Honestly, I'm fine. I'm just a bit pissed off he's got the nerve to do that in front of all our work colleagues. I'm going to be the subject of the gossip for the next few weeks. Unless you can get Beth to take another swan dive into a stack of glasses. She might take some convincing though. She looked like she was drinking orange juice. You might need to spike it...and then give her a push. And probably create a stack of glasses, seeing as I didn't see one. Actually, I'm disappointed, Tristan. What happened to the penis ice sculpture? That would have been a perfect opportunity. Unless you really are saving it for your wedding. I—"

Realizing I was rambling to cover my embarrassment, I stopped talking abruptly, glancing over at Tristan. The set of his jaw while he navigated the car away from the curb was a dead giveaway that he was angry.

"Are you annoyed at me? I told you, you didn't need to leave the party. Just drop me off here." I began to fumble at my seatbelt. "And I'll get a cab and—"

Tristan reached over, folding his hand over mine and preventing me from undoing the seatbelt. "Why would I be annoyed at you? I'm annoyed at Adam for being such a shit!"

I relaxed slightly, relieved the anger wasn't aimed at me. "Would you really have punched him if I asked?"

"Yes." There was a long pause. "I'm glad you didn't take me up on the offer though. His face looked hard. I probably would have hurt my hand. And then there's the fact I've never punched anyone before. I probably would have made a complete fool of myself."

"There's also the fact I don't think you're meant to go around punching your employees."

Tristan smiled. "Probably not. And as for the gossip, I wouldn't worry. The only person who's going to come out of this looking bad is Adam."

I leaned my head back against the comfortable seat. The car still smelled new. It must have been a recent acquisition. "Doesn't mean I'm happy to have people talking about me."

"Ignore them." Tristan slowed the car before pulling over in front of a pizza restaurant. He got out before I could protest. "Wait here. I won't be long."

As soon as he'd gone, I closed my eyes, only opening them again at the sound of the car door opening. Tristan was clutching a couple of pizza boxes, beer, *and* a bottle of whisky. "Tristan, you need to go back to the party. You're the boss. You have to be there."

He shrugged, reaching over to to place his stash on the back seat. "Yeah, later. I'm hungry. They only had tiny canapes at the party. We're going to go back to yours and eat pizza first."

"What about the alcohol? You need to be able to drive yourself back to the party."

"I'll get a cab. Stop worrying."

I did as ordered and sat back, attempting to avoid thinking about Adam or the party during the drive back to my apartment.

Chapter Eighteen

Tristan was already halfway through his second bottle of beer, the first having been consumed in a matter of swallows. He probably needed it to wash down the huge quantity of pizza he'd devoured. In contrast, I'd barely scratched the surface of my first one. It had seemed churlish to refuse after it had already been opened and handed to me. Plus, there was concern that rejection of the beer would have meant having whisky foisted on me as an alternative. It was definitely the lesser of two evils. I took another sip. I lounged at one end of the sofa with Tristan at the other. Unusually for him, he was silent. He was probably calculating his best option for making a quick escape, now he'd eaten. I picked up my phone. "I'll call you a cab so you can get back to the party."

Tristan shook his head emphatically. "Not yet."

I paused, my finger hovering over the button to connect the call to a local cab firm. "Are you sure? I promise you I'm absolutely fine. You don't have to stay."

Tristan turned his head sideways and gave me a long searching look. "Are you going to give him another chance?"

"Adam?"

He nodded.

I placed my phone back on the table, leaving the call unmade. I was reticent to admit just what a non-relationship I'd actually had with Adam. "You think I'd give a guy who embarrassed me in front of our mutual work colleagues another chance?"

Tristan shrugged. "Maybe. If you...cared enough about him." He'd turned away again, and seemed intent on peeling every strip of label from his now nearly empty beer bottle. I watched as a piece floated slowly to the carpet. Lacking the energy to kick up a fuss about the mess, I refrained from commenting on it.

Suddenly, it all clicked into place. "I get it!"

My sudden exclamation wrested his attention back from the beer bottle. "Yeah. Do you?"

I nodded, smug in the knowledge I'd worked him out. "This was your first matchmaking attempt, so you don't want it to fail." I waved a finger at him. "You want to convince me to give Adam another chance. That way I can't claim your matchmaking skills are rubbish."

Tristan shuffled closer along the sofa, shaking his head and frowning. "No. That's not it at all. He doesn't deserve you. He..." He stopped, seeming to catch himself. "Of course, it's your decision. Your feelings."

For some reason, Tristan looked more miserable than I felt. Maybe he was feeling guilty for pushing us together in the first place. "It was hardly the romance of the century."

Tristan shuffled closer still, a strange, unreadable expression on his face. "Really? I thought you were getting on well."

"We got along fine, but it wasn't..." I trailed off, trying to work out how much I was going to admit.

"Wasn't what?"

"It wasn't really going anywhere."

"But you'd slept together?"

I raised an eyebrow at Tristan's inquiry. "Remind me to start asking personal questions about you and Maria. Oh, shit. Maria! Was she coming tonight? She's going to be pretty pissed if she gets to the party and you're not there. Check your phone. Check you haven't missed a call."

Tristan's gaze didn't leave my face, and he made no move to follow my suggestion. I was used to him acting weird, but this strange level of intensity was a first, even for him. I couldn't work out what was bothering him. He finally responded. "Maria wasn't coming tonight. Office parties aren't really her style."

I'd started to lose count of the number of times Tristan had said that while talking about his fiancée. I was beginning to wonder what in the world was her sort of thing.

Tristan had moved closer. I really should talk to him about personal space. Now he was barely inches away. He was beginning to remind me of those angel statues in *Doctor Who*, the ones that moved as soon as you looked away.

He took a drink of beer. "You haven't answered my question."

"Which question?"

"The one about Adam?"

"Oh, the personal one. Well!" I was caught for a moment between lying completely or telling the truth. I sighed. "No. We hadn't. Nowhere near."

Tristan's expression turned from strangely pained to a look of relief. Neither made sense. I was genuinely concerned. "Tristan, are you okay? You're behaving really weird. Well, weirder than usual tonight. Has something happened?"

He ran a hand through his hair. It disrupted the slicked-back style, causing a few locks to flop across his forehead. "It's not the right time. I know that. I should wait a week...or probably a month, really. No, that's probably too long." He looked at his watch and grimaced. "Definitely longer than a hour though, that's for sure. Even if you weren't really—"

I didn't have a clue what he was talking about. It didn't help that he'd turned away again, so I couldn't read anything from his facial expression. Never mind the fact he was talking in riddles. "Wait for—" I didn't get a chance to finish the question before Tristan swung around, closing the remaining space between us. His lips met mine. I froze, too shocked to react in any way. I just sat there and was kissed.

It wasn't until his hand came up to cup the back of my head at the same time as I felt his tongue make an exploratory foray against the tight seam of my lips that I snapped out of it. I pushed him back, tearing my lips away from his.

"What the fuck, Tristan!" My voice came out in a squeak. I stared at him as if he were an alien. I expected him to look apologetic, or shocked, or a damn sight drunker than he'd appeared five minutes ago. For all I knew, he'd been knocking back shots at the party before I arrived. My subconscious successfully buried the knowledge he'd been completely sober during the drive back here. He looked none of those.

I continued to gawp at him, waiting for some sort of explanation. None was forthcoming. He pressed forward, searching for my lips again. Turning my head to the side in an effort to thwart him meant his lips met my neck instead. He didn't appear to mind, seeming quite content to nibble, nuzzle, and lick his way along its length. I suppressed a shudder of desire. If he knew

I was enjoying this, I'd never get him to stop. Did I want him to stop? Of course I did. I just needed to push him off again, be a lot firmer this time.

I was so lost in thought about what I should be doing that it took a moment to realize Tristan was speaking. The words vibrated against my skin. "I know you were attracted to me before...at the hotel in Brighton. You tried to kiss me. So, I'm hoping—"

I made a half-hearted attempt to push him away, which came to nothing. "I was drunk!"

I felt the smile against my neck. "There's a bottle of whisky in the kitchen. Do you want some? I can get you drunk again, if that's what it takes."

"That's not—" My words were cut off as his teeth scraped sensually against the sensitive skin behind my ear. This time I couldn't hide my sharp intake of breath.

"Oh, that's the spot, is it? I can work with that." For the next few minutes, he was true to his word, using lips, tongue, and teeth to work the sensitive place until I was a quivering mass of jelly. When my head was turned back to center for a kiss, I had no resistance, meeting his tongue enthusiastically with my own. I entwined my hands in Tristan's hair, trying to get closer, working to deepen the kiss. The spark that had been so absent in all my kisses with Adam was most definitely there.

I could hardly believe I was kissing my boss. My straight boss. My *engaged*, straight boss.

"Oh, fuck!" I pushed him off with such force, he almost fell off the sofa. He regained his balance and shot a wounded look in my direction.

"Dominic! There's no need to be so rough."

"You're engaged!" I almost hissed the words at him. He reached for me. I pushed his hands away. "Don't touch me! I don't kiss engaged men. You're getting married in a couple of months."

Tristan reached for his beer bottle, swigging the last couple of swallows. "Ah, about that." He stared off into the distance for a few seconds before swinging his gaze back to mine. "I'm not engaged anymore. I haven't been for a while, actually. So you don't...you know...that's not something you need to worry about."

After a bombshell like that, I expected some sort of elaboration. Eventually, I had to prompt him. "Since when?"

"Erm..." Tristan was trying to bring some semblance of order back to his hair. It resisted any of his efforts to return to being slicked back. After a few attempts, he gave up. I swallowed thickly as I realized it was my hands that had wrought most of the damage. "A few weeks."

"And you didn't bother mentioning it?"

He shrugged and leaned in again. I held him back with a hand on his chest. "Why? Did she end it?"

"No. I did." Tristan covered my hand on his chest with his own, moving it so it lay over his heart.

Feeling the firm beat under my palm, I fought to concentrate. "Why?"

Tristan's heart sped up slightly. "I liked spending time with you more than her."

I laughed, not believing him for one minute. He obviously didn't want to divulge the real reason. Maybe she'd cheated on him.

"So anyway, I'm not engaged in any way—" Tristan's lips hovered nearer. "Shape or—" He kissed my ear. "—form."

I made an effort to squirm away. "You may not be engaged, but you're still straight. I don't kiss straight men either."

"Not that straight. Obviously."

I pulled back and eyed him suspiciously. "You've been with a man before?"

Tristan started to unfasten his tie. "Not yet." He removed it, throwing it carelessly over the back of the sofa. I couldn't see where it landed. Then he started on the buttons of his shirt. "I'm working on it." He started to shrug the shirt off, revealing a tanned, sculpted chest. "But he's proving difficult to convince."

I averted my eyes from his bare chest. "Why are you taking your clothes off?"

"I'm trying to use all my powers of seduction." He finished taking his shirt off, and it went the way of his tie. Bending over, he began to unfasten his shoes.

"What! By getting your forearms out?"

His movements stilled and he paused to look back, quirking an eyebrow in my direction. "My...forearms?" He held them out in front of him, staring down at them in puzzlement. "What about my forearms?"

I glared at him. "Nothing. There's nothing interesting about them. Stop going on about them."

I watched him flick first one shoe across the room, and then quickly follow it with the other.

"Stop messing my apartment up!"

His look held a clear challenge. He slowly unrolled his left sock, throwing it in the opposite direction to where the shoes had gone. My glare intensified as he did the same with the right one. It hit a lamp, dangling precariously and creating an interesting shadow on the wall.

I kept my gaze fixed solely on his face, scared by the temptation of looking anywhere else. "You're not going to take your trousers off, are you?"

He glanced down at the only item of clothing he was still wearing. "Not yet. You can do it later."

I swallowed with difficulty. "I don't want to take your trousers off."

Tristan looked thoughtful. "You might change your mind."

"I won't." I watched him like a hawk, waiting with trepidation to see what he would do next. I still wasn't adequately prepared to stop him when he moved suddenly, grabbing my thighs and pulling me down the sofa. I slid toward the center of it on my back. Before I could recover and maneuver myself back to a sitting position, he came down on top, his weight holding me in place. "What are you doing?"

He gave a long-suffering sigh, like *I* was the one being extremely irritating. "I already told you, seducing you. Now will you just lie still and be...bloody seduced?"

"Why?"

"Why what?"

"Why are you seducing me?"

His hair fell into his eyes as he loomed over me. I stared at the darker blue flecks in his eyes. I'd never been close enough to notice them before. Tristan's gaze held mine. "I like you. A lot."

He shifted, pinning me more firmly in place. It brought his cock into contact with my thigh. Even through his trousers, there was no disguising the fact he was hard. Despite his words and actions, the physical evidence came as a shock. I lifted my hand, brushing the hair back out of his eyes. I figured, given the position we were in, it was stupid to try to resist the temptation.

When my hand dropped back down, it curled around the back of his neck of its own volition. "This is a really bad idea."

Tristan simply stared. "Okay."

I echoed his response. "Okay. So you're going to stop. You're going to get off me and put all your clothes back on."

He shook his head slowly. "No. We can talk about it being a bad idea tomorrow."

"But—" I never got to finish my latest protest before his lips covered mine again.

It suddenly became difficult to remember all the reasons I should be pushing him

off. I gave up thinking about it.

Chapter Nineteen

Somehow, and I still wasn't exactly sure how, I found myself lying naked across the bed. Tristan had been right; I had changed my mind about removing his trousers. As a result, I had an equally naked Tristan draped across me, his chin resting on my hip as he stared intently at my erect cock. "You were right. Your hair's that color naturally."

"I know. I told you that."

"I like your hair."

"Thanks. I think."

"I mean the hair on your head, not...not that there's anything wrong with... You know what I mean."

There was a long pause while he continued his scrutiny. I shifted restlessly, conscious of a cool draft from the open window ghosting across my naked body. My movement seemed to shock him back into speech.

"Does it come with instructions?"

Subconsciously, I'd been waiting for this: the moment where he came to his senses and realized what he was doing. Probably quickly followed by a freak-out and a quick exit, not necessarily in that order. I was surprised it hadn't happened earlier during our extended kissing and groping session in the living room. But no matter what I'd touched, caressed, or licked—and there had certainly been a lot of places—he'd seemed completely at ease. It had been his suggestion to move to the bedroom. His insistence I got naked. But I guess you couldn't pretend anymore once you were faced with the unequivocal proof you were indeed with a man.

"Forget it." I reached for the sheet, intending to pull it over and cover myself.

Tristan frowned, his hand shooting out to stop me. "Hey! Don't be like that. I'm allowed to worry about getting it right, aren't I? I don't want to mess up."

"You've got one yourself, you know. Just do what *you* like. I'm sure I can't be that different."

Tristan didn't respond, his gaze still fixed on my throbbing erection. I was beginning to feel like some sort of freakish art exhibit. I brought my arm up, intending to take matters into my own hands, quite literally. I'd barely made contact before Tristan grabbed my wrist, pinning my arm onto the mattress. "Oh, no you don't."

"Well, excuse me! I was getting bored, lying here with nothing happening."

I brought my opposite hand up, knowing full well what would happen even before it met the same treatment as the first one.

I smirked up at Tristan, flexing my arms half-heartedly to test how firm his grip was. The answer was pretty damn firm. He wasn't letting go anytime soon. "Now what are you going to do? You've got no hands left."

Leaning over me, he quirked an eyebrow. "If you want me to blow you, you just need to ask. We don't need to go through all this elaborate role play to get there."

My cock twitched at the thought. Would he? He'd obviously never done it before. Would he chicken out? Where the hell were we even going with this? I should tell him to use his hand. A hand job would be fine, and I had a greater chance of him seeing it through to completion. I stared up at him, thoughts and doubts whirring chaotically in my brain. Tristan licked his lips. I wasn't sure whether the gesture was intentional or not, but I suddenly wanted nothing more than to feel those lips and that tongue on my cock, even if it was only for a few short moments. Then I'd let him use his hand. "I want you to suck my cock."

I watched him closely. He simply nodded. His face didn't alter expression. If there'd been a trace of anything resembling doubt, I would have relented. He kept a tight hold on my wrists as he leaned forward. I held my breath, waiting expectantly to see what he was going to do. He stopped, barely an inch away from contact.

"Biting's out, right?" He chuckled at the sudden panicked expression on my face.

I bucked, making a determined effort to release my arms, but he was far too strong. "You're not funny."

He hung his head, still laughing. "Sorry. I couldn't resist it. Your face was a picture." He coughed. "Right. Back to the serious business." He leaned in again. When his tongue darted out, touching the tip of my cock, I wasn't sure what affected me the most: the sight or the feel. I squirmed, unsure whether I was fighting to get closer or to move farther away. My reaction seemed to bolster his confidence, and he moved in for another taste.

Before long, he'd worked himself up to licking from base to tip. I closed my eyes, content to simply feel as his tongue went to work. His lips finally closed around the shaft, taking it in. I groaned as he took more, feeling the sensitive tip of my cock nudge the back of his throat. Suddenly there was nothing but air on my erection, and Tristan was choking. I tried not to laugh, I really did, but I lost the battle.

The coughing fit meant Tristan had let go of his grip on my wrists. I took advantage of the freedom of my hands to wipe away the tears streaming down Tristan's face. I waited while he regained his composure. He collapsed next to me on the bed. "Sorry. That went much better in my head. I thought it'd be easier."

I swiveled my head to meet his gaze. "It was good, you know, right up until the choking part. I'll admit that's not the sexiest thing I've ever seen. That was probably karma for the biting comment, you realize that?"

"Probably. Maybe I'll leave blow jobs for now." He rolled closer, exploring my chest with a sure but delicate touch, his lips meeting mine.

As our tongues dueled, he reached down, wrapping his hand around my cock and beginning a firm stroke. I thrust into the tight grip, content to get off that way. I figured I'd return the favor, or maybe blow him. I could show him how it was meant to be done. I moaned, my orgasm creeping closer. Gripping his neck, I crushed our lips together, encouraging him to pick up the pace. My balls drew tight, and I was seconds away from coming, when he suddenly halted and pulled back, staring at me intently.

I panted, frustrated I'd come so close and then been denied at the last moment. Was this some sort of twisted game he was playing? "Tristan, I really need to come." I made a grab for his hand, pulling it back onto my throbbing cock. He let me, but didn't pick up the movement again. "Tristan?"

"Have you got condoms? Where are they?"

I stared at him, gauging the seriousness of his question. "Condoms? Yes. But...it doesn't matter where they are. We're not going to be needing them. We're not. That's not happening."

Tristan rolled me under him, his stiff cock throbbing against my own. "Of course not. But let's say we were. Which we're not...obviously, but if we were, and we did need them, where would they be?"

My glance towards the nightstand gave away their location without words. He made no move toward it, but I still wanted to clarify anyway. "We're not doing that. That would be a very bad idea."

He began to grind his erection against my hip. "You keep saying that. Who are you trying to convince? Me or yourself?"

"You don't want to fuck me. Not really."

Latching onto the sensitive spot behind my ear again, he whispered straight into my ear, his voice husky with arousal. "Of course not. Why would I want to be inside you? Why would I want to find out what that feels like? Why would I want to see what you look like when you get fucked? I can't think of anything worse." He pulled back, looking me straight in the eye, his gaze roving hungrily over my body. I suddenly felt like the most attractive man alive simply from the way he was looking at me. He smirked. "No. I'm lying. I really, really want that. What can I do to persuade you? I could suck your cock again. I promise I'll do a better job this time. Just tell me what you want."

Stunned by his words, I kept silent while I scrutinized him. His body really was perfection, each muscle perfectly defined. He obviously hadn't been joking when he said he spent a lot of time at the gym. My gaze dropped lower, lingering on his thick cock. No doubt it would feel fantastic inside me. "You really want to fuck me?"

He gave a tight nod, his hands ghosting over my ass.

I reached over, pulling the drawer on the nightstand open and withdrawing a condom and lube. He gave a sharp intake of breath as I passed them to him. I rolled face down, head buried in the pillow, throbbing erection pressed into the bed below. "Just so you know, if you ask me for instructions, I *will* change my mind."

"I'll work it out. It can't be that different."

I lay there listening to the rustle of the condom wrapper. "Use lots of lube and take it slow."

He covered my back with his body until I could feel the length of his latex-covered cock throbbing against my ass. "I thought you weren't giving instructions."

I squirmed back against him, suddenly really damn eager to have him inside me. "I said you couldn't *ask* for instructions. I'm telling you things that are an absolute must-know."

He wrapped himself around me, his body covering mine from head to foot. He nuzzled my neck. "I see. So I can't ask if I need to use my fingers first? I don't want to hurt you. I've done some research but—"

I turned my head sideways on the pillow in an effort to meet his gaze. I'd intended to ask what kind of research he'd done, and more importantly why the hell he'd been looking up anal sex. But all thoughts abruptly fled from my head as I felt his cock graze my asshole. "No fingers. Just slow." I turned back to the pillow and concentrated on relaxing and taking deep breaths.

Even relaxed, the sting was considerable as he breached me in one move. His idea of slow and my idea were obviously two completely different things. At the feel of my body stiffening, and the gasp I hadn't been able to hold back, he halted. "Sorry. I—"

Panicked he might be about to withdraw as quickly as he'd entered, I hissed out another instruction. "Just don't move!"

His body stilled immediately, his cock fully embedded. At least I knew he was listening.

"What did I do wrong?"

"Too fast."

"Sorry. I thought that was slow. God! You feel good. How long do I have to wait? I'm not sure I can wait, you feel too good. So tight, so hot!"

He began to thrust, and I knew there was no slowing him down. Just as I was contemplating telling him to stop, pain turned to pleasure. My body relaxed, and his pace quickened. I stifled a moan when a particularly deep thrust grazed my prostate.

I should have guessed that sex wouldn't put an end to the talking. He kept up a constant running commentary of his thoughts and feelings. "Dominic, you're so gorgeous. I've wanted to do this for ages, thought about it for weeks. You feel fantastic. I can't believe you're letting me do this. I didn't know it would feel like this. You're going to make me come so hard."

I tried not to listen, and what I did hear, I didn't take seriously. He wouldn't be the first man to rattle off meaningless words with an orgasm in sight. Turning my head sideways brought a muscular forearm into view, flexing with each thrust. I gasped. Figuring I may as well make the most of the strange kink I'd developed, I bucked up off the bed, pushing my body backward to a position where I could see both forearms and entwining my fingers with his.

The change in position glued us even closer together. In between kisses on my neck, Tristan was still talking. "I hope this feels as good for you as it does for me. I want to feel you come. Feel what it feels like to be inside you when you do. I'm so close." He thrust harder. I was close myself, pushing back with every thrust, forcing him as deep as possible. Fingers still entwined with his, I tried to summon up the willpower to let go in order to stroke my cock. There was no way I could come without direct contact.

Tristan nudged me forward, another deep thrust grazed my prostate, and I came instantaneously without touching myself. Riding the crest of an extremely satisfying orgasm, I was barely aware of Tristan reaching his own until he collapsed over me, muscles straining and shaking.

With the release of orgasm, cold, hard reality crashed down almost immediately. I'd just had sex with my boss. Not just my boss, but the boss of the whole bloody company, which I had no plans to leave any time soon. I quickly disengaged myself from Tristan. Ignoring his mumbled protests, I maneuvered myself to the other side of the bed, covering my naked body with the sheet. I couldn't bring myself to look at him.

The bed shifted and, a few seconds later, the bedroom door creaked open. I assumed he was getting rid of the condom. It would make perfect sense for Tristan to collect his clothes and leave while he was out there. No doubt he'd be freaking out about what just happened. That made two of us.

As the seconds ticked by, I convinced myself that was exactly what he'd do. I listened carefully, waiting for the tell-tale sound of the apartment door closing to announce his exit. Once I heard that, I could relax. I could try and scrape my addled wits together and work out how the hell I was going to deal with this at work.

The bedroom door creaked open. I steeled myself to look over. Expecting a fully clothed Tristan, I wasn't prepared for the sight of him strolling across the room, still naked. He grinned as he approached the bed, completely unabashed. So much for freaking out and leaving. He placed one hand on the other side of the bed, about to pull the covers back.

I leaped across the space and held the blankets down with one hand. "What are you doing?"

"Getting in." He gave the sheet an experimental tug, trying to pull it from my grasp.

I held on tighter. "You can't."

He quirked an eyebrow. "Why not?"

"You need to leave. I can't...I don't have people stay over."

He cocked his head to one side as if giving the thought great consideration. "You don't? Huh! So, ask me to leave."

"Would you leave?" I added a please as an afterthought, hoping politeness would seal the deal.

He straightened up. I relaxed slightly. Seeing this, he made a dive for the covers, yanking them successfully out of my hand, before climbing under them. "No, I won't leave. It's late. I'd have to get dressed, call a cab, because I've been drinking, and wait for it to arrive. Not to mention the fact I'd have to leave my car here, which means another cab to get me to work in the morning. Then I'd have to come all the way back here tomorrow to get my car." He lay down, plumping the pillow underneath his head until he was satisfied with its shape. "That wouldn't make any sense." He closed his eyes.

I glared at him, hoping the action would cause him to change his mind. He remained oblivious. "You can't just refuse to go."

"I just did."

"I could throw you out."

He smiled without bothering to open his eyes. "What? Bodily? You could try, I suppose." He pulled the covers up higher. "Now shush. I need to sleep. Some of us need our beauty sleep." He shifted his head on the pillow, finding a more comfortable position. "That was great, by the way. More than great, actually. Thank you."

Lost for a suitable response, or any response, really, I reluctantly lay back. I couldn't think of any way of getting rid of him. I kept my gaze fixed on Tristan, worried he was likely to spring up at any moment and do God knows what. He didn't move, and after a while, it became clear he was already asleep. Turning over so I had my back to him, I attempted to get some sleep myself.

Chapter Twenty

I hadn't slept well. I'd spent most of the night keenly aware of Tristan's presence in my bed. It wasn't that he'd done anything to warrant it: he didn't snore, he hadn't stolen the covers, he hadn't taken up the whole bed. He didn't encroach onto my side of the bed at all. In fact, a sleeping Tristan seemed to have far more respect for personal space than a conscious one. He was just there, breathing and emanating heat and acting as a constant reminder of last night's mistake. It was almost a relief when morning finally came and I was able to get up for work.

I waited till I was showered and fully dressed before attempting to wake Tristan. I tamped down on the overwhelming temptation to fill a bucket with cold water and tip it over his head, settling for making a cup of coffee instead. Congratulating myself on my sheer generosity, I carried it into the bedroom. He was still asleep. I called his name, and he stirred.

I watched nervously while he stared sleepily around the room, trying to orient himself. His gaze eventually settled on me, and he smiled. I held out the cup of coffee. Sitting up against the headboard, sheet dropping dangerously low, he took it, placing it on the nightstand next to him. I took a step back, wanting to put as much distance as I could between myself and all that distracting bare skin. It didn't stop him from slowly perusing my body. "You're dressed."

"Ten out of ten for your observational skills, Mr. Maxwell." Okay, that sounded completely wrong, given the current circumstances and what we'd got up to the previous night.

Amusement flared in Tristan's eyes. He patted the bare expanse of bed next to him, which I'd vacated earlier. "Come back to bed. I'll even let you call me Mr. Maxwell, if that's what does it for you."

I backed away even farther. "I need to get to work. *You* need to get to work."

Tristan winked. "I know your boss quite well. He told me you don't need to. He thinks you should ring in sick and then come back to bed." Tristan reached out, making a clumsy grab for the corner of my suit jacket. I narrowly managed to evade it. No way was I going to let him drag me back into the bed.

I put as much conviction into my voice as I possibly could. "You need to get dressed. You've got fifteen minutes before I need to leave and catch the train."

Tristan looked puzzled. "Why do you need to catch a train? My car's outside."

I stared at him like he was insane. "I'm hardly going to travel into the office with you, am I?"

He sighed before sinking back down on to the pillow. "In that case, I'm going back to sleep. I've got zero meetings scheduled, and I've got this exceptional personal assistant who can handle anything else with ease. He's great. You'd like him."

Successfully ignoring the personal assistant comment, I focused on the words at the beginning of his speech. "What! You can't."

Another wink. "I can, and I am."

"You can't just bloody stay here. This is my apartment. You need to leave." The exact same words I'd said the previous night. I suspected they'd have as little impact now as they had before. "Tristan, please?" Even I could hear the imploring note in my voice.

Yawning, he rolled onto his side, the untouched mug of coffee still on the nightstand beside him. It would have been better to go with the bucket of water after all. "You wore me out last night, Dominic. The least you can do, if you're not going to join me, is not throw me out when I clearly need more sleep. Don't worry. I'll let myself out without stealing anything."

"But—" I stopped when I realized his eyes were already closed. It really was a replay of the previous night. I waited for a moment. Then I conceded defeat and left the bedroom.

IT SHOULDN'T HAVE COME as any real surprise to find myself completely out of sorts that day. The third time I knocked over the same pile of papers, I left them lying on the floor of the office. Lack of sleep probably didn't help matters. By the time I'd lied through my teeth for the fifth time when confronted with the "Where's Tristan?" questions, I was ready for the day to be over, and it wasn't even lunchtime. At half past eleven, the text messages started.

Tristan: *I know I've said it before, but I really like your apartment.*

Staring at the screen of my phone didn't cause the message to disappear. I knew what I needed to ask, but was incredibly apprehensive about the answer. Sighing, I typed it anyway.

Dominic: *You've left there, right?*

Tristan: *Your bed's really comfortable, and your shower's great. Much better than mine.*

Dominic: *What time did you get home?*

Tristan: *I'm coming round to shower at yours in future. You can scrub my back. ;)*

Dominic: *Did you check the door was locked when you left?*

Tristan: *You need to go shopping though. It took me ages to find something to eat for breakfast. Oh, and your milk is off. You need to get more.*

I counted to ten. It didn't work, so I started a slow count to fifty. I'd reached forty when my phone chimed again to announce an uploading photo. What the hell had Tristan sent a photo of? The message linked to the photo came before the picture.

Tristan: *I like this. It looks good on me.*

My confusion lasted until the photo finally materialized. In it, Tristan wore one of my shirts.

Dominic: *TAKE IT OFF!*

Tristan: *Oh like that is it? Okay.*

In less than a minute, another photo arrived. This one downloaded much quicker. I stared in disbelief at the phone screen, my eyes automatically flicking to the office door, paranoid someone could see what I was looking at. The door remained closed. I turned my attention back to the screen. In the new picture, Tristan sprawled across the bed provocatively, wearing nothing but a pair of white briefs and a sexy smile. I'd been trying to avoid thinking about details from the previous night. At the sight of Tristan's near-naked body, it all came rushing back: the feel of Tristan's muscles beneath my fingers, the taste of his skin, his throaty gasp as he came. Under the desk, my cock told me exactly how much it liked the image I couldn't seem to tear my eyes away from.

Tristan: *Better?*

I knew I should just ignore him. The best way to get him to stop was to stop giving him attention. I was just feeding the flames by replying. He was taking absolutely no notice of anything I was saying. With shaking fingers, I still found myself typing.

Dominic: *No. GET OUT OF MY APARTMENT.*

Tristan: *Didn't you like the picture? I take requests. Where do you want me? Am I wearing too many clothes?*

Frustrated beyond belief, I dropped my head onto the desk with a *thunk*. I'd be lying if I said there wasn't a small part of me that could think of a thousand requests, all of them wholly inappropriate. The devil in me couldn't help wondering how he'd respond if I suggested something particularly lewd. Would he really do it? Sighing, I fought the temptation and lifted my head to type one more message.

Dominic: *Tristan, this isn't funny. Please leave.*

There was a long pause while I dreaded the reply.

Tristan: *On my way out. :) Xx*

I switched my phone off. At least that way, if he hadn't really left, I'd be none the wiser. In a crisis of indecision, I was just toying with the idea of switching it back on when Paul walked through the door. He gestured at the adjoining office door and lowered his voice to a whisper. "Is he in there?"

I shook my head wearily. "I really wish he were."

Understandably confused by my answer, Paul frowned. "What?"

"Nothing. What can I do for you?"

His frown deepened as he found himself having to step gingerly over the pieces of paper littering the floor before perching against the edge of my desk. "I came to see how you were. You know, after last night?"

"Last night?" My voice came out higher than usual. For one horrifying moment, I thought he knew about Tristan.

"Yeah. Adam—the idiot! Just so you know, everybody is completely on your side. They think he was completely out of order. Apparently, the other guy was really drunk. I don't think he even knew Adam had been seeing you. Now he knows, he's apparently worried about bumping into you. Go easy on him, if you see him. Lon, that is, not Adam. Adam deserves everything he gets. So anyway, are you okay?"

I nodded. It was obviously less than convincing. Paul leaned in, peering closely. "You look really tired. Don't say you lost sleep over Adam."

When I didn't offer a response, Paul carried on talking. "Anyway, everyone thought it was really sweet that Tristan was your knight in shining armor last night."

"What?"

"Russell said he got you out of there, away from Adam's public display of 'I don't give a fuck about you.' He didn't use those exact words. Obviously, the last part of it is me...paraphrasing. I can't remember the exact words he used."

"Russell exaggerates everything. It wasn't quite like that."

"So you didn't leave together?"

"Well, yes, but—"

"You were seen getting into his car."

"Was I?" *Fucking fantastic!* "He gave me a lift home."

"Then what did he do?"

I suddenly became incredibly interested in a pen on the table. "Sorry. What?"

"Everyone thought he was really sweet helping you, but they were pretty pissed off when he didn't bother coming back to the party."

"Didn't he?"

The pen was suddenly snatched out of my hand. I cast around for something else to fix my attention on. Paul leaned in, eyes narrowed suspiciously. "You're such a bad liar. You already knew he didn't come back. But then how would you know that?" He sat back looking thoughtful, gaze still fixed on my face. I knew how a butterfly pinned in place must feel. I tried not to squirm and failed miserably. "Why are you going red?"

I stared at the office phone, silently begging it to ring. Of course it didn't. It had been ringing non-stop all bloody morning. Now, it stayed persistently and maddeningly silent. Maybe if I refused to answer Paul, he'd get bored, or the fire alarm would go off, or the phone would finally ring, or the world might end. Unfortunately, none of those things happened. In the face of silence, Paul changed his question. "What did you do?"

My gaze shot to Paul's face. "What do you mean? What did I do? I didn't do..." My words tailed off. Even I couldn't tell a lie quite that blatant.

He continued to study me, trying to extract the truth simply from searching my face. "Did you do something stupid? Oh my God! Did you—" He stopped short, as if considering his next words carefully. "I mean, I don't want to bring up this old argument, given how we nearly fell out over it before, but you're clearly flustered and blushing—which is not like you—and you obviously know something about why Tristan didn't come back to the party. And you look like you haven't slept. Which I find it hard to believe is about Adam. I know you never slept with him. So I know that you're nowhere near as cut up about what happened last night as everyone expects you to be. Which incidentally sucks for Adam, because he's going to be painted as a much bigger villain than he actually is. He was just convenient." He paused for breath. "Anyway, all this makes me think—"

I stared at the phone harder, doing my best to tune Paul out. I wondered absently if anyone was close to inventing time travel. Perhaps some mad scientist tucked away in some dark, damp cave could magically transport me back to the previous afternoon, with a warning to go straight home and give the party a miss.

Paul grabbed my chin, forcing me to look at him. "Did you try and seduce him?"

I yanked my head away. "Of course I bloody didn't! I'm not insane." I suddenly wanted, maybe even needed, someone to confide in. "It was all him. He's the seducer. He's—" Remembering where I was, I abruptly stopped talking. Paul's eyes widened dramatically. Under other circumstances, I would have found the expression on his face hilarious. "Can I talk to you after work? This is, you know, not really the best place. But I do need to talk to somebody."

Paul nodded, still wearing a look of shock. "Do you...erm...want to come to the mail room?"

I didn't even attempt to hide my sarcasm. "Yes, Paul, the office where anybody could walk in is a really bad place to discuss it, but the mail room where even more people might walk in would be so much better."

He smiled sheepishly. "Yeah, of course. Where do you want to go?"

"How about the bar down the road? Six o'clock?"

He pulled a face at the mention of the bar. I had no idea what that was about. We'd gone there numerous times after work. Despite his apparent misgivings about the venue, he nodded reluctantly.

He'd barely been gone from the office for two minutes when the phone rang.

I'D ASSUMED TRISTAN would take the whole day off. After all, he'd been the one to point out that everything was taken care of in his absence. So, when he waltzed in just before two o'clock, all I could do was stare. No words came to mind, no matter how much I searched for something, anything to say. He, of course, had to look his usual gorgeous self. He was wearing a different designer suit from the day before, so had obviously returned home at some point. I found myself picturing what lay beneath the suit. I froze as he sauntered across to my desk and deposited a coffee with a smile. "What have I missed?"

I finally managed to find my voice. "Nothing." I studied the polystyrene container of coffee. I wasn't sure how you conversed with your straight boss the day after letting him fuck you. I guessed there weren't too many advice books out there to cover such an eventuality. Maybe there was some sort of internet problem page where I could drop them a line and they'd get advice to me within the hour.

"Have you seen Adam?"

I glanced up at the sharpness in his voice. Shaking my head, I went back to staring at the cup.

"Are you going to drink it?"

I nodded. I could certainly do with the caffeine.

"It's not laced with anything."

"What?"

"You're staring at it like it's going to explode or I've put something in it."

There was a long pause. I risked a glance at Tristan. His head was cocked to one side, a mixture of confusion and concern aimed in my direction. He took a step forward. "Are you okay? You seem... Did something happen?"

I gave myself a mental shake. Last night had happened. I couldn't change it. Tristan didn't seem unduly worried about it, which somehow made it worse. I would be stupid to let him get under my skin. I had to get my head back into the mindset of being at work, and this being my boss standing in front of me. Raising my head, I finally wrapped my hand around the container and took a sip of coffee, forcing myself to look him right in the eye.

"I'm just fed up. A day of fielding enquiries about your whereabouts, while you send messages to deliberately wind me up, is not my idea of a good time. It's been a long day." Tristan opened his mouth to speak, but I interjected. "It would have been useful if you'd let me know you were coming into work after all, before I told people you weren't. I might be your temporary personal assistant, but I still want to look like I know what I'm doing."

Tristan looked momentarily taken aback. "I didn't come here to work. I came in to talk to you. You stopped answering my messages."

"I switched my phone off. It's hardly the place is it, to talk about..." I ran several possibilities for finishing the sentence through my brain—*what happened*, *us having sex*, before leaving it hanging.

Tristan looked like he really wanted to object. He checked his watch. "But after work. We can go somewhere else and talk?"

"Sure!" Tristan looked pleased as the lie rolled easily off my tongue. Even if I hadn't already agreed to meet Paul, I would have found some other way to avoid the conversation. Tristan continued to stand there. I raised the coffee in a salute. "So. Work now. Talk later." He took the hint and disappeared into his office, muttering something about talking somewhere with food. I breathed a sigh of relief before switching my phone back on and bracing myself to read back through the messages.

12:28p.m.

Tristan: *I didn't mean to upset you earlier. Sorry. Xx*

12:31p.m.

Tristan: *I left your apartment tidy, and yes the door was locked when I left.*

12:33p.m.

Tristan: *I hung your shirt back up.*

12:35p.m.

Tristan: *Dominic? Talk to me.*

12:45p.m.

Tristan: *Are you ignoring me?*

12:55p.m.

Tristan: *We need to talk about last night. I don't want you getting the wrong idea.*

I re-read the message a few times, trying to read between the lines to find the hidden meaning.

13:10p.m.

Missed call from Tristan.

13:15p.m.

Missed call from Tristan.

13:17p.m.

Missed call from Tristan.

13:30p.m.

Tristan: *I'm coming in so we can talk, seeing as you're not answering my calls. I'll see you soon. Xx*

Chapter Twenty-One

Paul was over by the bar. He'd gestured for me to sit down, saying he'd get the drinks and bring them over. I'd chosen a table tucked away in a corner. Given the conversation we were about to have, the fewer ears in the vicinity, the better.

The bartender was flirting outrageously with Paul. I watched with barely concealed amusement. Normally, he would be well up for responding in kind. For some reason, my friend's body language today screamed impatience and annoyance.

Drinks finally obtained, he navigated toward me. He eased himself into the seat opposite, dropping the beer bottles onto the table with a clink. Smirking, I inclined my head toward the bar. "Cute."

Paul's head immediately swiveled back in that direction. The bartender leaned casually on the bar, watching Paul. He blatantly ignored customers, who were waiting to be served, while he looked his fill. My smirk grew more pronounced, while Paul's frown increased tenfold. "How can you tell under all the tattoos and piercings?"

"He obviously likes you."

Paul shrugged. "Not my type. Besides, he's like that with all the customers. He's got to get his tips somehow." He took a drink of his beer before focusing his attention on me. "Speaking of tattoos and piercings, does Tristan have any hidden away?"

I sat back with a sigh, taking a large gulp of my own beer. "I assume you don't actually want an answer to that question?"

Paul looked intrigued. "Why. Does he?"

I shook my head. "No."

"So you saw enough to know?"

I shot a glare in Paul's direction.

He simply quirked an eyebrow. "*You* were the one who said you wanted to talk about it."

I took another large gulp of beer. At this rate, I was going to need another one in under five minutes. In an effort to slow down, I slid it away from me across the table. "I probably shouldn't have said anything. I mean it's not... I can't... I don't know..."

Paul smiled at my nonsensical stuttering. "Well, that's clear. I tell you what. I'll make it easier for you. I'll guess at what I think might have happened, and you can just agree or disagree."

I nodded my agreement, shifting slightly in my seat when I felt my phone vibrate in my pocket, announcing a message. I'd had the good sense to put it on silent before meeting Paul. I had a sneaky suspicion that my early, and unannounced, exit from the office might just have been rumbled by Tristan.

"So..." Paul leaned in. It was reminiscent of the earlier interrogation in the office. "He drove you home. He obviously came in with you. You both had a fair amount to drink." I shook my head. Paul carried on with a surprised look on his face. "You were both sober?"

"He had a couple of beers. I don't know what he'd had to drink at the party, but he'd driven, and he seemed fine. I hadn't really had anything." I pointed at my beer bottle on the table. "Less than I've had just now."

"You said earlier, he...came on to you?"

I nodded. "He was...erm...quite insistent." My phone vibrated again.

Paul raised an eyebrow. "He's hardly the first straight guy to be tempted into a blow job from a gay guy. That's as far as it went, right?"

I looked everywhere but at Paul.

"Okay. It went further than that. You had sex!"

I swiveled my gaze back to his. "Is that a question or a statement?"

"Both. Neither. Shit!" He drank the rest of his beer in a series of swallows. "He fucked you?"

I polished my own beer off before nodding.

"You fucked the boss!"

I shushed him. He'd almost shouted it. I quickly checked the bar for any sign of employees from the same company. I was relieved to see there were none.

Paul's chair squeaked as he pushed it back. "We need more beer for this."

I was hardly going to argue with that statement. "Make sure to flirt with the cute bartender. You could ask him where to get a tattoo done."

I chuckled at the middle-fingered salute he offered on his way back toward the bar. Making the most of the brief opportunity for privacy, I checked my phone.

Tristan: *Where did you go? Have you left? I thought we were going to talk.*

Tristan: *I'll come round and see you. Xx*

Glancing over to check Paul was still otherwise occupied, I typed a quick response. The last thing I needed was Tristan hanging about outside my apartment, waiting for my return home.

Dominic: *Sorry. I forgot I was meeting a friend. I couldn't get out of it. I won't be home till late. I'll see you tomorrow.*

I kept hold of my phone, waiting for the reply whilst observing Paul becoming increasingly more irritated by the flirty bartender. I didn't have to wait very long.

Tristan: *I see. You could at least have come and told me. I looked for you for twenty minutes.*

Dominic: *Sorry. I didn't want to disturb you.*

No further response came. Seeing Paul was returning, I slipped my phone back into my pocket, not wanting him to ask who I was messaging.

Paul was grumbling even before he took his seat. "He's a complete dick. Like I'd ever go on a date with *him*. If we have any more drinks, you're getting them. I'm not going anywhere near him for the rest of the night."

I hid my mirth at his reaction behind my hand. It was so uncharacteristic, I began to suspect some sort of back story I wasn't aware of. "Do you know him? I don't see why going on a date with a cute barman would be such a problem." It seemed clear that the barman's presence had been the reason for Paul's earlier reluctance to come here.

"I told you. He's a dick! Thinks everyone in the entire world finds him irresistible. Anyway—" He clinked his beer bottle against mine. "Cheers. Now let's get back to discussing the important matter at hand." He fixed me with a steady stare, and I got the pinned-butterfly feeling again. "So you had sex. I assume it must have been pretty damn awful? You know, straight guy who didn't know what he was doing. It was embarrassing and awkward, right?"

I considered lying, but if I was going to admit last night had happened, I might as well be honest. "It should have been, but it wasn't. It was..." I searched around for a suitable adjective. "Pretty fantastic, actually."

"And how did you leave things last night?"

"Last night?"

"When he left."

Paul obviously read the answer on my face.

"He didn't leave." He sighed. "You never let anyone stay over. I always wind you up about how you're never going to manage to have a long-term boyfriend if he's not even allowed to stay under the same roof. Yet, you let Mr. Straight Guy, the guy you claim not to like, stay over."

"It wasn't like that. I tried to get him to leave, but he wasn't exactly cooperating. Tristan can be...difficult."

Paul folded his arms in front of him. "So he stayed the whole night. And what do you think he told his fiancée about his whereabouts?"

I sat up indignantly. Although I hadn't mentioned it, I'd assumed Paul knew me better than that. "I wouldn't have slept with someone who's getting married in a few months! He's not engaged anymore. He broke it off. Or she broke it off. I'm not sure."

Paul had a stubborn set to his jaw. "Says who?"

"Well, he said—"

"And you believe him?"

"What?"

"You know how gossip spreads around the building. I haven't heard any mention of his engagement ending. His fiancée is some big-shot model, right? So you'd think it would be splashed all over the newspapers."

"Oh come on. You really think he'd lie about something like that?"

Paul looked suddenly weary. "I don't know, Dom. Probably not. I just think you should be questioning it or something, rather than just taking everything at face value. You know, Google it. Turn your bullshit filter back on. You seem to have a strange blind spot when it comes to Tristan."

I knew what he was saying made some sort of twisted sense. "Okay. Sure. I'll do that."

Paul suddenly chuckled around the mouth of his beer bottle. I waited to find out what could possibly be so amusing. He wiped his mouth with his sleeve before sharing. "Are you at least going to admit you have a crush on him?"

I sighed. "Well, I would hardly have sex with someone if I didn't find them attractive, would I?"

Paul smirked. "Halle-bloody-lujah! He finally admits it."

I looked around for something suitable to throw at him, but the only thing to hand was the three-quarter-full beer bottle. I settled for taking a drink instead. "So why do you think he—"

"Slept with you?"

I nodded. Paul looked thoughtful. "I don't know. Some sort of experiment, maybe? What's he said since?"

"He wants to talk to me. He sent a message saying something about not wanting me to get the wrong idea."

I cringed as Paul pasted what he obviously thought was an empathetic look on his face. "Just be careful, Dom. I don't want you getting hurt."

I DON'T KNOW WHAT I'D expected my apartment to look like when I got home, but it was almost anticlimactic to find it looking exactly the same as it normally did. Even last night's beer bottles had disappeared from the living room. I hadn't thrown them away, so I could only surmise Tristan had done it this morning before leaving. Thinking about what Paul had said, I gave the bedroom a wide berth and sat down at my computer. Before I could change my mind, I typed "Tristan Maxwell Maria Rivera engagement" into the search bar.

It immediately flashed up numerous hits. Clicking on images brought up hundreds of photographs of Tristan and Maria at various parties and gatherings. In most of them, she was draped across him possessively. I hovered the cursor over a particularly intimate image of the two of them. I clicked on it and it enlarged, filling my screen. They were dancing: her arms entwined around his neck while his arm encircled her waist, palm resting on the shapely curve of her lower back. They were both smiling. The photo had been taken six weeks ago.

I clicked onto news and was immediately assailed with article after article announcing their engagement. Not bothering to read any of them, I altered my original search term to "Tristan Maxwell Maria Rivera end of engage-

ment." I pressed return and scanned the results. Nothing. All the same arti-
cles had come up. Not one of them said anything about the engagement ending. I clicked on the next page. Same result. Paul was right; I was a complete
gullible idiot. I'd let my boss use me for some sort of pre-wedding experiment. That was the only feasible explanation I could think of that explained
his actions.

I spent ten minutes staring into space, head swirling with unwanted
thoughts. I probably would have spent longer, if it wasn't for my phone. I
knew who it would be even before I read the message.

Tristan: *Just wanted to say good night. Xx*

I wondered if he'd sent the same message to Maria. I didn't bother to reply. All I wanted to do was sleep and spend a few hours ignoring how badly
I'd fucked up. It wasn't till I crawled between the sheets that I realized they
smelled of Tristan. I was too tired to do anything about it.

Chapter Twenty-Two

I arrived at work half an hour late. I would have felt bad if it didn't feel like a monumental achievement to have turned up at all. Twice, I'd picked up the phone to call in sick, and both times I'd ended up not making the call. It wouldn't have surprised me to find Tristan waiting at the door, but the entryway and my office were both blessedly clear. Even better, the adjoining door was firmly closed. The relief faded when I noticed the handwritten note placed carefully in front of my computer. I read it reluctantly.

YOU'RE LATE!

You left early yesterday and you're late coming in today. Tut tut, Dominic.

Let me know as soon as you get here.

I need the following things done today.

I browsed the list Tristan had included. There was nothing particularly urgent on it. My eyes unwillingly returned to the penultimate sentence. Gritting my teeth, I pressed the intercom.

"Morning, Tristan. Sorry I'm late. I..." A potential list of excuses flashed through my mind. "I wasn't feeling well. You wanted me to let you know when I got here. Is there something you needed me to do that's not on the list? If not, I'll just get on with the rest of it."

"What's wrong with you?"

"What?"

"You said you weren't feeling well." Even through the intercom, I could hear the concern in Tristan's voice.

"I'm fine."

"Are you sure?"

"I'm fine. So I'll just get on with these tasks. Oh, and I'll work through lunch to make the time up. And stay later to make up for yesterday."

"I need to see you in my office."

"Can it wait?"

"No. Straight away, please."

"Okay. Give me a minute."

I eyed the door to Tristan's office like it was a portal to hell. Mentally preparing myself, I schooled my face, opened the door, and walked through it. The preparation time was wasted: no amount of prior thought could have prepared me for being immediately grabbed the moment I set foot in the door. I was spun around, slammed against a wall, and thoroughly kissed. The gasp of shock at the jarring contact with the wall made it all the easier for Tristan to deepen the kiss.

His body pressed insistently against mine, pushing me firmly back against the solid surface behind and making escape impossible. Dazed, I brought my hands up with the intention of pushing him off. Instead, I found my fingers gripping the lapels of his suit jacket. He insinuated his thigh between mine, pressing our groins together, the heat of his body leaching through both our suits. Finally coming to my senses, I wrenched my mouth away, breathing hard. I foiled Tristan's attempts to seal our lips back together by turning my head to the side.

"Stop." My protest sounded weak even to my own ears. I repeated the word with more conviction. He stopped but didn't move away. When I shoved at his chest, he finally seemed to get the message, easing back slightly but keeping me trapped against the wall.

"What the hell, Tristan? We're at work. You can't just—"

He didn't look remotely remorseful. In fact, he looked horny as hell, his lips swollen from kissing and his pupils dilated with arousal. Whatever kind of experiment this was to Tristan, he was obviously under the impression it was going to last longer than one night.

He loosened my tie and undid the top button, giving him enough room to slide his hand into the open neck of my shirt. "You didn't leave me a lot of choice. You sneaked out yesterday. You won't reply to my messages. What am I supposed to do?" He undid another button. For some reason beyond my comprehension, I let him. His hand felt warm against the skin of my bare chest.

"I don't know. Take a hint, maybe?"

He reeled back as if I'd hit him. "So you admit you're avoiding me?"

I let my head thunk back against the wall. Another dent wouldn't hurt it. I still hadn't had the ones inflicted by the impromptu office golf session fixed.

"I don't know what you want from me. You can't just do what you want and tell lies and—"

"Lies! What lies? I haven't told any lies."

Grabbing Tristan's wrist, I finally summoned up enough willpower to extract it from my shirt. "I'm not stupid, Tristan. I'm referring to the so-called end of your engagement. Funny, how when it was announced, it was splashed all over every single newspaper. I think there were even a few in different languages I couldn't read. I guess Maria's got a bit of a following abroad. Yet, there's not even the slightest mention of it ending...anywhere. I looked. There were lots of pictures though of the two of you together. Recent pictures where you looked perfectly happy."

I tried to ignore the hurt plastered all over my boss's face as he took a step away from me. At least I could think more clearly without him pressed against me. "It's fine. You had some sort of pre-wedding freak-out, I guess." I started to re-fasten the buttons he'd undone. "But it ends now. Before anyone gets hurt. I'll keep my word. I'll carry on working for you until after Christmas, then we'll find a replacement, you'll get married as planned..."

"And what? You'll never talk to me again. I'm glad you've got my whole life mapped out. There's just one big problem with that whole scenario."

I lifted my head from re-fastening my tie to find Tristan's gaze locked onto mine. He looked mighty pissed. "What's that?"

"I'm not engaged. I didn't realize you needed a front-page headline to believe it. I thought you'd take my word for it. So, I'm not going to be getting married. And as for the pictures, they can't have been that recent, because I haven't seen Maria for over three weeks."

I didn't know what to think anymore. I glanced longingly toward the door. It wasn't even fully closed. The whole incident had taken place with the door ajar. Anyone could have seen us. Maria herself could have walked in. Unless, of course, Tristan was telling the truth and they really weren't engaged anymore, then there probably wouldn't be any reason for her to be here. I was so confused. I should have followed my instincts to call in sick. I glanced toward Tristan. He stood immobile in the middle of the office, regarding me with a frosty expression. I'd finally managed to annoy him. I cleared my throat. "Erm...was there anything...workwise you needed to talk to me about...or?"

Shaking his head, Tristan didn't say a word.

I nodded. "Okay, so I'll..." I gestured toward the door before edging closer. Tristan finally spoke as I reached for the handle.

"As long as you realize this conversation isn't over. I obviously need to sort some stuff out before we can talk properly. But then we'll definitely talk."

I left the office and returned to my desk, my head still swimming. There was very little contact between us for the rest of the day. Any instruction or question from Tristan was delivered in a curt but professional manner. I responded in kind. It was hard to believe the same man had had his tongue down my throat hours earlier.

At three o'clock, Tristan left for the day. He didn't provide any explanation for his early departure, and I didn't ask.

Chapter Twenty-Three

I jumped when a newspaper came skimming none too gently across the desk toward me. After throwing it, Tristan sank wearily into the seat opposite. I'd heard nothing from him the previous evening: no phone call, no messages. Nothing. I'd convinced myself that was a relief. And if I'd checked my phone frequently throughout the evening, well, that was just a sign of how surprised I'd been. Nothing else.

He gestured at the newspaper, which I still hadn't touched. "Present for you."

Regarding him cautiously, I took in the dark smudges under his eyes. He looked like he'd barely slept. "I prefer coffee."

"Sorry. No coffee today. Hopefully you'll believe me now."

Confused, I continued to stare at him. He waved a hand at the newspaper again. I slowly unfolded it. The front-page headline detailed an elderly couple's narrow escape from a tsunami while on holiday. "What exactly am I meant to be looking at?"

Tristan offered a wry smile. "I bought this one for a reason. They didn't deem it newsworthy enough for the front page. Maria will no doubt be devastated. Turn to page seven."

I flicked through the pages until I'd reached the right one. It was a double-page spread, the headline proclaiming, *COLD-HEARTED BUSINESS-MAN JILTS SEXY MODEL*. The picture below the headline was the same one I'd seen a couple of days ago: the one of Tristan and Maria dancing together. I started to read through the story. It didn't exactly paint Tristan in a good light, making it sound like they were hours away from marriage rather than months. According to the story, he'd cruelly dumped her weeks ago, breaking her heart in the process. She was apparently so devastated by the split, she was in a secluded hideaway in France.

When the familiar sound of my ringtone broke the silence, I absent-mindedly answered it while continuing to read the story. Paul's voice reverberated in my ears. "Holy shit! You should see the amount of press camped outside the building. You've heard right, about Tristan?"

Conscious of the man himself less than a meter away, I made sure my response was deliberately vague. "I'm aware, yes."

Paul continued to ramble excitedly in my ear. "There's reporters from just about every newspaper here. Some magazine columnists as well. I'm sure I saw someone from *Vogue*. Apparently, they all arrived when Tristan did, like they followed him from home or something." I pressed the phone closer to my ear, concerned the sound might carry. "Anyway, Russell was late in. Think he had a doctor's appointment or something, so he was there. He said Tristan didn't say anything to them, just shoved his way through and said 'no comment.'"

I knew Paul would go on and on if I didn't stop him. "I can't really talk now."

"Is he there? Are you with him now? Is he okay?"

"Yes, yes, and...I don't know. Listen, I'm going to have to go."

"Fine. But I'm coming to get you for lunch, so we can talk properly. We'll go out. Then you can see all the reporters."

"Why would I— Never mind. Fine. I'll see you at lunchtime."

I took a while hanging up, trying to work out how much of the conversation Tristan had heard and what I was supposed to say to him. I was saved from having to come up with anything when he spoke first. "So the gossip mill has started then?"

I nodded, finally lifting my gaze back to his face for the first time since he'd directed my attention toward the article. "Sorry, I shouldn't have answered my phone during work hours. I wasn't thinking. I was a bit..." I pointed at the newspaper story, as if that explained everything. "A bit harsh on you, isn't it?"

Tristan looked pained. "That was the only way I could get Maria to agree to leak it now. She's got a big catwalk show coming up in Milan next week. She wanted to avoid being hassled by paparazzi while she was there. We'd already agreed to wait and announce it afterward. Anyway, I managed to convince her I couldn't wait until then." Tristan's expression made it clear it had taken a great deal of effort on his part to get to that point. "She had a few conditions. That was one of them. That whatever she says to the press, I don't argue with it."

I stared at him aghast. "Why the hell would you agree to that?"

Tristan looked momentarily taken aback. He frowned as if I'd asked a really ridiculous question. "You didn't believe me! I figured you couldn't argue with it in black and white."

"It doesn't matter what I think. That's hardly a reason to let them do a complete hatchet job on you."

Tristan shuffled his chair farther forward and leaned across the desk, his gaze fixed on mine. "Of course it matters. I—"

I automatically reached for the phone when it started to ring. Tristan's hand shot across the space between us, knocking my hand away. "First rule of press intrusion. We don't answer the phone. That way, you don't have to claim you don't know where I am, or lie, or hang up on them."

I eased back in my seat, grateful to put some space between us. "So I can't answer the phone all day?"

Shaking his head, Tristan stood up. "I'd like to say we could go out to lunch, but leaving the building for me isn't really an option today, unless I really have to. Besides..." His brow furrowed. "You already have a lunch date. Who *was* that on the phone? Please tell me it wasn't Adam."

I snorted. The notion seemed ludicrous, given I still hadn't heard a thing from him. I knew I'd been going to end it myself. But, at the very least, I'd figured I'd get some sort of an apology, or at least an acknowledgement of his behavior being out of order in front of all our work colleagues. But it had been complete radio silence. I'd toyed with calling him myself. Things felt strangely unfinished between us at the moment. "It wasn't Adam. It was Paul. He works—"

Tristan finished my sentence. "In the mail room, I know. You introduced me a while ago." He sighed. "Now if you don't mind, I'll be sleeping in my office. Only disturb me if it's of crucial importance. Or for food. You can always disturb me for food. Or for—" His slow perusal made me feel naked. I shifted uncomfortably, heat immediately rushing to places thankfully hidden beneath the desk. He grinned, leaving the sentence unfinished, and disappeared into his office.

"I THOUGHT YOU WERE exaggerating."

Paul turned and flashed a grin in my direction. "When do I ever exaggerate?"

"Frequently."

We were still in the foyer of the building where we both worked. The fact the whole front of the building was entirely made of glass gave an unobstructed view of the chaos currently taking place outside. The door was completely surrounded by a throng of assorted reporters, all jostling and vying for a good position. Disgruntled security kept clearing them to a safe distance, only for them to gradually creep forward again. Venturing out of the safety and security of the foyer for lunch suddenly seemed like a really bad idea. "Maybe we should forget this. I've got a sandwich back in the office. I'll just eat that."

Paul shook his head. "No way! I need to talk to you. Besides, they're not remotely interested in us. They're only interested in Tristan." He paused for a moment, as if something had just occurred to him. "Actually, they probably would be interested in you, if they knew you were his personal assistant." He frowned. "But there's no way they could know that, right?"

When I realized it wasn't a rhetorical question, I responded. "Kevin's still listed officially, so I doubt it. Not unless someone that works here has told them. Did Russell talk to them?"

Paul shrugged. "Doubt it. I expect he just ran away." He looked suddenly mischievous. "Of course, they'd be incredibly interested in you if they knew about the other night." He raised an eyebrow. "Just think of the money I could make selling that story." Laughing, he feigned a step toward the reporters.

Glaring at him, I surreptitiously checked no one was in ear shot of our conversation. Good job we were separated from all the tape recorders and notebooks by the thick sheet of plate glass. "You're not funny at all."

Paul chuckled to himself. "Yes, I am. I'm the funny one. You're the serious, sarcastic one. That's why we get on so well. We cancel each other out."

"I think you mean we complement each other."

"That's what I said."

We both went quiet while we stared at the assorted press. Finally, with a loud exhale, Paul began a determined stride across the foyer. A brief glance over his shoulder, along with an incline of his head, indicated I should follow. Ignoring the temptation to run in the opposite direction, I fell into step behind him.

The reporters were on us the minute we exited the building, firing questions without pausing for breath. "Do you know Tristan Maxwell? Do you know Maria Rivera? Do you know why he dumped her? When was the last time you saw them together? Is he seeing someone else? Did he cheat on her? What do you think about the end of the engagement? Do you think they'll get back together?" We pushed our way through, both of us looking straight ahead and avoiding eye contact. Halfway through the crowd, Paul suddenly stopped dead. I narrowly avoided walking into the back of him. "Tristan Maxwell, did you say?"

The nearest reporter swooped immediately. "Do you know him?" I held my breath, wondering what the hell Paul was playing at.

Paul paused dramatically, leaning closer to the microphone that had been shoved into his face. "Never heard of him. Who is he? Is he famous or something?"

The reporters lost interest immediately, muttering among themselves and turning their interest back to the office building. Paul grinned in my direction, waiting until we were out of earshot to make a comment. "Gullible lot, aren't they?"

Relieved to have navigated the craziness and come safely out the other side, I refrained from offering my opinion on the intelligence of the journalists, instead concentrating on working out where we were going for lunch. After a brief discussion, we discounted most of the food places in the area. They were all invariably frequented by people from the same company, which seriously curtailed any possibility of a private conversation. With few options left, I'd finally suggested the bar we'd visited the previous night. Paul's face had said it all. But unable to make a better suggestion, he grudgingly agreed.

The bar was fairly quiet and thankfully again completely empty of anyone we knew. I was amused to see the same barman leaning casually on the bar. As soon as he spotted Paul, he winked, his eyebrow piercing glinting in the sunlight streaming through the window.

He barely spared a glance in my direction, greeting Paul as if he were an old friend. "Hey, sexy. I don't normally get to see you during the day. It's obviously my lucky day." Paul stiffened, his response decidedly frosty. I studied the barman while we ordered our food and drinks. Up close, it was easy to see the reason for all the tattoos and piercings: he'd be far too pretty without them.

By the time we were seated, Paul was positively glowering. Unfortunately, that just served to amp up my amusement even more. Paul got on with everyone. I'd never seen him react to anyone this way before. There was definitely a story there. I'd let it go far too easily the other night, but he wasn't getting away with it so easily this time.

"So, the barman? What's the story?"

He looked away. "No story."

"Right. Course there isn't."

I waited. Paul studied his glass as if he'd never seen one before. Eventually, as I knew he would, he caved. "Do you remember Stephen?"

"Of course I do." Stephen had been Paul's last serious boyfriend. They'd been together a year, had lived together for the last six months of that year.

"Remember he cheated on me?"

I could hardly forget. Paul had come home early from work one day to find Stephen fucking someone else in their bed. He'd rung me angry and upset, calling Stephen all the names under the sun. I'd done what any good friend would do and offered him a shoulder to cry on, a bucket full of alcohol, and enthusiastically joined in with calling Stephen names. "Yeah, the bastard! But what's that got to do with—"

Paul inclined his head toward the bar, a strained expression on his face. I was slow to make the connection. When it finally dawned, I nearly choked on my drink. "No! No way! That was the guy Stephen was fucking? The one you caught him with?"

Paul simply nodded.

"But he keeps flirting with you. That's a bit... He's got a bloody nerve, hasn't he?"

Sighing, Paul rolled his eyes. "Sickening, isn't it? He seems to think it's in the past and I should just let it go."

"How do you let something like that go?"

"Exactly."

Our conversation paused as our food was delivered to the table. Luckily, by someone other than the barman. I eyed my plate, thinking the large portion size would be right up Tristan's street. I'd have to suggest this place to him.

Paul took a bite of his burger, wiping a stray drip of ketchup from his chin. "So, what the hell's going on with Tristan?"

I put my burger back on the plate, still untouched. "I'm not sure."

Paul shot me a look of pure disbelief. My phone chimed. I pulled it out of my pocket and checked the screen.

Tristan: *You're not at your desk. Have you gone for lunch? Where have you gone? What are you eating? I'm hungry. Can you bring me something back? Xx*

Smiling at the sheer predictability of the man, I typed a quick response.

Dominic: *Bar down the road. Don't worry. I'm not drinking. Eating a burger. Deserve it after navigating through your reporters.*

Tristan: *Hardly my reporters. Need to give a statement to them. Hopefully, that will get rid of them. Trying to work up to it. Xx*

Tristan: *Can't do it on an empty stomach. Xx*

Dominic: *Okay. I can take a hint. I'll bring something back for you. Look in my desk drawer. There's probably some chocolate or something.*

Tristan: *:) Xx*

Tristan: *Don't rush your lunch. Take as long as you need. Xx*

I startled, a loud cough from the other side of the table suddenly reminding me I wasn't alone. Raising my head, I found Paul watching me, a strange expression on his face. "Sorry, I just needed to...you know..."

Paul raised an eyebrow. "Who are all the messages from? You know you're smiling like an idiot, right? Is it Tristan?"

I nodded sheepishly, embarrassed at ignoring him when we were meant to be having lunch together. Speaking of lunch, I took a quick bite of my rapidly cooling burger.

Reaching a hand across the table, Paul snapped his fingers. "Hand it over."

I paused mid-chew. "What?"

"Your phone."

I knew that determined look. He wouldn't rest until I'd given in to his demand. Assuming his intention was simply to hang on to it, to keep my attention on him, I passed it over. Expecting Paul to place it on the table next to him, I couldn't hide my shock when he started reading through the messages. "Hey! You can't—"

Paul's glare could stop traffic. "Shush. Eat your lunch. I can't get anything remotely honest out of you. You've left me no choice but to resort to underhand tactics. I don't know if you're doing it deliberately or you're just in denial. I need to find out what's going on."

I chewed mechanically, barely tasting the food, keeping one eye on the man currently taking his time studying my personal messages. His expression barely altered as he worked his way through them. He wasn't giving anything away.

"Paul, I don't think—" I stopped mid-sentence as his eyes dramatically widened in an expression of shock. Too late, I remembered what else he could see besides messages.

Paul raised his head for a millisecond. "Holy shit, Dominic!" He went back to staring intently at the screen. I knew he was staring at the photo Tristan had sent; the photo I probably should have deleted but hadn't quite been able to bring myself to. Cheeks burning, I reached across, attempting to snatch my phone back from Paul's grasp. He drew back, easily keeping it out of reach. "No way! I need to look at this for a bit longer. I've often wondered what his body is like under that suit." He gave a long, low whistle. "Damn, he's hot! Shame he's got shorts on. Can you get him to send one without next time?"

"There won't be a next time."

Paul placed my phone back on the table. I was relieved to see the messages screen was now closed. "Why not?"

"You know why not! You were the one who told me the other day to watch myself."

Paul sat back in his chair, looking thoughtful. "I didn't have the full story the other day. I thought he was lying about the engagement and you were stupid to believe him." He silenced me with a pointed look before I could comment. "But obviously he wasn't, so you weren't stupid at all. I also didn't know about *all* these messages between the two of you."

"There's not that many."

"Of course not." Sarcasm dripped from his voice. "Just several every night. For the past few weeks."

"Not *every* night."

Paul's look was scathing. "Just about. Not to mention you apparently meet up in diners, and he comes around for cozy DVD-watching sessions, which you've never bothered mentioning either."

"They're just messages." Even I could hear the defensive tone in my voice.

Paul sighed wearily. "He's obviously into you. He messages you all the time. He signs every bloody message with a kiss." He lowered his voice. "He had sex with you. You can't be that blind."

I ignored the warm glow the words evoked, pushing the feeling back before I could even start to consider it might be true. "He's straight."

Paul pulled a face. "I've never been that keen on labels. They don't fit the majority of the time. Eat up. We need to get back to work. We're already late." He winked. "Oh, sorry, I forgot. Your boyfriend, the boss, said we could take our time."

"He's not my boyfriend."

Paul smirked.

I glared at him. "He's not!"

The smirk grew more pronounced. "So, we'll just go straight back. Nowhere else we need to go, right?"

I finished my meal, pushing the plate away from me and getting to my feet. "You've read my messages. You know I said I'd get Tristan something to eat."

Paul marched determinedly past the barman, steadfastly ignoring his attempts to try and catch his eye. "One boyfriend meal coming up."

Chapter Twenty-Four

Finding Tristan at his desk, I deposited the bag of food in front of him. He wasted no time in poking through its contents and ripping open the wrapping on the store-prepared sandwich. "Dominic. You're an angel."

"I know." Acting on a whim, I seated myself on the chair on the opposite side of his desk.

He smiled around a mouthful of sandwich. "And I get the pleasure of your company too. Just when I thought this day was going to be shit from start to finish."

I shifted uncomfortably on the seat. "You can tell me to go and do some work. You're the boss, after all." He shook his head emphatically, mouth too full to speak. Relaxing slightly, I distracted myself by staring around Tristan's office. I really needed to get someone to come and sort out the dents in the wall.

My gaze swung back to Tristan. He took a momentary break from wolfing down the sandwich. "Of course I want you to stay. I've been trying to pin you down for days." He waggled his eyebrows in a suggestive manner. "Literally and figuratively." I looked away again. Paul's words coupled with a flirty Tristan were doing strange things to my brain, making me believe things that weren't true.

I changed the subject. "Are you really going to give a statement to the press?"

Tristan's lip curled. "They won't go away until I do."

"They'll get bored eventually. They can't stay outside the building forever."

Tristan pulled an apple out of the bag and frowned at it. "What's this?"

"It's an apple. They grow on trees. I thought you might want something healthy."

He pulled a face, rolling it across the desktop toward me. I plucked it off the lacquered surface before it could fall to the floor and took a bite of it.

There was no point in letting it go to waste. "What are you going to say to them?"

"That I'm a bastard. That I didn't treat Maria like she deserved to be treated. That I cruelly dumped her because I was seeing someone else. That I—"

I discovered a sharp inhale of breath while chewing a piece of apple was a really bad idea: the apple lodged in my throat, and I coughed in an effort to dislodge it, dissolving into a choking fit. Tristan came up out of his seat and hammered me on the back. I was in no fit state to stop him. He passed his coffee across, encouraging me to take a drink. Accepting it gratefully, I pulled a face at the strength of it. "Who? I mean...I didn't realize...when...shit!"

"What?" Tristan hadn't returned to his seat. He perched on the corner of the desk, rubbing soothing circles on my back. At least, I assumed it was meant to be soothing. In reality, it was just distracting. I shifted away from his touch. "Sorry, it's none of my business."

Tristan's brow furrowed. "What isn't?"

"Who you're seeing. I'm just surprised you'd...with me, when you're seeing someone else. Christ! You're quite the player, aren't you?"

"Am I?" Tristan looked momentarily astounded before breaking into a laugh. I really didn't appreciate him finding the situation funny. Annoyed, I made an attempt to get out of the chair.

"I've got work to do. I'll leave you to it."

He leaned over, still laughing, gripping the arms of the chair. It left me boxed in and unable to go anywhere. "Hang on. Wait. Don't run away. Just to be clear—you think I had a fiancée, then I started seeing someone else so I dumped Maria, then I decided to sleep with you. Is that right?"

I gave a tight nod. "It's fine. It's really none of my business."

"You're an idiot."

Reeling back at the insult, I glared at Tristan. Coming from the usual cheerful, unflappable man, it packed an extra punch. "You're probably right." I turned my head, fixing my gaze on the wall so I didn't have to look at him. If he was going to sit there and be smug about how easily he'd gotten me into bed and what an idiot I'd been to fall for it, well I'd just ignore him.

Tristan kept talking. "When I told Maria I was seeing someone, I was talking about *you*. I don't know why this is a surprise. I told you the other night."

I shifted my gaze back to him. At least he'd stopped laughing. "Told me what?"

"You asked why my engagement had ended. I told you I'd realized I preferred spending time with you."

It was my turn to laugh. "That's hardly true though, is it?"

Satisfied I was no longer going to make a run for it, he released the arms of the chair and sat back. "Of course it's true. We were spending most of our evenings together, seeing each other all day at work. I was spending far more time with you than Maria. When I wasn't with you, I was thinking about you. You must have seen that from all the messages I kept sending you."

His take on the messages was pretty similar to what Paul had said to me less than an hour ago. "That doesn't mean..."

Tristan had a thoughtful look on his face. "It didn't hit me until the day we were meant to be going for lunch. You know, the day Maria turned up and you tried to cover for me. I was sitting opposite her, this gorgeous woman who I was meant to be getting married to, wishing she was you. Thinking I'd be having a much better time if I'd been with you. I could hardly go on and marry her after that, could I? I ended it with her that evening."

I remembered how distracted he'd been the next day. It had been the same day he'd invited himself around to watch *Game of Thrones*. I was still struggling to make sense of the things he was saying. "You told the press you were *seeing* someone else. We weren't seeing each other."

Tristan smiled wryly. "Weren't we? Once I took my head out of my ass, it felt an awful lot like dating to me. At least on my part."

"Why didn't you tell me any of this before?"

Tristan shot me a wry look. "You were seeing Adam. You let me think things were more serious than they were. I thought you were a couple. I could have kicked myself for putting you together in the first place. Talk about providing your own obstacles. I couldn't say anything, even when I'd finished things with Maria, because of him. I didn't want to mess things up for you."

I took a moment to digest his words, seizing on the part that made little sense to me. "We weren't seeing each other."

"I said it felt like it on my part. I don't know about your feelings. I still don't know about your feelings. You keep running away, and you're really bloody difficult to read. I've spent two days trying my best to have this conversation. I—"

"You're straight." My words came out a little more accusatory than I'd intended.

"So you keep telling me."

"You said you didn't want me getting the wrong idea."

"I didn't want you thinking it meant nothing. It did mean something. It meant a lot...to me." Tristan looked suddenly nervous. "What did it mean to you?"

"I don't know."

The clear disappointment on Tristan's face did strange things to my stomach. I felt inexplicably guilty. "I need some time. To get my head around what you've said. I don't...I just need time. This is...this is all—"

Tristan nodded slowly. "Okay. I guess."

There was a long, awkward pause where I looked everywhere but at Tristan. When my gaze slid sideways to the door, Tristan immediately leapt off the corner of the desk, traversed the office in a matter of strides, and locked the door. He leaned back against it, smiling mischievously.

I gaped at him in shock. "What are you doing?"

"You're obviously desperate to leave. You can—of course. But there's one condition."

Standing up from the chair, I approached him warily. "What condition? Actually, don't tell me. I don't want to know. Just unlock the door."

"One kiss then I will."

"That's your condition?"

He nodded.

I fixed him with the steeliest stare I could muster. "Unlock the door."

He shook his head, seemingly unmoved by my attempt at displeasure. "Come and unlock it yourself."

"What happened to giving me time to think?"

"I will. After."

I stared at him, feeling like I was in some sort of dreamworld. I didn't have a clue how to handle him. What was it about Tristan that threw me off so badly? Maybe it was the model good looks? Or the nagging itch at the back of my mind where I still thought of him as straight? Maybe it was the undeniable fact he was my boss, and I shouldn't be touching him with a bargepole? Although it was probably a little late to be worrying about that one. Maybe it was the fact he'd just declared he had feelings for me, and I didn't have a clue what to do with the information.

He crooked a finger in a provocative come-hither gesture. Despite knowing I should return to the desk, sit down, and refuse to move until he opened the door, I found my feet moving toward him. I stopped a few steps away. He made no move to touch me.

"One kiss?"

He nodded.

I took another step forward. "You realize you are the most irritating, annoying man in the world."

"Probably, but kiss me anyway."

"And then you'll open the door?"

"Of course. You're not my prisoner."

Sighing, I closed the remaining space between us. I leaned in, fully intending to deliver a brief peck on the lips and then insist I'd met the condition. But I wasn't prepared for his arms to immediately snake round my waist, pulling me flush against him, while his lips immediately opened under mine. Heat engulfed me, and suddenly the only thing that mattered was getting as close as possible and exploring his mouth fully. I let out a moan as his hands skimmed below my suit jacket to grasp my ass. Lost in the moment, it took longer than it should have to become aware of a sound from the adjoining office. My office. I pulled away with a gasp, holding Tristan at bay when he immediately tried to initiate another kiss. Panicked, I tried to put some space between us, but Tristan's arms were like a steel vise around my waist.

Tristan stared down into my face, his brow wrinkled with confusion. "What! What's wrong?"

I shushed him, gesturing at the door behind his head and whispering as quietly as I could. "Someone's in the office."

He cocked his head, amusement twinkling in his eyes. His whispered reply felt like I was being humored. "So? The door's locked. Whoever it is can't come in here."

"Who is it?"

Tristan twisted slightly, aiming a brief glance at the solid door at his back. "I don't know. I can't see through wood."

I jumped when a firm knock suddenly reverberated off the surface next to Tristan's head. It was closely followed by the sound of a voice. "Tristan, are you in there? I thought I heard voices. I'm looking for Dominic."

Recognizing the familiar voice, I mouthed the word, "Adam."

An unprecedented scowl immediately graced Tristan's handsome features. He ducked his head, whispering right into my ear. "Do you want to talk to him?"

I glanced down to where the fit of my jacket didn't quite manage to hide the state of my arousal. "Like this?"

Tristan smirked, then held his finger to his lips while we both listened carefully for further sounds. Finally, there was the tell-tale sound of footsteps retreating and the click of the external office door closing. I exhaled noisily. "Now unlock the bloody door. I've got work to do."

Miraculously, Tristan did so without argument. However, he made no move to open it or even to step aside. "Can I come round to your apartment tonight?"

I was shaking my head even before he'd finished the sentence. "Give me time, Tristan, please."

He nodded his acquiescence, backing it up by pushing the door open. After a long, searching look, he moved out of the way. Entering the office, I half expected to find Adam still waiting, but the office was blessedly empty.

It was mid-afternoon before I saw Tristan again, and even then it was only briefly on his way out to talk to the press. There wasn't a lot I could say or do apart from wishing him good luck. He responded with a tight smile.

Ten minutes later, footsteps sounded outside the room. Assuming it was Tristan, I raised my head with a smile, ready to try to cheer him up after his grilling by the reporters. The smile faded quickly when Adam strolled through the door. If he noticed my lack of pleasure at seeing him, he chose to ignore it

"Hi, Dominic. I looked for you earlier but you weren't here. I tried to talk to Tristan to find out where you were, but he didn't answer." He rubbed a hand through his hair as I continued to simply stare at him. "It was weird, though. I thought I heard you in there. I could definitely hear voices."

My voice came out flat. "He was probably on the phone. And you didn't hear me. I wasn't there." I didn't feel remotely guilty about lying to him.

He shrugged and then smiled. "Anyway—"

I waited, drumming my fingers impatiently on the desktop. He stood there, still smiling, not saying a word. Eventually, I cracked. "What do you want, Adam?"

"We need to talk."

"About what?"

"You know what. The other night. I'd had a lot to drink, and you weren't there, and Lon had been making eyes at me all night. It just happened. And it's not like we ever said we were exclusive, so—"

I held a hand up as a signal for him to pause. "Hang on. I'm confused. Shouldn't we have had this conversation two days ago? I've heard nothing from you. Not even a phone call or a text."

Adam shifted uncomfortably. "I thought I'd give you a couple of days to miss me. Anyway, like I said, it didn't mean anything. I'm not even sure Lon's gay. I think he's just confused." He smiled again.

"What are you expecting me to say to that?"

"To be honest, Dominic, you know things between us... I wasn't sure what the hell was going on. You were quite... So you can hardly blame me for having a bit of fun. But, you know I do like you. It just depends if you're going to carry on playing hard to get. If you actually relaxed a bit, then I'm sure we could have a bit of fun without all this drama. What do you say?"

"No way!"

For a moment, I thought the words had come out of my own mouth. I'd been about to say the same words, or at least something incredibly similar. It wasn't until Tristan came into view over Adam's shoulder that I realized the words had come from him.

Adam turned with a frown. "Oh, hey, Tristan. This is kind of a private discussion. So if you don't mind..."

Tristan raised a disbelieving eyebrow. "You're ordering me out of my own office?"

Adam visibly paled. "Oh, no, of course not. It's just..."

Tristan folded his arms, pinning Adam with a stony gaze. "Good! Because that probably wouldn't be the best idea. You know, considering I'm the boss and—" Tristan made a big show of checking his watch. "—it's in work time, and you're harassing my staff. Did you not embarrass him enough the other night in front of his work colleagues?"

"It wasn't. I didn't. I just explained to Dominic what happened. I just wanted a few minutes to—"

"To convince him it was his fault you were getting it on with another guy?"

Adam shook his head. "Of course not. It was entirely my fault. Dominic's just a bit of a challenge. You know what I mean, right?" He smiled at Tristan like they were sharing some sort of inside joke.

Tristan met his gaze head on, his expression not changing one iota, before slowly turning my way, a clear question in the look. "Dominic, do you want to talk to him?"

"Not particularly."

Tristan swung his gaze back to Adam. "You heard the man."

Adam took a step toward the desk. I had no idea why he was pushing this. He'd pretty much said himself that I was too much hard work. Did it sting his ego that much that he hadn't managed to get me into bed?

"Shall I give you a call, Dominic? Then we can talk properly. See what we can do to sort things out."

I glanced at Tristan. He stood as still as a statue, watching the interchange between the two of us closely. As invested as he was in the outcome, I knew he'd give me privacy if I asked for it.

Returning my attention to Adam, I tried to make my words as clear as possible. The last thing I wanted was for either of the men watching to misunderstand my feelings.

"There's no point in us talking, Adam. Listen, I can't really blame you for the other night. We were nowhere near as serious as everyone else seems to think. But that doesn't mean I'm not annoyed about you putting on a show in front of colleagues at the bloody Christmas party. I really could have done without being the subject of gossip. I'm not going to—" I deliberately avoided looking Tristan's way. Maybe I should have requested some privacy. "—sleep with you. You're a nice guy. But there's no real spark there. And I'm sorry if you feel like I've been stringing you along. I didn't mean to. But even if I was more into you than I am...was, there's no way I'd ever give anyone another chance who showed so little regard for me in front of my whole workplace. I'd look like a total mug to everyone."

It was lucky Adam's gaze remained fixed in my direction during my speech. It meant he missed the smirk of satisfaction that briefly crossed Tristan's face before he masked it.

Adam opened his mouth to say something. Before he could, Tristan held the door open, in a clear instruction to leave. Adam took the hint, leaving without another word.

LOUNGING ON THE SOFA, I fiddled with my phone, contemplating the events of the day. After Adam's departure, I hadn't really gotten a chance to speak to Tristan due to the fact he'd been called away to an unscheduled meeting. I'd heard through the grapevine that his interlude with the press had been particularly grueling. It seemed at least three members of staff had sneaked out to witness it. The gossip had spread round the building like wildfire detailing what a terrible fiancé he'd claimed to be. I'd been fighting the urge to message Tristan for the last thirty minutes but with no real idea what to say, I hadn't gotten any further than thinking about it. I nearly dropped the phone as it chimed in my hand.

Tristan: *I'm not messaging you, because I'm giving you time to think. So you're imagining this. Xx*

I couldn't hold back the smile. It was a typical Tristan message.

Tristan: *I've just got home from the gym.*

Tristan: *Intensive workout. I worked out my forearms.*

Tristan: *For you ;) Xx*

Dominic: *I don't know why you're telling me that.*

Tristan: *No reason. Just making conversation. Xx*

Tristan: *Can I tell you something?*

Dominic: *If I said no would it make any difference?*

Tristan: *You like my forearms. I really, really like your...*

I waited a few minutes for the next message, knowing full well he was doing it deliberately.

Tristan: *hair. Xx*

Dominic: *My hair!!!!!! Are you winding me up?*

Tristan: *No. It's the color. It's unusual. I keep picturing it draped over my*

He'd finished the message with an eggplant emoji. I stifled a laugh.

Dominic: *If it's gone purple, you really need to visit a doctor.*

Tristan: *I've got a better idea. You can examine it for me. Just be gentle. Xx*

Dominic: *You're insane. X*

Tristan: *I got a kiss! I finally got a text kiss from you! I'm as happy as a teenage girl. XXXX*

Dominic: *Shut up.*

Tristan: *:(*

Tristan: *Anyway, you need to be thinking, so I'm going to leave you alone. Good night. Sleep well and I'll see you in the morning. XXX*

Dominic: *You too. X*

Chapter Twenty-Five

I'd barely taken two steps into the office before I stopped dead. I blinked, expecting the image in front of my eyes to disappear. It didn't. The entire surface of my desk really was covered with a huge flower arrangement, the computer shoved to one side to make room. I approached it slowly. Circling the desk cautiously, I jumped when Tristan burst out of the adjoining room. "Hey! What do you think?"

"What do I think?" I continued to stare at the floral tribute. It was mainly constructed of white flowers with the odd touch of red. In its center was a large heart with an I and a U surrounding it. "What's it doing here?"

Tristan moved in close. "They're for you. I wanted to get them delivered later, while you were here. But for some reason—I think it was something to do with the size—the florist said they could only deliver early. Something to do with the availability of the van. I don't know. It didn't make a whole lot of sense. But by then it was too late to order from anywhere else."

I was still fixated on the flowers. "Why?"

"Why?" I could hear the frown in his voice, even without turning. "I'm romancing you. I gave you time to think, now I'm...you know. Do you like them?"

I finally turned to face him, trying to gauge whether he was serious. His face exuded complete sincerity. I bit back the sarcastic comment hovering on the tip of my tongue. "Tristan, what do you think the purpose of these flowers is?"

His brow furrowed. "The purpose? I told you. I'm romancing you."

"Not *your* purpose. The original purpose?" I stepped out of the way, allowing him an unobstructed view of the flowers. "Where have you seen flowers like this before?"

He studied them carefully. I waited patiently for the penny to drop, but when no dawn of realization came, I prompted him. "Maybe in the back of a car? A long, black car. Or at a church?" He continued to stare blankly at them. I ran out of patience. "Oh, for God's sake, Tristan! They're funeral flowers. You've given me flowers meant for a dead person."

He reached out, lightly touching the edge of a petal. "Are you sure?"

"Quite sure. Now will you help me get the bloody thing off my desk? I can hardly get any work done if I can't even get to my computer."

It took a while, but between us we finally managed to wrestle the oversized monstrosity to a new position, leaned up against the wall.

Tristan stared at it with a look of sorrow. "So you don't like them?"

Picking loose petals from the sleeve of my suit jacket, I could only manage to shake my head in absolute bewilderment.

THE LOUD, ENTHUSIASTIC—AND not to mention persistent—knocking on my apartment door could only belong to one person. I wrenched the door open to find the predictable, smiling figure of Tristan. From the fact he still wore a suit, I would have deduced he hadn't been home, if it weren't for the large earthenware pot cradled in his arms. He held it out. "I cooked for you."

"You...*cooked* for me?"

Taking advantage of my surprise, he breezed past me, heading straight for the kitchen. Left with very little choice, I closed the door and trailed after him. I found him rifling through the drawers. Pulling a spoon out with a flourish, he slid the lid off the pot. "It's my mum's recipe. You'll love it."

I had to admit the aroma coming out of the pot did smell great. My stomach rumbled in appreciation. "What is it?"

"Thai vegetable broth." Tristan dug a large spoonful out. "Try it."

Remembering the sandwich incident, I took a step back, putting a safe distance between myself and the proffered food. "Hang on. What's in it?"

"Ginger, chili, lime, vegetables, tomatoes." He thought for a while, obviously trying to recall any ingredients he'd missed. "Oh, coconut milk, lemongrass. Erm...garlic. The green bits on the top...that's coriander."

"Anything else?"

Tristan shook his head, holding the spoon out again. Remembering how I'd rejected his flowers earlier that day, I didn't have the heart to do the same to his food. I took the spoon, obediently swallowing the contents. I drew the line at letting him feed me.

"What do you think?"

I was about to answer with a positive affirmation, when the all-too-familiar sensation hit me: my throat tightened, and my heart began to pound. Something must have shown on my face, as Tristan moved forward with a look of concern. "What's wrong? Did you swallow the wrong way? Need me to pound you on the back?"

"It's got fish in. You didn't say that."

"A teaspoon of fish sauce. It's only a tiny bit."

My head swam, and my breathing became labored. My voice came out in a gasp. "Allergic."

Tristan prised the spoon out of my hand. I hadn't even realized I was still holding it. "Shit! Just a bit though, right? You're going to be okay?"

Shaking my head, I struggled to get words out. "Anaphylaxis. Need...epi pen." I bent over, clasping my thighs, putting all my concentration into breathing as deeply and as slowly as I could.

Tristan's panic was clear to see. "Where is it?"

"Night...stand."

He was out of the room even before I'd finished speaking. In a matter of seconds, he was back. I was greatly relieved to see him clutching the epi pen. "I don't know what to do!" The anguish in his voice was clear, even though I couldn't see his face. I gestured for him to hand it over, immediately removing the lid and jabbing it into the upper quadrant of my thigh. I waited a minute, ignoring Tristan pacing in the background. Finally, he came to a halt beside me. "That's it, right? Now you're going to be okay?"

My breathing had eased enough to enable me to stand upright, but it was still an effort. "Now...I need to go...to the...hospital. Can you ring...an ambulance?"

"Hospital? Are you winding me up?"

I managed to summon enough energy to glare at him. "Right. Can barely breathe...but—"

Giving up on the insult—it was hardly the biggest priority—I headed for the living room, where I remembered leaving my phone. Tristan grabbed my hand before I could pick it up.

"Sorry. I thought. My car's outside. It'll be quicker. I'll drive you."

Nodding, I allowed him to lead me out of the door, lock my apartment, and steer me to his car. Once safely ensconced in the passenger seat, I closed my eyes and leaned my head back. Tristan started the car, and I felt it pull away from the curb. "I'm so sorry, Dominic. This is all my fault. You should have told me you were allergic to fish. Is it all fish, or just some? Don't answer that now. You just need to concentrate on breathing and not—"

I answered without opening my eyes. "Dying?"

"Don't say that word!"

I smiled. Even my current incapacitated state didn't prevent amusement at his reaction. "I assure you, my number one priority is not to die."

"Good." There was a pause. I assumed he was navigating his way through traffic. A wave of nausea hit. It was hard to tell whether it was a result of the anaphylaxis or a side effect of the medication. I focused back on Tristan's voice.

"But you should have told me. This is a major thing. Aren't you meant to wear some sort of medical bracelet or something? Sorry, I shouldn't be having a go at you. After all, you did ask me about the ingredients. But if I'd known why you were asking, then I would have remembered it had fish sauce in. Then I wouldn't have done this to you. You're the last person I'd want to hurt. Dominic?"

When I didn't answer, he repeated my name with more urgency. "Do you need me to pull over?"

Assuming he was looking in my direction, I shook my head. The movement did nothing for the nausea. "Just get to the hospital. If I lose...consciousness before...we get there, tell them...severe fish allergy...anaphylactic shock. I've had one shot of epinephrine."

"You're going to pass out?"

"It's a possibility."

"Shit! I wish I'd never bloody cooked anything."

You and me both. I felt the car lurch forward as he stepped on the accelerator.

Chapter Twenty-Six

The familiar smell of disinfectant tickled my nostrils. It didn't make any sense: I couldn't even remember cleaning. Even stranger, someone was holding my hand, their thumb gently stroking the back. I enjoyed the sensation for a minute. Then curiosity forced me to open my eyes. Blinking against the bright light, I struggled to make sense of my surroundings. The grip on my hand tightened. I turned toward its source. Tristan! That's right. The Thai broth, complete with fish sauce, had sent me into anaphylactic shock. My voice came out in a croak. "Hospital?"

Tristan leaned forward and smiled reassuringly. "Yes. You passed out. Scared the absolute shit out of me. I got you here as quick as I could. They gave you oxygen and fluids. I think they gave you another shot of adrenaline. How do you feel?"

I considered his question. "Like I've been run over by a truck. How long was I unconscious?"

"About an hour. Not too long."

I shifted slightly, taking care to avoid dislodging the IV, which was in the opposite arm to the hand Tristan still had hold of. "So you've just been sat here waiting for me to wake up?"

Tristan frowned, casting a barely susceptible glance over to the far wall before quickly looking away. "Of course. Where else would I be?"

I turned my head to the side in an effort to see what he was avoiding looking at. In the center of the wall, minding its own business, sat a fairly small spider. "There's one of those things we don't mention the name of over there."

The grip on my hand tightened considerably before relaxing again. "I know. I'm aware of that."

I couldn't hold back the smile. "I thought you were holding my hand to comfort me. Now I'm not so sure it's not the other way around."

"I can neither confirm nor deny your theory."

The door to the room squeaked open before I could offer any further response. I raised my head slightly to see who it was, watching as a heavyset nurse bustled into the room. I let my head drop back to the pillow with a *thud*, the effort too great.

She walked over to the bed, placing herself back in my line of sight and offering a smile. "I see the patient's finally awake." I saw her frown slightly at the sight of our joined hands. Turning her attention to Tristan, she fixed him with her best no-nonsense stare. "I need to speak with Dominic in private. Can you give us five minutes?"

Tristan bristled immediately. "I'm not leaving him alone."

It was obvious something was bothering the nurse. Wanting to find out what it was, I pulled my hand from Tristan's grasp. "I'll be fine, Tristan. It's just for five minutes. Just do as she asks."

Reluctance clearly etched into his face, he got up. "Five minutes, and then I'm coming back." Giving the nurse a prolonged, hard look, he left the room. The nurse, Gloria according to her name badge, waited until the door had fully closed. Confused by what could be so important she needed to talk to me alone, I tried to read her face without success. "Is something wrong?"

She placed her hand on her hip. "You tell me. Your boyfriend brings you in muttering about giving you funeral flowers and poisoning you. We couldn't get any sense out of him." She stopped, as if considering her next words carefully. "If he's been making threats to you, and he's deliberately hurting you, then you need to speak to someone. I can give you the number of a helpline or put you in touch with people who can help. I can also get security to remove him from the building, or at least this room. I can't promise he won't sneak back into the hospital. But we can get him away from you. You just need to say the word."

I stared at her aghast. Tempting as it was to see Tristan's reaction to security manhandling him out of the room, even I couldn't be that mean.

Gloria completely misread my silence. "I know it's difficult, sweetheart, to admit when things are... Well, when things don't go to plan. That you may have made some wrong decisions. You're not the only one to have found yourself in that position. It—"

"He's not hurting me."

She raised a disbelieving eyebrow.

"And he's not my boyfriend. Not really. At least I don't think so. I think he wants to be, which is...weird." I paused at the expression on the nurse's face. "But, you don't really need to know that. You just need to know...this—" I gestured at myself lying in the hospital bed. "—was nothing more than an accident."

Gloria looked less than convinced. "Why is he sending you funeral flowers? If it's not meant as a threat, then what's that all about?"

I laughed. "Because he's an idiot who's not used to having to handle daily menial tasks, like ordering flowers for himself. He has a personal assistant who handles all that stuff for him." I decided against sharing the information that I happened to be that personal assistant. "God only knows what he actually asked the florist for. But there was obviously some sort of mix-up. He didn't intend to give me funeral flowers. He didn't even realize what they were. I had to point it out."

"He said he'd fed you fish sauce."

"Not deliberately. He cooked for me. He didn't know I was allergic to fish. I hadn't told him. I probably should have mentioned it. So you could say it was my own fault. I really appreciate your concern though."

Her face relaxed slightly. "You promise you're telling the truth?"

I smiled at her. "I promise."

She nodded, finally accepting my assurances. "Okay. Well, let's get on to the medical side of things then." Leaning over, she checked the IV. "We'll keep infusing fluids for about another hour. Then I should be able to take this out."

I interjected, "Then I can go home?"

She gave me a knowing look. "Nice try. You know you'll need to stay here overnight for observation."

I sighed. I had known that, but I'd been hoping that perhaps hospital policy had changed since my last allergic episode. "I feel fine now. I'm just tired. I'd sleep much better in my own bed."

Ignoring my pleading, she wrapped a blood pressure cuff around my arm and proceeded to take a measurement. Apparently satisfied with the results, she wrote on the chart at the end of the bed. "I'll be back to check on you in an hour. Anything else I can do for you before I go?"

I shook my head and she walked away, getting as far as reaching for the door handle. "Hang on! Wait!" She turned back, an enquiring look on her face. "There's a spider on the wall over there. Could you possibly get rid of it? He's...*I'm* not exactly a fan of them." She nodded, strolling over and efficiently evicting it out the window.

Within a minute of the nurse leaving, Tristan was back. If it weren't for the polystyrene cup in his hand, I would have assumed he'd been hiding somewhere, waiting for her departure. He reclaimed his seat by the bed, immediately leaning forward with a look of concern. "What's wrong? What did she need to talk to you about? Are there some sort of complications? You have to tell me."

Wanting to see his face when I told him, I rolled over onto my side. "She wanted to rescue me. From you. She thought you'd been making death threats, and that you'd tried to kill me."

His brow furrowed as he digested my words. "You're winding me up, right?"

I allowed myself a smirk. "Afraid not. You shouldn't have dragged an unconscious man into a hospital, talking about funeral flowers and being poisoned. It brings out the suspicious side in people."

"I didn't." He paused for a moment, scratching his head. "Did I? I can't really remember. It's all a bit of a blur. I was so scared you were going to die."

"Anyway, she was lovely. She offered to get security to throw you out of the hospital."

Tristan's gaze immediately flicked to the door, clearly expecting them to burst through at any moment. "You put her straight though, right?"

I left a dramatic pause before letting him off the hook. "Of course I did."

Tristan plucked my hand from the sheet, resuming the same rhythmic stroking from earlier. Dismissing the brief urge to protest, I relaxed, closing my eyes at the soothing touch. If he kept that up, he was going to send me to sleep.

The peace only lasted a few moments. My eyelids crashed open when Tristan none too gently snatched his hand back. It meant I could witness his dramatic leap from the chair. The momentum sent it crashing to the floor. He stood, looking wildly around, panic etched into his features. "Where is it? Where's it gone? Oh, Christ!"

I reached out with the intent of calming him down, but my hand only grasped at thin air. He was too far away. "Tristan, calm down. What's wrong?" I'd only ever seen him this wild-eyed once before, back in the hotel room. That was when I realized what the problem was. "Tristan—the...it's gone. I got the nurse to put it out the window."

He eyed the underneath of the bed suspiciously, like he expected it to have grown twenty times in size and come hurtling out from under it. "Are you sure?"

"Quite sure. Sit down."

"You saw it go out the window?"

"Yes. I promise."

Seemingly placated, he sat back down. "Sorry. I could just about handle it when it was over there. I could see it, but it wasn't moving. I even thought it might be dead. But not knowing where it is but knowing it's here some-where..." He gave a shudder. "I really hate them." He took a deep breath. "I'm meant to be making you feel better, not freaking you out. Sorry."

"Stop saying sorry."

"Sorry."

We both laughed at his automatic apology. "Tristan. Why don't you go home?"

He shook his head emphatically. "No way. I'm not leaving you alone."

"But I'm probably just going to go to sleep, and you've already sat here for over an hour. It was nice of you to stick around until I woke up. You even..." I gestured toward the now blank expanse of wall. "Put up with facing your fears to stay with me. That's really sweet of you."

He shrugged. "It's the least I could do. You wouldn't even be here if it weren't for me. Anyway, I'm not just going to abandon the man I love, am I?"

I replayed his words several times. They came out sounding exactly the same. "Pardon?"

"Hmmm...what? I said I'm not leaving you."

I made an effort to heave myself semi-upright up on the bed. I managed to lever myself onto my elbows so I could look properly into his face. "Not that bit. The other bit."

"I don't know what you—"

"Oh, for God's sake! You said the L word. You can't just throw that out there and then carry on like nothing's happened."

Tristan shuffled his chair closer to the bed. "I already told you that."

I stared at him. He seemed sincere. "I think I'd remember if you'd told me something like that."

"Well, I didn't exactly *say* it. But I did tell you."

"What is this? Cryptic comments? If you didn't say it, how can you be claiming you've told me? And don't look at me like I'm stupid."

Tristan smiled. "I'm not." He held his hands up in mock surrender. "I would never be that mean to someone lying in a hospital bed. I told you with the flowers."

"The funeral flowers?"

Tristan grimaced. "Yeah, thanks for reminding me of that fact."

I thought back to the flowers from that morning. They had indeed spelled out "I love you," only with a heart replacing the word *love*. I'd just assumed that was all part and parcel of the same mistake. "How was I meant to know that bit was intentional? What exactly did you ask the florist for, anyway?"

"I don't know." He thought for a moment. "Flowers that say I love you for someone I miss." He paused. "I suppose I can kind of see why they assumed you were...that you weren't around anymore."

I sank back into a horizontal position on the bed. The same nurse from earlier popped her head around the door. "Visiting hours are over in five minutes." She turned her attention to Tristan, obviously reading his desire to protest in his expression. "And no, there is no point arguing it or asking for longer." She took a good, long look at the way Tristan was dressed. "And don't offer a large donation to the hospital, either. That doesn't work. I've heard it all before." Tristan opened his mouth to speak and then just as quickly closed it again. "Good man. Now say goodbye to your friend, and be ready to leave in—" She checked her watch. "Four minutes now." She disappeared back through the door.

Tristan let out a whistle. "Wow, she's... I should employ her to make deals for me. She'd terrify everyone." He looked down at me. "I suppose I have to go. Are you going to be okay?"

"Of course I am. I'm just going to sleep, and then when I wake up, it'll be time to go home. I guess I can't work tomorrow. Sor—"

He laid his finger on my lips. "Don't even mention work. You're not setting foot in there until I say so. I'll ask what time they're going to discharge you in the morning. I'll come and pick you up and drive you home."

"You don't have to do that. You've got work. I can get a cab."

Tristan crossed his arms. "You're not getting a cab. Promise me you won't."

I rolled my eyes. "Fine. If it makes you happy, you can come and pick me up."

He dropped a chaste kiss on my forehead. "It'll definitely make me happy. I'll see you tomorrow. Sleep well."

Chapter Twenty-Seven

Morning found me shivering outside the hospital in just a T-shirt. It was a shame I hadn't been wearing a jacket, or anything with long sleeves, before Tristan had called round and my whole evening had gone to hell. I made a feeble attempt to rub some feeling back into my arms. It didn't really help. A glance at my watch revealed I'd already been here for close to ten minutes. Maybe they'd told Tristan a different time? Or maybe I was just incredibly stupid, trustingly waiting for the man I constantly had to remind to do the simplest thing. Yet I still stood here, simply because I'd made a promise. Laughing at my own naiveté, I turned, ready to head back into the hospital, just as a familiar car drew up at the curb.

Hurrying round to the passenger door, I climbed in. "I thought you weren't coming. I was just about to give up on you and call a cab."

Tristan looked suitably contrite. "Sorry. There were unscheduled roadworks. It meant I had to take a diversion, so it took longer than I'd anticipated. I got here as fast as I could. I tried ringing you, but I guess we left your phone behind yesterday." Tristan glanced across, frowning at the sight of the shivers I couldn't suppress, despite the interior of the car being considerably warmer than the frigid air outside. He shrugged out of his suit jacket, passing it across. "We also didn't bother to make sure you were dressed appropriately for December. Why were you waiting outside? You should have waited inside the hospital. I would have come and got you."

I hesitated for a moment before accepting the jacket and putting it on. It smelled of Tristan. Wrapping it around me, grateful for the warmth, I relaxed back into the seat. "I don't know. I guess I'm not thinking clearly."

Tristan started the car. "Not surprising, really, considering the last twenty-four hours." He reached over, turning the heat up to maximum.

We were both quiet throughout the journey to my apartment. I was content to warm up and watch the world go by. Why Tristan was so uncharacteristically silent, I wasn't sure. Maybe he was regretting offering to collect me from the hospital? That reminded me. "You're going to be late for your meeting."

Tristan threw a quick smile in my direction, before focusing back on the road ahead. "Stop worrying. You're not allowed to think about work today. Besides, I got it put back by an hour." He glanced at the clock on the dashboard. "I should get there with plenty of time to spare. There's not much point in being the boss if I can't rearrange stuff to suit myself, is there?"

Taking it as a rhetorical question, I returned to staring out of the window, watching the familiar buildings come into sight the closer we got to my apartment. I released my seatbelt and turned as Tristan brought the car to a stop. "Thank you for coming to the hospital. You didn't have to, but it is appreciated." Realizing I was still wearing Tristan's jacket, I began to shrug my arms out of the sleeves.

Tristan looked momentarily perplexed, reaching over and tugging the jacket back over my shoulder. "I'm not just dumping you out here and leaving you. I'm coming up."

"That's not necessary."

He raised an eyebrow in challenge, daring me to argue. "It's entirely necessary." I followed Tristan as he headed toward the trunk of his car, still talking. "Besides I've been through your kitchen cupboards. Unless you've actually been shopping in the last couple of days, which I doubt, there's very little for you to eat." He heaved two large, heavy-looking grocery bags from the trunk. "So I got you a few essentials."

It looked like more than a few essentials. His thoughtfulness left me flustered. "What did you get me? Let me guess—crabsticks, fish fingers, and a lobster?" My attempt at a joke as a means to hide my discomfort fell completely flat, an immediate look of hurt crossing Tristan's face.

"I read all the labels. I'm ninety-nine percent sure there's absolutely nothing here with fish in it or that has ever been anywhere near fish. I'll check again when we get inside."

He spun on his heel, heading at a fast pace in the direction of the apartment building door, a grocery bag in each hand. Forced to break into a jog to catch up, I had to grab his shoulder to bring him to a stop.

"Tristan, I'm sorry. That was just a joke. A bad joke. And it's probably too soon to be joking about it. You shouldn't have gone to all this trouble getting groceries for me, but it's really considerate of you. I know exactly what I can and can't eat when it's in a packet or can. It's only restaurants and things that people cook that can cause a problem."

Tristan swung round to face me. "And I kept making you go out to eat. Why didn't you tell me?"

I shrugged. "I don't know. I've got it under control, so, you know... I guess I don't like to make a fuss. Or bore people silly with the details."

ONLY TWO HOURS SINCE I'd gotten home from the hospital, and I was already going absolutely stir crazy. If I could, I'd go into work. How strenuous could answering the phone and responding to a few e-mails possibly be? But I knew I'd be lucky to get one foot in the door before facing the wrath of Tristan. I wouldn't put it past him to have had a word with security, so it was entirely feasible I wouldn't even get into the building, never mind the office.

Smiling, I remembered his panic from that morning when he'd walked into the kitchen with the groceries. He'd taken one look at the abandoned Thai vegetable broth still on the kitchen counter and immediately barred me from going any farther into the room. Then he went one step further and ushered me back outside. Hovering outside the door, I'd tried to explain that it was unlikely to jump from the kitchen counter and contaminate me; that there was only a problem if I ingested it. It had fallen on deaf ears. I spent the next ten minutes listening to various scrubbing and clanking sounds. Tristan had finally appeared, clutching a black plastic bag with the remnants of the broth inside.

Spotting the look of amusement on my face, he'd frowned before announcing we weren't going to take any risks. Then he'd disappeared into my bedroom, appearing a few seconds later with an armful of bedding. Depositing it on the sofa, he'd bundled me under it like a child. Still amused, I'd allowed it without protest. Only after he'd bustled around the apartment, gathering various items he thought I might need and placing them all in arm's reach, had he finally left. I still hadn't worked out what I was meant to do with the scissors and glue.

Two hours of watching daytime TV later, and I was already climbing the walls. It didn't help that it provided plenty of time to dwell on Tristan's strange declaration of love the previous evening. I didn't know what to make of it. There was no way his feelings could be genuine. He was obviously just confused. Every time I let myself consider the remote possibility they could be, my gut filled with a mass of squirming snakes. I knew I needed to have a proper conversation with Tristan. It wasn't as if he hadn't been trying. I was the one who'd kept using evasive tactics. I reached for my phone. One message couldn't hurt. He was probably far too busy to answer anyway.

Dominic: *How's work? Are you managing without me?*

The response came almost immediately. So much for him being busy.

Tristan: *Forget work. How are you feeling? Have you had lunch? Xx*

Dominic: *You're meant to say you're struggling without me.*

Tristan: *I have a temp. She's surprisingly good. Not as good as you of course. But better than the usual temps. Xx*

Dominic: *Is she hot?*

I regretted the message as soon as I'd pressed send. I sounded like some sort of possessive, jealous idiot.

Dominic: *Stupid question. Sorry. Ignore it.*

Tristan: *So you don't want an answer to it then?*

Dominic: *No. Like I said, it was a stupid question.*

Tristan: *So you don't want to know she's in her fifties? Or that she showed me a picture of her grandchildren?*

Dominic: *Are you making that up?*

Tristan: *Honest truth, I promise. I love the fact you care though. Now don't spoil it with a jokey offhand comment where you pretend you never did and I just misunderstood. Xx*

What the hell was I meant to say in response to that? I was damned if I did, damned if I didn't. And he was using the bloody L word again. Not in the same way, but it was still there in black and white, messing with my head. I was saved from trying to think of a suitable response when my phone chimed immediately with another message.

Tristan: *Serious question. I want to come and see you after work and spend time with you. Will it be the usual battle, where you try and get rid of me? I have visions of standing outside your door while you ignore me.*

Dominic: *You make me sound like an ungrateful idiot.*

Tristan: *I don't want your gratitude. And you're avoiding my question.*

Dominic: *I'll let you in. We do need to talk.*

Tristan: *Sounds ominous. I'll see you later. Get plenty of rest. Xx*

Chapter Twenty-Eight

Tristan turned up far earlier than I'd anticipated. I took a moment to surreptitiously admire him as he stood on the doorstep. At least, I thought I hadn't made it obvious; his pleased smirk as he edged past me made me suspect I'd been less than successful. He headed straight for the couch, taking a seat at one end and patting his lap in clear invitation.

I stopped mid-stride. "What?"

He smiled. "Come and lie down." He patted his lap again. "Put your head here."

"Why?"

"I'll give you a head massage while we talk." He smiled. "I've never done it before, but it can't be that difficult." He held up his hands, waggling his fingers. "I've got magic hands."

I remembered those magic hands all too well from our night together. Thinking about it triggered an immediate swelling in my groin. Worried Tristan would notice, which would no doubt cause a great deal of smug satisfaction I could well do without, I disguised it by lying on the sofa in the position he'd requested. Ordering me to relax, he immediately sank his fingers into my hair and began a slow massage. It felt surprisingly good.

I closed my eyes. "Do you remember the message you sent, where you said you had a thing about my hair?"

Tristan made a sound I took as an affirmation.

"Was that the truth?"

I got the same sound again.

"So this is just an excuse to fondle my hair, then?"

Tristan chuckled. "Definitely. I'd try and fondle something else, but you're still recuperating, so I'll have to make do with your hair for now."

I ignored his last comment. I'd only just convinced my cock to calm down. "What did I miss at work?"

Sensing his hesitation, I opened my eyes to squint up at him. "What? What happened? What don't you want to say?"

He smoothed the lines from my brow. "Shhhh. You're meant to be relaxing. I was going to tell you later."

"Tell me what?"

He sighed. "Paul just got a bit upset about what happened last night. He...had a bit of a go, but—"

"What!" I made an effort to sit up, but immediately found myself pushed back down with a firm hand on my forehead. "How did he even know? I haven't spoken to him."

"He came to find out why you weren't at work, so I explained about last night, and the hospital, and you being unconscious when we got there."

I groaned. I dreaded to think how he'd phrased it. Given the wrong idea he'd managed to give the hospital, it shouldn't have come as too much of a surprise that he'd done the same with Paul. "Then what happened?"

There was the hesitation again. "He said some stuff."

His fingers kept up the steady massaging of my scalp. I could get used to this. "What stuff?"

"That I was an idiot. That I could have killed you. Oh, then he told me if I ever hurt you again, I'd have him to deal with."

"Shit!" I let the ramifications of Paul threatening the boss sink in. "Did you fire him?"

The fingers stilled for a moment. "No."

I craned my head back so I could see his face. "Are you going to?"

Tristan looked thoughtful. "I'll admit I thought about it. But I figure it's a personal thing rather than a work thing. It just happened to occur at work. Anyway, firing your best friend would only cause problems for the future."

I thought about his comment for a moment. "What do you mean?"

"Well, it'd be awkward, wouldn't it, every time our paths cross, if your friend and your boyfriend have that sort of history?"

I sat up. This time Tristan didn't try to stop me. "Do you want coffee? I'll make coffee, and then...then...we can talk." I felt like I needed to do something to break the intimacy between us prior to having a straight-talking conversation. Tristan looked less than pleased at the obvious delaying tactic but gave in gracefully. I was grateful when he didn't try to follow, instead remaining in the living room while I took my time making two cups of coffee. I carried them back through, finding him in exactly the same place as when I'd left.

He accepted the coffee with a smile. Instead of seating myself alongside him on the sofa, I pulled a chair across to position myself opposite. Wrapping my hands around the mug of coffee, I steeled myself to start the discussion. "Okay, so we need to talk."

Tristan nodded in response, gaze intently fixed on my own. "We both need to agree to be 100 percent honest, though, and feel free to discuss anything we need to."

"Sure." I narrowed my eyes at his immediate look of pleasure. What the hell was that about? I racked my brains, trying to work out what I'd just given him carte blanche to ask. I drew a complete blank. "Okay...so..." I really needed to find another way to start sentences. I was beginning to sound like a broken record. "Last night, you said...erm...you know, you said..."

Tristan smirked, and I wanted to slap him. Either that or go outside, find the biggest spider I could, and throw it at him. He leaned forward. "I said I loved you. Is that what you're trying to say?"

I nodded. The offhand way he said it was even more irritating. Maybe I'd make it a tarantula. "You know that's not possible, right? We've had sex once. People don't fall in love with other people when they've only had sex once."

"Don't they?" Tristan raised an eyebrow. "How many times?"

"What?"

"How many times do they have to have sex before they can fall in love?"

"I don't know."

"Interesting." Tristan affected an exaggerated thinking face. "But you know it can't happen after one time?"

I took a slow sip of my coffee, giving myself time to formulate a response. Tristan hadn't even touched his. "Okay...so..." Same bloody words again. "We've established it's not possible."

Tristan laughed. "We've established no such thing. You're talking rubbish. If you want to know the truth, I'm pretty sure I was already in love with you *before* we had sex. You keep telling me I'm straight. Well, I'd have to have pretty strong feelings to decide to sleep with a man for the first time, right?"

"I suppose."

Tristan sighed. "I've done nothing but make my feelings toward you clear. I don't mind repeating it over and over again, if that's what you need to hear. But...I need something back. At the risk of sounding about twelve years old, do you even...like me?"

My head snapped back. "Of course I like you. I mean...you're—" I waved my hand up and down, trying to convey in actions what I couldn't easily put into words. "You're...you know—"

"That's just a physical thing. There's more to me than that."

"I know that."

He gave another long sigh and finally took a drink of his rapidly cooling coffee. "I know I keep messing up, what with the flowers and the broth, but I'll do better. And I know there's things I need to work on in bed. I probably gave you the worst blow job you've ever had." He directed a long, lingering look at my groin. "You know what they say. Practice makes perfect."

I shifted uncomfortably, willing the blood away from my cock. "It's not that."

"Then what is it?"

I chose my words carefully. "What happens in a few weeks' time, when you're done with experimenting, when the novelty wears off, when you realize people might find out we're having sex? I mean, I can't imagine your parents being too happy to discover you've gone from being engaged to a gorgeous model to doing God knows what with an average personal assistant—"

"They're fine with it."

It took a moment to digest Tristan's words. "What do you mean?"

"My parents don't care. I mean, I'll admit they were surprised when I told them, but they just want me to be happy."

"You—told—your parents about me?"

Tristan nodded enthusiastically. "Of course I did. We're a close family. We tell each other everything. They really want to meet you. I've told them you might not be able to come for dinner before Christmas, which they totally get, so they've said we can sort something out between Christmas and New Year. Or failing that, I suppose after New Year, but that means I'll spend the whole time being interrogated. I'll have to at least take a photo of you or something."

I watched with amazement as he pulled his phone out of his pocket and proceeded to do exactly that. I wrestled it out of his grasp and deleted it. "What the hell are you doing?"

Tristan frowned. "I told you. Taking a photo. So I can show it to my parents. I'm only going to have to take another one if you've gotten rid of it."

I glared at him. "How are you going to be able to do that with a broken phone?"

"It's not broken. It's—oh, I get you. Okay, no photos. When can I tell them you'll come round for dinner?"

I sat back, a hundred and one thoughts swirling around my brain. "So—" At least I'd managed to leave the word *okay* out of it this time. "You want to have...a relationship with me? You really think you're in love with me? You broke your engagement because you wanted me?"

Tristan's gaze locked steadily on mine. My heart was pounding, and my palms were suddenly sweaty as I waited for his response. "Yes. Yes, and yes."

I suddenly lost the ability to breathe. The most gorgeous guy I'd ever seen seemed to be 100 percent genuine. For the first time, I allowed myself to imagine the possibility of the two of us being together. Every obstacle I placed in the way, he just shrugged off or acted like it wasn't even a consideration. Lost in my own thoughts, I didn't realize I hadn't said a word until Tristan spoke again.

"Shit!"

My eyes snapped to his. "What?"

"You're trying to work out how to let me down gently. You really don't want me."

I was already shaking my head halfway through his sentence. "No. I do. I'm just finding this difficult to get my head around."

Tristan's beaming smile was infectious. I found myself returning it. He leaned forward, moving in for a kiss, but then pulled back at the last moment. "Hang on. You're not distracting me that easily. I had stuff I needed to clear up."

"Like what?"

Tristan cocked his head to one side, a look of mischief written all over his face. "Why did you hate me when you didn't even know me?"

Shifting uncomfortably, I avoided his eyes. "I don't know what you mean."

"Liar! You expect me to be honest, and I have been. Now it's your turn. I want to know why, when I was perfectly friendly toward you, I got death glares back, not to mention you shutting elevator doors in my face. It was pretty hurtful."

I rolled my eyes at the look of pseudo-hurt on his face. I really thought I'd convinced him he'd been imagining the elevator part. "Let's get one thing clear. I didn't shut the elevator door. I just didn't stop it from closing. There's a difference."

He folded his arms. "I'm still waiting for the explanation part."

I took a deep breath. "You can't expect to give an interview like you did, and everyone be fine with it."

"What interview?" I stared at him steadily. He didn't so much as blink. He cocked his head to one side. "Seriously. What interview?"

"The interview where you called all your staff minions and said that you don't have to work hard because you pay people peanuts to do that for you. There was other stuff you said, as well. But that's probably the statement that annoyed me the most."

A look of comprehension dawned. "Oh, that interview! The one where they completely misquoted me and I'd actually said only about ten percent of the words they printed. You didn't believe that, did you?"

My face obviously gave me away.

"You did! You've worked with me for weeks. Is that the attitude you've seen from me?"

I ducked my head, my cheeks flaming. Well, when he put it like that... "Well, no...but—"

"I can understand you believing that crap before you knew me." He shook his head. "But to still believe it now? Why didn't you just ask me about it?"

"I don't know. If it wasn't true, why didn't you sue?"

"It's not worth it. If they print a retraction, it's usually so small that no one sees it anyway. Or even worse, people see it and then go and read the original article when they wouldn't have seen it otherwise. You end up making a big deal out of something that anybody that matters knows is utter bull-shit."

"What did you say? You must have said something. They can't just make everything up." I knew I was taking a defensive stance but couldn't stop myself. If there wasn't even a seed of truth in it, it meant I'd been an absolute idiot. I remembered Paul's offhand dismissal of the article. He'd been able to see through it. Why hadn't I?

"I don't know. It was ages ago. I certainly didn't use the word minions. I probably talked about the fact that my staff were so hard-working, I was lucky if they left me anything to do. I didn't say they were paid peanuts either."

I sat back, feeling like an idiot. "Sorry."

"Was that it?"

"Mostly?"

His eyebrow quirked in a question.

"I'm scared if I tell you the rest, your already large ego will swell to gargantuan proportions."

A smug look crossed his face. "Oh, God! Were you trying to get me to notice you? Was it like when you're at school and you're only mean to the people you really, really like?"

"Hardly."

"Well, what then?"

"I just thought you were too irritatingly perfect." Suddenly, I had the urge to see his reaction when he found out what I used to call him. "I used to call you Mr. Fucking Perfect."

His eyebrows shot up. "Is that meant to be an insult? Because I have to tell you, people commenting on my perfection"—he paused to wink—"normally get rewarded."

I scowled. "You're not perfect. I said I *used* to think you were. Now I know you, well..."

"I could have told you that. Saved you all the hatred bit." He leaned forward again. This time it was me holding him back with a hand on his chest.

"There's something else we need to discuss. If you're serious about us having a..."

Tristan filled in the missing word. "Relationship. Surely it's not that hard to say."

Steadfastly ignoring him, I soldiered on. "Then I can't be both your personal assistant and your..."

"Boyfriend?"

"Yeah."

"So I have to choose. Is that what you're saying?"

I nodded, mouth suddenly dry.

Tristan rubbed his chin thoughtfully. "Well, that's a difficult one, isn't it?"

"Is it?" My voice came out lacking emotion. Which was ironic considering the churning, nauseous feeling which had taken over my whole body.

"Yeah, I mean, I've had far more experience of you as a personal assistant, and you are a really good one. Everything's always well organized. Reports never have any mistakes in them. You're really good at putting together my schedule. I've had PA's in the past who just don't bother to factor in getting from one place to another. They arrange for one meeting to start at the exact same time as they've scheduled the previous one to finish. I mean, you tell me how I'm meant to travel ten floors in under a minute. I don't really know what you're like as a boyfriend. How long have I got to think about this?"

I rocked back in my chair, hurt clawing at my insides. Eyes fixed on the floor, I didn't know what to say or do. Without looking at Tristan, I got up and headed for the kitchen. I had no idea what I was going to do once I got there. It just provided much-needed space between us. Space to gather my thoughts and put my protective armor back together. Or at least it would have, had Tristan not followed.

He grabbed my arm, turning me to face him. "I'm joking, Dominic. I didn't think you'd take me seriously. You asked a stupid question, so I gave a stupid answer." He cupped my cheek, ensuring I had to look at him. When I did, I was shocked at the blatant look of adoration directed my way. "Of course I'm not going to choose having you as a personal assistant over having you as a boyfriend. What part of me being in love with you are you still not getting? I won't pretend I don't want both, but I can see where you're coming from. I didn't have you down as being so insecure. Which, while we're on the subject, don't ever describe yourself as average again. You're gorgeous!" He stopped. I assumed, he needed to take a breath.

I took the opportunity to get a word in edgeways. "Sorry. I guess I need to be less sensitive."

His thumb stroked my cheek. "You don't need to be less anything...or more anything. You just need to carry on being yourself. I like your snark. I like your attitude. I like the fact you're hard work." He leaned forward so his forehead was resting against mine. "I like you."

I shifted the angle so our lips met. What started as a chaste press of lips soon deepened and accelerated until we were both left gasping into each other's mouths.

He was the first to pull back. "No sex tonight. You're still recuperating. And if we carry on like that for much longer, I'm going to forget all my good intentions."

I curled my hand around one of his biceps, using the grip to tug him back toward me. "I'm absolutely fine. I want you to stay."

A small smile played around his lips, betraying his pleasure at the invitation. "Oh, I am staying. I'm not going anywhere. But much as I want to, we're not doing anything tonight."

Chapter Twenty-Nine

I fumbled for my alarm clock, desperate to halt the incessant noise that had roused me from a deep sleep. Despite my rolling over and hitting the button, it continued. I hit the alarm clock again, this time so hard it bounced off the nightstand and crashed to the floor. Yet still the noise continued.

"Phone."

I jumped at the sound of the husky voice behind me. Rolling my head to the side, I met the gaze of a sleepy-looking Tristan. He looked gorgeous, even first thing in the morning, with his hair sticking up in all directions and his eyes half closed. "What?"

The noise stopped. Tristan smiled. "It's your phone, not your alarm clock. Correction. It *was* your phone." He closed his eyes again.

"Right. I knew that." I turned away again, peering over the side of the bed to take stock of the various pieces of plastic now littering the floor. "I think I need a new alarm clock."

Tristan's arm snaked around my waist, pulling me back against him, his warmth leaching into my back. "I'll buy you one, if you promise to put your phone on silent or call whoever it was back *before* they can ring and wake me up again."

"Deal." I relaxed back into his embrace, enjoying the feel of the taut, muscled body pressed against me. For a recently straight man, intimacy with another guy didn't seem to be an issue. He'd kept to his word the previous night. We'd both stripped down to boxers, and then he'd smiled and said good night before turning off the light. I'd lain awake long after Tristan was already sleep, trying to get my head around why it suddenly felt perfectly normal—no, not just normal, but nice—to share a bed with him.

I reached for my phone to check the caller display. Paul. What the hell did he want so early in the morning? Pressing the button to return the call, I ignored both the exaggerated groan against the back of my neck and the muttered words that he hadn't expected me to take the second option. I shushed him before Paul answered with a tired-sounding hello.

"Do you know what time it is, Paul?"

"Sorry. But I needed to talk to you. How are you? I heard what happened. I should have called you yesterday, but—"

I cut him off. "Well, that would definitely have been preferable to half-past five in the morning. I'm fine."

"Good." There was a long silence.

"Well, I'm really glad we had this conversation at half-past five in the morning, Paul. Did I mention it's not six o'clock yet?" A muted chuckle vibrated off the back of my neck. Tristan threaded his fingers with my free hand. I had to make a concerted effort to focus back on Paul again.

He seemed to be struggling with his words. "Sorry. Did you...erm...happen to...erm...talk to Tristan last night?"

"I did, and yes, he did tell me what happened between the two of you. What were you thinking, Paul?"

There was a muttered curse from the other end of the line. "Are you pissed at me? That's why I didn't call last night. I figured if you were, I'd give you a chance to calm down."

I answered honestly. "I'm not sure. I don't know whether to be angry you did such a stupid thing without even hearing my side of the story first or pleased you'd risk your job to stick up for me."

"Can you go for the latter option, please, so I can ask a huge favor?"

I had to admire his nerve. "What?"

"You're coming in to work today, right?"

"Definitely."

"Well, obviously I need to apologize to Tristan. I was wondering if you could butter him up for me first. You know, take him some doughnuts or something. You know him better than me. You must know a way to get him in a good mood. Please, Dominic. I'd do the same for you."

I dragged out the silence just long enough to worry Paul that I was going to say no. "I'll have a go. I can't promise anything, though."

Paul's sigh of relief was audible even over the phone line. "Thanks, Dominic. I'll see you at work later. I'll let you know how the groveling goes. Hopefully, I'll still have a job."

I mumbled my goodbyes, hung up, and placed the phone back on the nightstand before considering the man currently wrapped around me. It should have felt weird. It should have felt like I needed to get out of bed and put some distance between us. Instead, I felt like I could quite happily spend the day like that. The possibility of having a relationship with Tristan was becoming more and more attractive the more consideration I gave it.

I'd assumed he'd gone back to sleep until he spoke. "What did Paul want?"

I answered honestly. "He wanted me to come up with some sort of plan to put you in a good mood. So that when he comes to apologize for his hasty words yesterday, you won't make him suffer too much."

I felt the smile on the back of my neck. "Waking up with you, without you running away or ordering me to leave, is already putting me in a good mood."

It was my turn to smile. Not that he could see it. "So you don't want to know what my plan is then?"

"Does it involve breakfast?" The hopeful note in his voice was typical Tristan. I wondered when I'd begun to find his obsession with food endearing.

"Possibly, after."

"After what?"

Squirming out from underneath his arm, I pushed him onto his back and quickly moved to sit astride him above the covers, my hands resting on his bare chest. He squinted up at me, his slight look of confusion causing a sudden, excruciating attack of self-doubt. "This is okay, right? If you meant everything you said last night, then I figured this...is okay."

"This?" The glint in his eye gave away the fact he knew exactly what I was talking about. Rolling my eyes, I shifted back slightly, bringing my ass into contact with his morning erection. He smiled. "You can do anything you want with me."

"Anything? Be careful what you agree to, Tristan." I watched his expression closely, deliberately setting out to shock him. "I might decide I want to fuck you. Then you'll soon regret saying that."

The only reaction I got was a slight shrug. "What makes you think I'm not up for that?"

Left speechless, I stared, mouth wide open. Tristan laughed loudly, clearly enjoying my discomfort.

Finally finding words, I summoned a glare. "You're winding me up, aren't you?"

Another shrug. "Not really. Assuming you're up for it, that's definitely something I want to try. Maybe not today. But definitely at some point in the future."

"Okay." I didn't know what else to say. Just the mere thought of burying myself deep inside Tristan's ass had an instantaneous effect on my body. Given the position I was in, it was impossible to hide. I saw the moment Tristan's eyes flicked down to the erection tenting the front of my boxer shorts.

He smirked. "I'll take that as a yes." Tristan rotated his hips, rubbing the length of his own rapidly swelling cock against my ass. "Anyway, I've distracted you. I thought you were meant to be offering me your body as a supreme act of self-sacrifice for the good of your friend's employment status."

I blinked at him. "What?"

"Too early. You look gorgeous in the morning, by the way. I wanted to tell you that, the other morning. But the way you were looking at me, I was worried you'd rip my head off if I tried for a compliment."

"Thanks." Blushing, I pulled the sheet farther down, uncovering more of Tristan's chest. The other night, stupid idiot that I was, I'd avoided looking for the most part. Now, I was determined to look my fill. The sight almost took my breath away. Grabbing his arms, I placed them behind his head, admiring the way it showed off his biceps. "Leave them there. I'm the one doing all the touching this morning."

Lust smoldering in his eyes, Tristan threaded his fingers together behind his head, anchoring them more firmly. "If you insist. I think I like this side of you. Maybe I'll give Paul a raise."

I pulled the sheet down another few inches, taking a moment to admire the tanned skin on display. Shifting back slightly, I kept going, revealing a taut stomach followed by a hint of pubes. "You're really going to let me do this?"

Tristan flexed his biceps. "Let you! I'm going to positively encourage it. In fact, if you stop, I might never recover from the rejection."

Reaching over to the nightstand, I extracted a condom and lube, placing them next to me on the bed. Tristan's eyes tracked my movements. Smoothing my hands over his chest, I bent forward, provocatively trailing my hair over one nipple. The resultant groan was music to my ears. The other night, caught up in denial, I'd been swept along. This time, I wanted to make the most of it.

Tristan lay silently gazing up at me, an unreadable expression on his face. His lack of words began to make me uneasy. "You would say if I did anything you didn't like?"

His lip quirked. "Didn't we just have this conversation? I said you can do anything you want to me."

"What if I've got some sort of hidden fetishes you don't know about?"

Tristan's gaze wandered down over my chest before finally returning to my face, while he pretended to consider my words. "Unless you're going to shove a ball gag in my mouth and tie me to a cross, I think I'll cope." He raised his head to take a cursory glance around my bedroom. "Nope. No crosses. I'm safe."

I let my fingers trail across his stomach, enjoying the feel of the muscles fluttering beneath my touch. "How do you like it? Fast, slow, hard, soft?

He didn't even pause to think about it. "Both. All of them. Either. Don't care."

"You're not helping."

"*You're* not doing anything."

I had a sudden idea. One that would hopefully serve to remove the lingering doubts still in the back of my mind. The doubts which kept me questioning my every action. "I'll tell you what. Seeing as this is meant to be about me softening you up, why don't you tell me exactly what you want me to do, and I'll do it."

Tristan's eyebrows shot skyward. "Really? Promise."

"Promise." A momentary flash of having handed my soul over to the devil hit me. What if he was the one hiding the strange fetishes? I didn't have much time to worry, as Tristan got straight into the swing of things with his first instruction. "Kiss me."

I hesitated. "Morning breath. I haven't—"

He brought his knees up, the momentum knocking me forward. I over-balanced, sprawling awkwardly onto his chest. His look held a challenge. "Don't care. Neither have I. Just kiss me. Remember, you have to do what I say." I kissed him. A tentative and brief kiss, which slowly turned hotter and deeper. He pulled back momentarily. "Lose the shorts." Hand cupping the back of my head, he locked our lips back together.

"How am I supposed to—" I would have thought my mumbled response was indecipherable, limited as it was by being kissed at the same time, if it wasn't for the slight smile I felt in response. Although he'd obviously heard, he made no move to release me. I reached down awkwardly with one hand, doing my best to squirm out of my boxers without breaking the kiss. I had a sudden empathy and respect for contortionists.

As soon as I'd finally managed to wriggle out of my boxers, Tristan let go, amusement written all over his face. I sat back, shooting him my best dirty look. "You're not meant to make your instructions difficult. That's not fair."

He laughed. "I wanted to see if you could do it." His gaze dropped, and we both stared at the contrast of the pale skin of my erect cock against the tanned skin of his torso. "Stroke yourself. Don't stop until I tell you to."

I opened my mouth to protest. I'd never done that for anyone before.

Tristan's expression turned pleading. "Please. You look gorgeous. I want to watch. See what you like."

Self-conscious, I took a deep breath and closed my eyes, wrapping one hand firmly around my cock and starting a steady, rhythmic movement. My abdominals quivered as Tristan's fingers lightly trailed across them. "Good?"

Without opening my eyes, I managed a one-word reply. "Dry."

I heard the rustle of a packet. My hand was briefly pulled away, the palm smothered in lube, before being guided back onto my cock. I laughed. "That's service for you." I gasped at the first slick slide of my hand, the lube making it ten times better. Relaxing into it, I was almost able to forget I was being watched. Only the constant soft touch of hands over my body serving to re-mind me. Lost in the ecstasy of a steady climb toward climax, I almost ig-nored Tristan's instruction.

I blinked my eyes open, panting. "What?"

A flushed Tristan gazed up at me. "I said stop."

I tried to steady my breathing, my cock throbbing. I knew all I needed was a few more strokes. "But—"

He pulled my hand away. "Get rid of the sheet and take my shorts off."

I did as he asked, my gaze fixed on the erection I'd uncovered.

"Put the condom on me."

My eyes flicked to his. "You don't want me to suck you?"

He shook his head, his breathing irregular. "I've had about all the foreplay I can take. Watching you like that was—" He swallowed, his throat convulsing. "Condom, please."

Taking him at his word, I scooped up the condom packet from where I'd left it earlier. Using my teeth to open it, I slowly rolled the latex down over his cock, taking the opportunity to palm his balls. His abdominals flexed with the effort of keeping himself in check. "Lube."

Noting with satisfaction the instructions were now down to one or two words, I added a generous amount over the surface of the latex. I waited for the next instruction.

"Sit on my cock."

I wasted no time following that one. Tristan watched in rapt fascination as I lowered myself slowly until my ass met his pubes. Breathing hard, I closed my eyes again while I adjusted to the stretch. Shifting forward slightly, I braced my hands on Tristan's chest, searching for the optimal balancing position. He moaned as I moved, letting me know how good it felt.

I waited, finally opening my eyes to find Tristan staring intently. I leaned forward to steal a kiss, my hair falling into my eyes. "Well?"

"Well, what?" His voice came out strained.

"I'm waiting for instructions."

He sucked in a breath. "No more instructions. Apart from—"

"Go on."

"Fuck me...and I want to come first. So then I can watch you."

Nodding my agreement, I started a slow rise and fall, taking his cock deep inside me before lifting almost completely off him. His hands came up to grip my ass, encouraging me to move faster and slam down harder. I was happy to oblige, his cock rubbing my prostate on every downstroke. Within minutes, his fingers tightened on my hips almost painfully. He bucked up, crying out, as he emptied himself into the condom. I could certainly see the attraction to watching the other person reach their climax. I sat still, fighting the urge to stroke my cock until he was watching.

It took a while for Tristan's breathing to return to normal. When it did, his eyes finally opened. Smiling, he relaxed back into the same position as earlier, hands locked behind his head. He gave an encouraging nod. Wrapping my fingers back around my throbbing cock, I rocked back on the still-hard length embedded in my ass. Within three strokes, I was coming, my spunk splattering his chest.

I collapsed over him, happy to lie there in a post-orgasmic trance. He stroked his fingers lazily through my hair, making no complaint about my weight. As the minutes passed and he still didn't say a word, I became uneasy. Rolling my head sideways to see his face, I found him deep in thought. Concerned, I reached up, attempting to smooth away the furrows in his brow. "What are you thinking about?"

He didn't answer straight away, giving me plenty of time to panic. Was this where he admitted he'd been stringing me along? Was he having second thoughts? Had I finally gotten used to the idea of having a relationship with him, only for him to kick me to the curb? He rolled slightly, getting rid of the condom while hoisting himself into a half-sitting position against the headboard. When I took it as a signal to give him space and tried to squirm away, he kept a firm grip, rolling me with him so I ended up half sprawled across his chest. "Do I have to stop eating fish?"

I pushed off his chest so I could look him in the eye. "What?"

"If I eat fish and then kiss you, what happens?"

"*That's* what you're thinking so seriously about?" I accompanied my words with a thump to his chest.

He grabbed my hand, preventing me from inflicting any more damage, in case I was tempted. "Ow! That hurt. What did you think I was thinking about?"

"I thought you were having second thoughts about this." I gestured to where our naked bodies were still entwined.

"Never. You haven't answered my question."

"Basically. If you've eaten fish, you need to let me know. So I can stay away from you, and yes, definitely no kissing."

Tristan raised his eyes skyward. "That's too much of a risk. I can't do any more emergency hospital visits. I'll give up fish. You could have told me last night that the choice was personal assistant, fish, or boyfriend, and I only get to pick one of them."

It seemed churlish to point out that if he'd chosen personal assistant, he could still have had two out of the three. Besides, I didn't want him changing his mind. His mention of the previous night's conversation prompted a question that had been niggling at the back of my mind. With other priorities, I hadn't got around to voicing it, but now seemed a good a time as any. I paused, trying to phrase it carefully. "Are you going to honor your agreement to find a new personal assistant?"

Tristan looked affronted. "Of course. Why would you think I wouldn't?"

I guessed there wouldn't be a better opportunity to investigate whether there had been any truth in Paul's musings. "Well. Someone said—" Bringing Paul's name into it was hardly going to help the situation between Paul and Tristan. "—that you were deliberately finding issues with the people you interviewed. Issues that were—"

Tristan raised an eyebrow in a clear question.

"—perhaps not true. I mean, I found it hard to believe you'd play me like that. But some of what you said about them did seem a bit odd. And I know some of the questions you were asking, weren't exactly...anything to do with the job. Like lizards. Why would you need to ask about lizards?"

"I only asked *one* of them about lizards. I like lizards." Tristan looked suddenly enthused, like a great idea had just occurred to him. "We could get a lizard...or a cat. I like cats. Or both. I suppose you can have both. One's in a tank, and one's not, so I suppose you can have both. Do cats eat lizards?"

"Tristan?" The warning note about changing the subject was clear in my voice.

He sighed. "I wasn't playing you. That makes it sound really manipulative. But what was I supposed to do? You were so dead set on not working with me. Which, incidentally, I still don't get. If I'd hired one of them, you would have disappeared back to your office and never bothered speaking to me again."

"Not true."

He twisted his head, maintaining eye contact and displaying blatant disbelief. I looked away.

"Okay, so probably true."

"It may have taken me a while to realize I had these sorts of feelings." His hand swept down our bodies, pausing to squeeze my ass. "But even before that, I knew I wanted you as a friend. I had to do something. I couldn't have you going back to glaring at me and pushing me down stairs."

I sat up. "Pushing you down stairs? I've never pushed you down any stairs."

Tristan grinned. "Not yet. But it seemed a natural progression from closing elevator doors in my face."

"I didn't close it—"

"I know, I know. You just didn't stop it from closing. Not a lot of difference, if you ask me. I've forgiven you. We've established you were just trying to hide your true feelings. These things happen when you become overwhelmed and you think there's no chance of them ever being reciprocated."

I offered no more than a slight eye roll as a response. I wasn't rising to the bait. "So, back to the personal assistant thing. What are you going to do?"

Tristan looked thoughtful. "Who was the lizard guy?"

"Matthew."

"I liked him. His resume was very impressive. He seemed like a nice guy. And he never so much as blinked when I spent the majority of the interview asking him about lizards." Tristan laughed. The memory obviously amused him greatly. "Do you think there's a chance he might still be interested in the job?"

I thought back through the conversation I'd had with him prior to the interview. "Maybe. I could call and ask him, if you're serious."

Tristan nodded his agreement before pulling me down into a kiss.

I tangled my fingers in his hair, returning the kiss enthusiastically, surprised to feel myself already getting hard despite an orgasm less than ten minutes before. Reluctantly, I pulled my lips away from his. "We don't have time. We have to get to work."

Tristan rolled me, using his weight to pin my body to the mattress. "We'll make time."

I stared at him. I knew he was expecting an argument. He probably expected a list of ten reasons why I couldn't possibly be late for work. I pulled his head down, pausing only to mutter about him being an incredibly bad influence before our lips crashed back together.

Chapter Thirty

I sighed, changing the channel again, unable to settle down to watch anything properly. It had been a week since my big talk with Tristan and the night I'd asked him to stay. Since then, he'd barely left. Sex had been frequent and incredible. So finding myself unexpectedly alone tonight had sent my brain into overdrive. Tristan had been on the phone when I'd left the office. I'd offered a wave and received a nod and a smile in return. I'd heard nothing since: no messages, no calls.

Half an hour ago, I'd cracked, sending Tristan a brief message asking him what he was up to. I hadn't received a reply yet. I checked my phone again: still no reply. Was he already bored? Was he just busy? Busy doing what? Why wasn't he replying? I changed the channel again, determined to stop thinking about Tristan's whereabouts. Christ! It was one night. It wasn't like we needed to be in each other's pockets. After all, I was the one who insisted we never arrived at or left the office together. Maybe, if I wasn't quite so adamant about sticking to that, I would have waited for Tristan to finish the phone call, and we could have left and gone somewhere together. Then I would have known exactly where he was. So I only had myself to blame.

I jumped at the sound of the doorbell. Could it be the very man I was obsessing over? Opening the door revealed it was indeed Tristan, a very sweaty Tristan. He'd obviously come straight from the gym, dressed as he was in tight-fitting shorts and tank top. At least that answered the question of where he'd been. I let my gaze travel slowly over the great deal of flesh on display.

Tristan raised an eyebrow at my lecherous look. "I had to go to the gym. Someone has distracted me this week from having a workout. Well, they've given me plenty of workouts"—he winked—"but not at the gym, if you know what I mean."

Laughing, I held the door open as an invitation for him to come inside. He wasted no time taking me up on the offer. "I need a shower. I could have gone home and had one, but your place is closer to the gym, and I wanted to see you."

"And of course they don't have showers at the gym," I teased.

Tristan took the bait. "But then I would have had to put my suit back on. Which just feels all kinds of wrong when I've been to the gym. Anyway your shower—"

I interrupted. "Is better. I know. You've told me enough times."

"Know what is especially good about your shower?"

I played dumb. "Water pressure, size of the cubicle, positioning of the soap, color of the walls?"

Tristan grinned. "All of those, plus the added bonus of hopefully having you in it, if I ask nicely."

"Go on then."

"What?"

"Ask nicely."

Tristan smirked. "I'm going to try a different strategy: taking off all my clothes and hoping you follow."

I folded my arms, schooling my face to look decidedly unimpressed while my heart rate immediately increased tenfold. With great willpower, I managed to avoid licking my lips. I kept expecting the illicit thrill of seeing Tristan naked to dampen, but so far it hadn't. "You could try that. Not sure how successful it will be." I leaned nonchalantly against the wall and waited.

He smiled wickedly before folding his arms and slowly pulling his tank top over his head. Dropping it on the floor next to him, he smirked. "Want to take a shower with me?"

I shrugged. "Not sure. I had one earlier. I don't really need another one."

Tristan took a few steps closer to my bathroom before toeing off his sneakers, removing his socks at the same time. "How about now?"

I screwed my nose up. "Feet don't really do it for me. That's not going to convince me."

He took another few steps, which left him standing in the doorway of the bathroom. His hand slid into the waistband of his shorts, toying with the elastic. "This is not going well. I've only got one thing left to remove to convince you." He turned round slowly, hand braced against the door jamb while he bent over and removed his shorts with the other hand. I found myself staring at his perfectly proportioned tight ass. I hadn't fucked him yet. He kept mentioning it, but as yet, it hadn't happened. Now, with this view, it was all I could think about. Tristan glanced back over his shoulder, no doubt to see the effect his little striptease was having on me.

I forced myself to look calmly back, despite the fact I was sure my flushed face—not to mention the erection in my pants—probably gave away my true feelings. "Seen it before."

Tristan straightened up, still looking back over his shoulder. "Never mind. I tried. I'll just have to have a long, lonely shower, all by myself, completely on my own, scrubbing my own back—" The words became more muffled as he disappeared around the corner, and I heard the water switch on. "—talking to myself, stroking my own cock, making myself—"

I made a beeline for the bathroom door, staying just outside, unable to keep a big grin off my face now he couldn't see me. I raised my voice so I could still be heard over the noise of the water. "What was that last bit? Something about your cock?"

There was a long pause. "Don't worry about it. I don't need you anymore. I've already started. My own hand is fine."

"It's my shower. If I want to come in, I will."

"Not necessary. I won't be long." Tristan gave an exaggerated moan. "Not long at all."

I stepped over the discarded shorts in the doorway, shaking my head at Tristan's constant need to litter my apartment with his clothes. I'd barely set foot in the already fogged-up room when an arm snaked out of the shower cubicle, dragging me under the water. I spluttered, genuinely shocked. "Jesus, Tristan! Still got clothes on."

He grinned at me, without a hint of remorse. That's your problem. You had plenty of opportunity to take them off. You shouldn't be such a tease."

I began to struggle out of the sopping-wet clothes. "I'm a tease? What does that make you?"

Tristan gestured down to his fully erect cock. "Frustrated."

I threw my sweater and T shirt out of the cubicle and onto the bathroom floor, starting work on my jeans. "Why? Who was at the gym?"

"Nothing to do with the gym. You see—" Tristan reached out, steadying me as I nearly toppled over in the confined space while trying to get one leg out of the jeans. "—I've got this really hot personal assistant. Like *really, really hot*. However, he's really uptight about anything happening at work. I'm not even allowed to touch him. I've spent most of the day fantasizing about fucking him over my desk. Or his desk. Any desk, really. I'm not that fussy."

Finally naked, I threw my jeans in the same direction as the previous items. They landed with a wet *slap* on the bathroom floor. "You hid it well."

Tristan sank to his knees, his cheek almost brushing my cock. "I didn't want to upset him. Besides, the anticipation just makes it better."

I didn't know about that. The anticipation of him sucking my cock was just about killing me. Over the last week, practice had certainly made perfect. He'd committed himself to improving his technique like the most dedicated student known to man. My head thudded back against the tiled shower wall as he yet again set out to demonstrate how much he'd learned.

TRISTAN SPRAWLED NAKED across my sofa, squinting down at his phone. "Hey! You sent me a message."

I threw a towel over his crotch, hoping it would ease the temptation of jumping on him. It had only been an hour since we'd indulged in mutually satisfying blow jobs in the shower. "I sent you a message hours ago, which, incidentally, you didn't reply to."

"I didn't see it. I was concentrating on getting here and working out my devious plan to get you into the shower." He frowned down at the towel on his lap, as if noticing it for the first time. "Why are you covering me up?"

Ignoring the last comment, I responded to the first one. "That must have taken hours to come up with: Step one, take off all your clothes."

He grinned. "Worked, didn't it?" He made sure I was looking his way before deliberately flicking the towel onto the floor.

I picked it up without saying a word and placed it back over him.

A spark of mischief flared in his eyes. He took hold of the corner of the towel, but at the same time leapt sideways, tackling me down to the sofa. Breathless, I found myself trapped under a naked, laughing Tristan, his elbow digging into my ribs and the towel back on the floor. He eased off slightly, giving me slightly more room to breathe. "You seem to have a phobia about my nakedness. You know what the best thing for a phobia is? Exposure to it."

I gaped at him, nodding slowly. It was hard to believe he'd walked into this one so easily. "Okay. So. I'll expose myself to your nakedness...for a while. And then we'll go outside and find a big, hairy spider for you." He paled immediately, and I felt guilty. When he tried to lever himself up, I pulled him back down, tracing soothing circles on his back. "Sorry. Quick, change the subject."

"To what?"

"Anything."

Tristan thought for a moment. "I know. If you could go anywhere in the world, where would you go?"

"I don't know. Why?"

Tristan maneuvered himself next to me on the sofa, assuming a more comfortable position. "I want to take you somewhere. You know, like a dream holiday. So name your place."

I shook my head. "That's really sweet. But I'm not going to let you do that."

"Why?" He seemed genuinely confused.

"There's a number of reasons."

"Like what."

"Well, money for one. I can't afford—"

"I'm paying."

"No, you're not!"

"Is that the only reason?"

"People might realize there's something going on if we're both missing from work at the same time."

Tristan rolled his eyes. "So you're planning on keeping me a secret forever?"

This wasn't exactly the first time we'd had this conversation. "Tristan, we've talked about this. It's—"

He rolled onto his back, staring at the ceiling. "I suppose the cat and lizard might be a problem."

I blinked, trying to follow his train of thought. I failed miserably, leaning up on one elbow to peer down at him. "What?"

He smiled. "When we go away, we'll have to find someone to look after the cat and lizard."

"We don't have a cat and a lizard."

Tristan shot me a look, as if I was the crazy one. "Well, not yet—obviously! But we will. Matthew might look after the lizard for us. After all, he's got all that experience with them. I don't know about the cat, though. Martin can't look after it. He's allergic. Would your sister look after it?"

"You want me to ask my sister if there's any possibility of her looking after an imaginary cat while we go on a holiday I've said I won't go on?"

Tristan nodded. "Maybe my mum would—"

I picked up the towel again. This time I draped it over his face. It didn't stop him talking. But at least the words were now decidedly muffled.

Chapter Thirty-One

"**S**o I just click here to transfer the files?"

"Hmmm...what?" I struggled to bring my attention back to Matthew's training. I needed to concentrate. It was the last day I had to bring him up to speed. Tomorrow, I would finally be back in my old office, back to the relative simplicity of working for John Stone. I attempted to drag my mind away from thoughts of Tristan and the intensity of the previous night. It was becoming clear that gym workouts left Tristan incredibly horny. He'd again turned up post-workout and after a shower—solo this time— he'd wasted no time in dragging me off to bed. Once there, I was subjected to an exploration by hands and mouth the likes of which I'd never experienced before. And that had only been a prelude to being expertly fucked. Apparently, his latest "research" must have been on orgasm denial. I'd called him all the names under the sun as he'd deliberately refused to let me come three times. The resulting orgasm had been well worth it, leaving me barely able to move for the next ten minutes.

After a takeaway, things had heated up again. With two fingers embedded in Tristan's ass and him all but begging me to fuck him, it was hard to work out how it hadn't actually happened, and which one of us had turned it back round to the usual order of things. I couldn't honestly say I minded when another mind-blowing orgasm had been the result.

I couldn't say everything was perfect. The work dispute still reared its head with increasing regularity. With him staying over every night, I'd given up on arguing about him driving me to work. However, I still insisted on being dropped off a few blocks away, where there was no risk of anybody seeing us arrive together. I didn't want anybody jumping to the right conclusion. Tristan couldn't seem to wrap his head around why it was such a problem for me. In turn, I couldn't understand how he could be so blasé about the possibility of people finding out we were sleeping together. He'd let slip that he'd told Martin, who apparently hadn't been that surprised. That had let to an awkward conversation when Martin had dropped by the office looking for Tristan. He hadn't said anything, but the perpetual smirk on his face had said he really wanted to. I assumed Tristan had threatened him with something horrible if he referred to it.

The other issue was Tristan's seeming inability to separate professional and private. It was a daily challenge to get him to keep his hands to himself at work. While it was of course incredibly flattering that he couldn't keep his hands off me, it did absolutely nothing for my paranoia about people finding out. At least after today, I'd be safely tucked away five floors below, with John Stone as a chaperone.

The impending separation for Christmas while we both spent time with our respective families was also on my mind. I couldn't decide whether it would be a blessing or a curse.

Bringing my attention back to the present, I got Matthew to repeat the question. I'd just about finished talking him through the process when Tristan strolled into the office, offering his usual cheery greeting. I mumbled something suitably vague before ducking my head and pretending great interest in the surface of the desk. I was finding it increasingly difficult to know how to treat him at work when other people were present. It was hard to have a normal conversation when you could picture exactly what lay under the suit and had spent hours mapping it with your hands and tongue. How the hell were you meant to talk to that person without giving away you were in an intimate relationship?

"Dominic, are you okay?"

I lifted my head to find Tristan staring intently at me.

Matthew flicked a glance my way. "He's been quite distracted today." I shot him a glare in response to his comment. He looked suitably chastened.

A look of worry crossed Tristan's face. "Aren't you feeling well? Have you eaten anything you shouldn't?" He directed his next comment over my head at Matthew. "He's allergic to fish. You should know that about him. He doesn't tell people, but it's important." He narrowed his eyes in an accusatory way. "Have you eaten fish today, Matthew? Are you breathing fumes all over him?"

I interjected before a slightly stunned-looking Matthew could respond. "Tristan. What the— If I want people to know that about me, *I'll* tell them. I don't need you to do it."

"Sorry. I—"

Whatever he'd been about to say, he seemed to realize it wouldn't be appropriate in front of other ears. He glanced at Matthew before stopping.

"So you're fine?"

"I'm fine." I checked my watch. "You have a meeting due to start in five minutes. You needed notes taken, right?" I stood, ready to accompany him. Maybe on the way, I could school him in not showing too much concern over supposed mere employees.

Tristan waved me back into the seat. "I thought Matthew could do it. He takes over permanently tomorrow. It'll be good experience."

I watched with mixed feelings as Matthew jumped up, almost bolting to the door to hold it open for Tristan. He certainly couldn't be faulted on his enthusiasm. With anyone else, the cynic in me would find it nauseating, but he was far too nice a guy to hold a grudge against. Tristan waved Matthew through the door ahead of him, waiting until he'd rounded the corner before aiming a wink my way, and saying he'd see me later. I got back to work, grateful for the solitude.

It was the clatter of high heels along the corridor that got my attention. At first, I dismissed it as one of the secretaries. It wasn't until it was combined with an all-too-familiar scent that alarm bells started to ring. By then it was too late: Maria was already through the door and halfway across the office. She strolled right up to the desk, resting her manicured hands on the polished surface. "Remember me?"

With a racing heart and a distinct lack of words coming to mind, I simply stared at the woman in front of me.

I struggled to find my voice, thoughts running chaotically through my mind about what her presence could possibly mean. The last I'd heard, she'd been hiding out in France. I wondered if Tristan knew she was back in the country. If so, I would have really appreciated the heads up. "Of course...you're—" How exactly was I going to phrase this politely? *Tristan's ex fiancée, the woman he was going to marry before he started fucking me.*

"—Maria." I made an attempt to sit up straight. Hopefully, she wouldn't notice how nervous I was. "Tristan's...erm...not here. He's in a meeting."

She shifted slightly, leaning over the desk. The movement displayed a generous amount of cleavage perfectly, and I wondered whether it was deliberate. If I wasn't gay, I probably would have been in my element admiring the view. Did she think I was straight? I guess the only way she would have thought otherwise would be if Tristan had told her while they were still together. The question was, if it was deliberate, why? What was she trying to achieve? She gave a half-hearted smile. "I didn't come to see Tristan. I came to see you. Well, whoever was doing this job. I wasn't sure it would still be you."

I could see her brain working overtime, desperately trying to remember my name. Miraculously, she dredged the memory up from somewhere.

"Dominic. You said you were temporary, so I thought it might be someone else. But it's you, so that's good." She forced another smile.

I swallowed dryly, hiding my sweaty palms beneath the desk. "You wanted to see *me*?"

Maria nodded. She leaned even farther forward. I deliberately kept my gaze on her face. She frowned slightly, evidently disappointed her womanly wiles were having so little effect on me. "I need information."

"Information?"

She eased herself into the empty chair, gracefully crossing her legs and showing a large amount of nylon-clad thigh. She'd obviously not given up on using her body to get her own way. I just wasn't clear what she was after. "You've been Tristan's PA for the last few weeks. You must know who it is."

I stiffened automatically before forcing myself to relax. Shit! She'd come here with the intention of finding out who Tristan was seeing. I played for time. "Who what is?"

She sighed. "You must know who he's been fucking behind my back. The...whore who thinks she can steal him away. The bitch who's stupid enough to think I'm not going to fight for the man I love. Who is it?" A tear glistened in her eye. Either she was genuinely upset or Maria was a first-class actress. She sniffed. "We were so happy together. Everything was set for the wedding. I had a beautiful dress, and you should have seen the place where we were going to get married. Then, he...he—" A tear rolled slowly down one cheek. Guilt gnawed at my insides. "He, out of the blue, says he's got feelings for someone else. He wouldn't even tell me who it was. He claimed nothing had happened, but I know that's a lie." She paused to sniff again, her voice increasing in pitch as she carried on. "Do you know what that feels like? To have your whole world ripped out from under you? Do you?"

I shook my head, watching as another tear tracked its way slowly through perfect makeup. "We were going to have children. Do you know what a sacrifice that is, for me to agree to that, with my profession?"

All I could do was shake my head again.

"Well, it is. So...I need to know who this woman is. I need to see this woman. I need to see what's so special about her. She can't be prettier than me. She can't have a better body than me. I don't understand what this...this...woman could possibly have that I don't have."

"I...don't...I—" I couldn't finish my sentence. I could do nothing but stare at her. She definitely wasn't acting. This was genuine anguish.

She dabbed at her eyes with a tissue. "So tell me who it is. I know you know. I can see it in your eyes. I understand you're loyal to Tristan, but I need to know. Does she work here?"

I felt lightheaded. What the hell was I supposed to say?

Maria gave an imploring look. "I'm not leaving till you tell me."

My voice came out in a whisper. "If I tell you, it won't make you feel better. It'll probably make it worse."

She frowned. "My heart is broken." She clutched at her chest as if to accentuate the point. "It's not possible for me to feel any worse. Just tell me. Please."

I think it was the please that broke me. Or maybe it was the fact the tears were now falling rapidly. "I'm sorry. It wasn't...I didn't mean to...but he...I—am—so—sorry!"

Maria sat up straight, confusion written all over her beautiful face. "Why would *you* be sorry? It's not like you—" She stopped, and I watched as she processed the words I'd said, the words I'd give anything to be able to take back. Her eyes narrowed, all evidence of tears suddenly gone. "You can't possibly be telling me that it's you." She gave a short, sharp laugh. "Tristan's not gay. Don't be ridiculous. I'd know if he was interested in men. He's not gay."

I fixed my gaze on a section of wall over her right shoulder, unwilling to look her in the eye. "I don't think he was before. I'm so sorry. I don't know what to say."

"You've been fucking my fiancé?"

Visibly wincing at the harsh bluntness of the words, I made a half-hearted attempt to defend myself. "It wasn't like that. I didn't—"

Even if I'd been looking her way, I doubt I could have moved out of the way fast enough as she flew out of the chair, delivering a vicious slap to my left cheek. There was enough force behind it to knock my head backward. She stood over me, breathing hard, fury etched into every part of her.

"You disgusting little shit! I'm part of the modeling world. I know all about predatory gays, swooping in and molesting their victims. But I thought Tristan was safely away from all that. What do you want from him? Money? A better job? The sick, perverted thrill of seducing a straight man? What?"

Shocked, I rubbed at my stinging cheek as she continued her diatribe. There was nothing I could say to calm her down or make it better. I tried anyway. "I don't want anything from him."

Her sneer of disbelief was a long way from the tearful woman she'd been less than five minutes before. "He's not really gay, you know. He may have had sex with you." She subjected me to a scathing look, as if she found that fact difficult to believe. "You're probably some sort of twisted experiment. He'll get bored of you. Sooner rather than later." Funny how she was echoing the exact thoughts I'd had myself a week ago.

"Have you met his mum yet?" She didn't wait for an answer. "I'm guessing not. You know what his mum wants more than anything?"

I pulled my hand away from my red-hot cheek, noting the tremor. I clasped it together with the other one in front of me in an effort to hide how much they were both shaking. I waited for her to answer her own question, knowing I wouldn't like whatever she was going to say. I steeled myself.

"Grandchildren!" She smiled: a self-satisfied, I've-got-you-over-a-barrel smile. "Can you give her that? Can you? Can you give Tristan the children he wants?"

My response came out in a barely audible mumble. "You know I can't."

"Ha, well, then, you—"

"Leave!"

My head whipped around as the single word sliced through the air. It came from the direction of the door. A clearly furious Tristan was framed in the doorway, his gaze locked onto both of us. For a moment, I thought the command was aimed at me. It wasn't until he strode across the floor, stopping just short of Maria, who was no longer looking quite as pleased with herself, and repeated the word that I realized it was aimed at her.

She turned to face him. "Your dirty secret's out, Tristan. I know you've been fucking your employee. And not just any employee, but a man. You should have told me that's what you were into. Is he the only employee that does additional duties for you? Or is this a new clause you've had put into all your employees' contracts?" I couldn't see Tristan's face. Maria was in between us, blocking my view. But I could imagine the comment would not go down well.

Tristan's reply, when it came, was surprisingly controlled in the face of such provocation. "I will only ask you once more. If you do not leave immediately, I will ring security and have you escorted from the building."

Her shoulders stiffened, and her voice softened. "Now, Tristan. We don't need to resort to that. I'm just upset. You can't blame me for that, surely? Especially after what I've just found out. Let's go into your office and talk. You can explain what you were thinking. I'm sure this has all been some horrible mistake. We can still sort things out. I'm a very forgiving woman. What do you say?"

Her honeyed tone was completely at odds with the way she'd been throwing insults out less than a minute ago. I couldn't keep up with the speed at which this woman segued from one attitude to another. She took a step forward, reaching her hand out to lay it on Tristan's chest.

Tristan took a step back before Maria's hand could make contact. "We have nothing to talk about. Dominic, ring security, please. Tell them there's an unnecessary disturbance on the top floor. We need immediate assistance and an escort from the building."

Reaching out obediently for the phone, I got no further than curling my fingers around it. Maria beat a hasty retreat from the office of her own volition. Her parting shot was to tell Tristan she'd be in touch.

Maria out of the way, Tristan's attention turned to me. As soon as his gaze met mine, I started apologizing.

"I'm sorry. I shouldn't have told her. I don't know why I did, but she'd come here to find out who you were seeing, and I didn't know what to say, and then she was crying, and it just came out. I shouldn't have said anything. It just made her worse."

Tristan crouched down in front of me. "It doesn't matter." A sudden look of alarm crossed his face. He turned my face gently to the side. "Shit! She hit you. Fuck! I can't believe she did that." He trailed his fingers gently down my burning cheek. "We'll go back to your apartment and put some ice on that. Then I'll take you out to dinner, somewhere nice that's never even seen a fish. You can choose the restaurant. I promise, I won't argue with your choice. And I won't eat your food."

Everything he was saying sounded really good. It was so tempting to give in to it, to let Tristan treat me like a prince, but Maria's words kept rebounding in my skull. *Can you give Tristan the children he wants?* I tugged my head away, breaking contact where his fingers still rested against my cheek.

"I can't do this."

"Okay. No dinner. We can order takeaway. That sounds good to me." Tristan smiled: a warm, reassuring smile. It broke my heart. "Whatever you want. Your apartment's good. We can have a chilled-out evening in front of the TV. I'll give you another head massage."

My head swam, his concern making it more difficult to do what I knew, deep down, needed to be done. It wasn't fair of me to take the chance of having children away from Tristan.

"No. Not dinner. This." I gestured between the two of us. "I can't have a relationship with you."

Standing abruptly, Tristan started to pace. "You're upset. Of course you are. You've just been attacked. If you're saying this because you're scared about what she might do next, you don't have to be. We'll go to the police, get them to take out a restraining order. I don't care if the media get hold of it. She should have thought of that before she was stupid enough to come here."

I took the opportunity to get to my feet. I felt like I'd been pinned to the chair, first by Maria, and then by Tristan for what seemed like forever. Tristan's pacing had paused momentarily. He watched me with a wary expression on his face.

"I'm not scared of Maria. It's not about that. I just think it's better...if we end this now."

"No! Absolutely not." Tristan's head shake carried a lot of conviction. "You're not thinking straight. If you need an evening on your own...okay, I can give you that. I don't want to. But if you need to get your head on straight, then okay. I'll give you some time. Then tomorrow, you'll have everything back in perspective, and—"

"I won't change my mind."

Tristan resumed his pacing, looking more and more frustrated. "What did she say to you? This morning we were fine. Hell! Two hours ago we were fine, and then suddenly you don't want to have anything to do with me. What the fuck, Dominic! This is insane. Surely you can see that? You can't just dump me for no good reason. You know how I feel about you!"

Tristan's voice had become increasingly louder and more distressed throughout his speech.

I avoided looking at him, determined not to let his obvious show of emotion affect my ability to go through with it. It was for the best. I knew that. He just needed some time, some distance, before he'd see the same thing. In a few months time, he'd be thanking me. "I'm sorry."

"You're sorry?" Tristan ran an incredulous hand through his hair. "Why? You haven't given me one damn good reason why you're saying this. Why are you doing this? Talk to me, Dominic. At least give me a bloody reason."

I was saved from having to answer when a flustered-looking Paul appeared in the doorway. "Jesus Christ, guys! Keep your voices down, or at least shut the door. You're broadcasting your relationship to the whole floor. The whole building's going to know about the two of you."

"I don't care." Tristan's reply was to Paul, but his gaze remained fixed on me.

Paul stepped into the room, closing the door behind him. The door, which, I realized, had been wide open ever since Tristan had walked through it. "You might not care"—he turned his attention to me—"but I know Dominic, and I know he doesn't feel the same. What's going on, Dom?"

He took a step closer, noticing my face for the first time. "Shit! What happened to your face?"

I brought my hand up to cover the offending cheek. It still felt hot to the touch. "It's nothing. And there is no relationship for the whole building to know about. Not anymore."

Ignoring Paul's open-mouthed look of shock, I grabbed my cardboard box of belongings—which thankfully I'd packed earlier—and exited the room. It took all my willpower not to respond to Tristan calling my name as I left. The note of pleading in his voice was like a knife to the heart. But somehow, I kept on walking.

Chapter Thirty-Two

Tristan—*missed call. 17:14*

Tristan: *Answer your phone. We need to talk. 17:22*

Tristan: *I just need to know you're okay. 17:24*

Tristan—*missed call. 17:35*

Tristan: *Dominic, please answer. 17:36*

Paul: *Dominic, what the hell is going on? You said yesterday that you and Tristan were doing great. What happened? I heard Maria was in the building. Did she hit you? It wasn't Tristan, was it? 17:42*

Paul: *I asked Tristan. But he didn't seem to know why you'd dumped him. He wouldn't tell me much. Said he needed to talk to you first. 17:43*

Tristan—*missed call. 18:02*

Tristan—*missed call. 18:30*

Tristan: *When are you going to talk to me? 18:35*

Paul—*missed call 19:01*

Paul: *You obviously don't want to talk. I just wanted to warn you that the secret's out and the gossip is all over the building. Call me if you need to talk. I'm a good listener. I can come round if you need me to. Is Tristan there? 19:10*

Tristan: *I've done nothing to deserve you treating me like this. 19:15*

I'd managed to ignore the barrage of messages. They'd started shortly after I'd left the office. I read them without responding. I watched my phone ring without picking up any of the calls. The last message, though, hit a nerve. He was right, of course. Reluctantly, I typed out a response.

Dominic: *I'm absolutely fine. You don't need to worry about me. You haven't done anything wrong. It's just better to end things now. Please don't call or text anymore. I won't answer.*

Tristan: *You're obviously not okay. Better for who? It's not better for me.*

Tristan: *I can't think what Maria could possibly have said to you to make you react like this. Please don't believe any lies she told you.*

Tristan: *Dominic, if you'd just talk to me. We can sort this out.*

210

Tristan: *We have a really good thing going. You know I love you. Xx*

Tristan: *If it's the fact everyone knows about us now, so what. I don't care, and you shouldn't either. Fuck them. I can always fire them ;) Xx*

Tristan: *This is like banging my head against a wall. You want me to give up. Fine. I'm giving up for tonight. I'd come round, but I know you won't let me in. But, WE WILL TALK. I love you. Xx*

EVER SINCE THAT FATEFUL morning I'd let the elevator door close in Tristan's face, only to find out minutes later I had to work for him, we hadn't arrived at work at the same time. So of course, it was Sod's Law that the one morning I would have done anything to avoid it, he was walking across the foyer. I leaned against the far wall of the elevator. It was already enough of a struggle to pretend I hadn't noticed the curious looks and whispers aimed my way from fellow employees obviously fully versed in the latest company gossip. Groaning inwardly, I averted my gaze from the door, praying it would swing shut before he reached it.

I could tell the moment they caught wind of his impending arrival in the elevator; the whispers increased in volume and excitement. They obviously couldn't wait to see what happened between the two of us. An obliging blonde woman slammed her hand onto the "door open" button. If thoughts could kill, she would have dropped dead there and then.

Out of the corner of my eye, I watched as Tristan stepped inside, smiling gratefully at the woman holding the door for him. She visibly preened under the attention. I stared resolutely ahead, willing the elevator to move. After what seemed like an age, it finally did. I counted the stops as it inched its way up floor by floor. How could one elevator ride feel like a lifetime? I swore I could feel Tristan's eyes burning into me, or maybe it was just my imagination. More likely, he was doing exactly the same as me—looking everywhere but in my direction. There was no point in giving the gossips any more ammunition. Although completely ignoring each other was probably doing exactly that. We couldn't win either way.

I breathed an inward sigh of relief as the elevator ground to a halt at my floor. I pushed my way out, keeping myself the maximum distance possible away from Tristan. The elevator, which had been deadly silent throughout its journey, suddenly seemed to spring back to normality as I exited and conversations seemed to re-start. I endured more curious stares on the way down the corridor to John Stone's office.

It was comforting to take in the familiar sight of John Stone at his desk. I stepped inside, and he waved me closer, pushing his glasses more firmly onto his nose before fixing me with an intent stare.

"Dominic, I can't tell you how good it is to have you back."

I managed a weak smile. "It's good to *be* back."

I had no preconceptions of any possibility the gossip hadn't yet reached his ears. The question was whether he was going to acknowledge it or not. He fiddled with a file on the corner of his desk, lining it up exactly so the corner of the file was in perfect alignment with the corner of the desk. He pulled his attention away from it, glancing at me before his gaze skittered quickly away.

"And, you're...erm...okay?"

"I'm fine."

Another quick glance. I knew I was lying. He knew I was lying. I just needed him to meet me halfway in the charade.

"Good. Good. Great." He offered a smile. "Well, there's plenty to do. I don't know what the temp did to your filing system. I can't find anything anymore."

"I'll sort it out."

"Great." He placed another file on top of the first one, taking the time to orient that one as carefully as the previous one.

"Well, if there's nothing else, Mr. Stone, I should get on. That filing system won't sort itself." Even I cringed at the false, cheery note in my voice. There went the planned acting career.

"There is one more thing." Another file joined the first two. I waited, knowing his reluctance meant I wasn't going to like it. That meant it must involve Tristan in some way. My brain went into overdrive. Had he demanded to see me? Would he play the boss card to force me to talk to him? Because if he thought that was going to work, he was going to be in for a shock.

"There's a...conference meeting at two. I need you to be present for it."

A conference meeting meant Tristan would be leading it. Not great, but not as bad as the scenario my brain had conjured up moments earlier. It wasn't like it would just be the two of us in the room. A conference meeting usually involved a fairly large group. I should be able to hide easily enough. "That's fine."

"Is it?" Without another file to line up, Mr. Stone concentrated on correcting the already perfectly placed files. On another day, I would have found his discomfort amusing, but my sense of humor was sadly lacking today.

"Of course."

With nothing else for either of us to say, I left his office to return to my own.

THE HOURS TICKED BY until two o'clock. I'd stayed in the office all day. A deliberate act to swerve any more unwanted attention. In a further act of avoidance, I'd deliberately left my phone at home. If I'd received any calls or texts, I remained blissfully unaware. The only blip so far in an otherwise peaceful day was a visit from Paul at lunchtime. He'd insisted on letting me know he was doing his best to correct any incorrect gossip he heard. Apparently some of the stories about Tristan and I making the rounds were mindblowing. If he was expecting me to ask what they were, he was disappointed. I made it clear I didn't want to know and had no interest in talking about it. He'd lingered for a few more minutes before taking the hint and drifting away.

I arrived at the conference room early. I figured if I got there first, I could position myself at the back, and if I was really lucky nobody would even notice I was there. My plan worked: the room was empty. A few people filed in soon after, including Martin, taking seats in front of mine. I slid down, trying to block myself completely from view and making sure I didn't meet anyone's eyes. Mr. Stone took the seat next to mine. A glance at the clock revealed it was a few minutes after two. I turned to John.

"Where's everybody else?"

John's brow furrowed. "This is it. We're just waiting for Tristan."

Great! I stared around the room at the largely empty seats. So much for being able to hide. Even with Tristan, there would be a maximum of six people in the room, including myself. I sighed. Mr. Stone shot me a searching look but refrained from making a comment.

Tristan arrived a few minutes later with Matthew in tow. Well, at least that was one extra person. Tristan took up his customary position at the front of the room. His gaze swept the room before coming to rest on me. I ducked my head, staring hard at the pad of paper in front of me, refusing to acknowledge him. I knew I was behaving like a child. After all, I'd dumped him. If anyone should be ignoring the other one, it should be the other way round.

The Tristan chairing the meeting was the one I found it incredibly difficult to recognize; the super-professional, efficient version who raced through several ideas in great detail at breakneck speed, paying little regard to others who couldn't keep up. Not the teasing, ditzy, seductive, obsessed-with-food, panic-at-the-smallest-spider version I was most used to seeing. Busy smiling to myself, it took me a few moments to register the mention of my name. I lifted my head, looking around quickly to try and work out who'd said it. Absolutely everyone in the room was staring at me. The voice of John Stone came from my right-hand side.

"Tristan asked if you can get a copy of the latest sales figures he's just run through, typed up and e-mailed to all the members of this meeting by the end of this afternoon."

"Erm..."

John peered over my shoulder, taking in the completely blank page on my notepad, apart from a detailed doodle in the top right-hand corner of a spider wearing a tie. The tie looked remarkably like the one Tristan was wearing today. The spider appeared to be riding a burger. It would be hard to type up a list of sales figures I hadn't bothered to write down in the first place or even bothered listening to. I shifted uncomfortably, unsure of what to say to explain my way out of not bothering to do my job. I still had six pairs of eyes all trained on me, waiting for an answer. Martin's gaze held a look of sympathy.

"That would be—"

As my gaze swept the circle of faces, a confused-looking Matthew offered a small, reassuring smile. I wondered what he'd made of the gossip. Maybe it wasn't a surprise. Maybe he'd already suspected. When I reached Tristan, the first eye contact I'd made with him all day, he seemed to detect something in my expression.

"Don't worry about it, Dominic. I'm sure you've got enough to do with settling back into your old role. I'll go through them again with Matthew when we get back to the office, and he can do it." He smiled, and I wanted to cry. "I have to get used to the fact you're not my...personal assistant anymore."

I nodded, wishing the ground would open up and swallow me. The last person I wanted coming to my defense was Tristan. I'd dumped him and refused to speak to him. It was my fault the whole building was talking about the two of us. Now, I couldn't even do my job properly, and he was still being nice. I dragged my eyes away from him with difficulty.

The meeting quickly re-convened, and I was relieved when the attention was no longer directed my way. Mr. Stone leaned over, whispering directly into my ear.

"Why don't you go? Your concentration today is obviously... Well, it's not as good as it usually is."

I whispered back, "You need me here."

He looked down at my notepad, which was still blank apart from the doodle. It now also had a hole in it where I'd pushed the pen really hard into the paper. "I think I can manage."

Humiliated, I waited for the next available opportunity. When the discussion became more lively, I picked my things up and quickly exited the room, looking straight ahead. It was clear in my mind what my next step had to be.

TRISTAN BLEW INTO THE office like a whirlwind. I'd expected it but not until the next day. He threw an envelope down in front of me.

"I'm not accepting this. This is bullshit!"

I stared at the envelope. I'd only handed it to John Stone an hour ago. He'd obviously run straight to Tristan. I was disappointed. Surely I'd earned a little more loyalty over the past year of working for him.

"You can't *not* accept it. It doesn't work like that, Tristan."

He picked my resignation back up from the desk. "Oh, yeah? Well, watch this." He proceeded to rip it up into tiny pieces, sweeping them from the desk and into the wastepaper bin. "Ha! What resignation?"

I massaged my aching temples. This had been a really, really long and stressful day. The only part that had made me feel any better was the part where I'd sat and written that resignation. After the disastrous meeting, it had seemed like the obvious solution, and Tristan throwing his toys out of the pram at someone daring to quit wasn't going to change that. It was lucky I knew him well enough to have guessed this would be his likely reaction, even down to the ripping up of my letter.

"I scanned it in and sent an additional copy to human resources. They'll have it on file, along with my resignation date. So"—I glanced toward the bin—"that copy doesn't really matter."

"You can't resign." Tristan's voice sounded less confident.

"I can, and I have."

Tristan began to pace. It was a repeat of the previous day, just in a different office. I prayed there was no reason for anyone to be coming to see Mr. Stone. This would feed the gossips even more. They were probably already having a field day over the news of my meltdown in the meeting. I may have handed in my resignation, but I still had to survive another month. Thank God for the impending Christmas and New Year holidays. At least that would take a few days away from the total.

Tristan turned my way. "Why?"

"You know why."

"Spell it out for me."

I chose my words carefully. "We're not together anymore. Which makes it awkward. The whole building is talking about us and watching our every move, which makes it even more awkward. Everybody here thinks I've been incredibly unprofessional. A belief I made even worse today by my ineptitude in that meeting. If I can't concentrate enough to do my job... Well, I need to work somewhere I can. Somewhere new."

"Why couldn't you concentrate? What were you thinking about?"

I shrugged, and then lied through my teeth. "Other jobs. What I needed to add to my CV."

"I don't believe you."

I raised an eyebrow.

Tristan reached into his pocket, producing a piece of folded paper and carefully unfolding it. He held it up, revealing the doodle I'd done earlier. I noticed he was holding it as far away from the spider as he could. "I think you were thinking about me."

Heart pounding, I forced myself to laugh. "That's a mighty big jump, Tristan. Some would say a pretty arrogant one."

"So you're denying that's a picture of my tie?"

I made an effort to deflect from the question. "Where the hell did you get that, anyway?" I cast my eyes about, spotting my notebook lying on the corner of the desk, where I'd left it after the meeting. "Did you go through my things? Because, I've got to tell you, that's out of order."

"I came to talk to you earlier, but you weren't here and I noticed—"

"So you went through my things?"

"I noticed it lying open on your desk."

I cast my mind back. Could I have left it open? Quite possibly. I hadn't exactly been thinking clearly. "You didn't have to look." The words were mumbled, but he'd obviously heard them.

"If you don't want people to look at things, don't leave them where they can be seen."

I glared at him before realizing that somehow I'd managed to get myself drawn into conversation with him.

He held up the piece of paper again as if presenting exhibit one in court. "Stop avoiding the question. I already know you're the master of avoidance. You avoid texts, you avoid calls, you avoid conversations. You're not avoiding this question."

I eyed the door. "What was the question?"

"You were thinking about me. All these pictures link to me."

"That's not a question. That's a statement."

He sighed, giving me a long, hard look. "Take your resignation back. The...personal thing between us is one thing, but this is your job, and you're bloody good at it."

I was shaking my head even before he'd finished speaking. "I wasn't today."

"That's one day, Dominic. Don't be so bloody hard on yourself. I'll stay away from you...*at work*...if that's what you really want, but—"

"My mind's made up." From the corner of my eye, I noted the adjoining door swinging open to reveal John Stone. His face flushed.

"Oh, I'm sorry. I didn't realize. Sorry." He scuttled back in so quickly, it was comical. I imagined him, trapped in his own office, trying to gauge when he was allowed to come out. Smirking, I turned back to Tristan, expecting him to share in my amusement. He was regarding me with a stony expression. My smile faded.

"You've made your mind up." His voice sounded flat. "You do that a lot, Dominic. And no one is allowed to have any input or offer any reasons why you might want to change your mind. You're stubborn to the point of..." He trailed off, shaking his head.

I felt slightly crushed by his words. "That's harsh. I don't think that's true."

Tristan didn't bother to answer. He gave one last indecipherable look before heading for the door. I was left wondering why him giving up on me was hitting me so hard when it was exactly what I'd been aiming for.

Chapter Thirty-Three

Sitting at my parents' kitchen table, I watched as my niece and nephew played happily with the Lego I'd gotten them for Christmas. I'd been here since Christmas Eve. I could have come earlier, having taken the coward's way out and rung in sick for a couple of days after the last conversation with Tristan, but it would have raised far too many questions with my family. Questions I really didn't want to answer or even think about, if I could help it. It had been nice to get out of London for a while, a much-needed respite from all the self-inflicted crap I'd left behind in the city.

Wrapping my fingers around the mug of coffee, I congratulated myself on successfully pulling the wool over their eyes through the whole of Christmas. To them, I was the same cheerful Dominic they were used to seeing. The table creaked slightly as my sister Charlotte sat down with a laptop in front of her. She turned it so the screen faced toward me.

"Do you think this dress would suit me?"

I stared steadily at her, barely giving the image on the screen a glance. "How many times do I have to tell you that me being gay doesn't automatically make me an expert on fashion?"

She smiled sweetly. The fact she was only a couple of years older meant we'd always been fairly close. "You say that, and then when I push you for an answer, you're always right. Do you remember those trousers? The ones you said the waistband wouldn't work for me? You told me not to buy them. I ignored you and bought them anyway. They made me look like I was pregnant again." She pushed the laptop closer.

Sighing, I studied the dress, flicking my gaze between her and the screen to imagine her wearing it. She waited expectantly for my verdict. "No. The sleeves are all wrong for you, and the neckline won't suit you."

Disappointment written all over her face, she turned the screen back to face her. "That's a shame. It was reduced in price."

"You've got lots of dresses."

She smiled brightly. "A girl can never have too many dresses."

I rolled my eyes and watched as four-year-old Lucy guided three-year-old Thomas as to which piece of Lego they needed to use to build whatever it was they were building. I couldn't quite work it out. I was about to ask Charlotte when she spoke first.

"So!"

Focusing my attention back on her, I waited for whatever it was she wanted to say. Knowing her, it would either be about shoes, the latest thing her long-suffering husband had done to annoy her, or computer advice. Two out of the three options just involved pretending to listen, with a few nods and smiles thrown in for good measure. I could cope with that.

Charlotte reached out grabbing a freshly baked brownie from the plate Mum had left in the middle of the table. God knows when she'd managed to bake them. I sometimes suspected she must get up in the middle of the night.

"Mum and Dad have agreed that now Christmas is over, I can broach the subject with you."

I frowned. "What subject?"

"The subject of what's wrong with you. Why you've been so down this Christmas. It's not like you. We're all worried about you."

My hand paused halfway to reaching for a brownie. So much for them all being taken in by my cheerful act. "I'm fine. And I don't really appreciate you talking about me behind my back."

Charlotte raised an eyebrow. "Well, tough! I told you we're concerned about you. I assume it's a guy. What was the name of that guy you were seeing when we last spoke? Andy? Aidan? Arnold?" She wrinkled her nose as she struggled to recall the name. "It definitely began with an A."

"Adam."

"Ha! Told you it began with an A." She waved her hand in a "told you so" gesture. Unfortunately, as it was the hand holding the brownie, it showered a flurry of crumbs across the surface of the pristine table.

"You better clean that up before Mum gets home."

"Yeah. Later. So, you and Adam stopped seeing each other?"

I nodded.

"And you're really upset about it?"

I shook my head.

She cocked her head to one side and waited. "You can either tell me now, or you'll have to deal with Mum asking you all the same questions." She paused for maximum effect, "And you know she's not as patient as me."

Unfortunately, I did know that. "It's a long story."

Charlotte folded her arms in front of her. "We've got time."

I gestured across to the two children. "You need to keep an eye on them. You don't want me distracting you."

"They're fine. The Lego you bought them has made sure of that. They'll be happy for hours."

I wondered if it was too late to claim there had been an emergency factory recall of the Lego. I could run over there, scoop it all back into the box, and then—well, that was about as far as I'd got with the plan. It would only delay the inevitable, so I started to talk.

"CHARLOTTE, DO YOU THINK you could stop staring at that picture? Please."

My sister kept her eyes locked on the Google image of Tristan she'd searched. "But he's gorgeous." She stroked the screen with the tip of one finger.

"Oh, my God, Charlotte! You're a married woman. Leave him alone."

She grinned wickedly. "Does it bother you, me touching him?" She deliberately did it again.

"Of course it doesn't bother me. I ended it. And it's a bloody picture!"

She let her hand drop from the screen. "So let's summarize."

"Do we really have to?"

She shushed me. "You dumped him, but you're sad, so, stupid move on your part. Even more stupid, you've resigned from your job, which you love, because it would make you too sad to keep on seeing him."

"That's not why I resigned."

She pulled a disbelieving face. "We'll agree to disagree on that one. You dumped him because, without even asking him, you've decided that he desperately wants children." She glanced across at the pair on the carpet. "He can have mine, if he's that desperate."

I snorted. "You don't mean that."

"All right, he can have one of them. I'll keep the other one."

"Which one?"

She held a finger up, wagging it in front of my face. "No subject change. You're clearly in love with him." She turned the screen so I was faced with a picture of a smiling Tristan.

I swallowed and looked away. "No, I'm not."

She smiled a knowing smile. "But you so are! You're sacrificing your feelings because you think that's the best thing for him." She clasped her hands together over her heart, "That's so sweet! My little brother has finally fallen in love."

"Shut up!"

She got up out of her chair and began to sway around the kitchen, arms outstretched. "Dominic's in love! Dominic's in love! Dominic loves Tristan! Dominic loves Tristan!"

I watched helplessly, knowing there was no stopping her when she was like this. The kids had stopped building and were staring open-mouthed at their mother. They began to giggle, and then, to my horror, joined in with the chant.

I shot my best, most venomous glare at her. "Charlotte, this is not funny." The only thing that could possibly make this situation any worse would be my parents choosing to return at that exact time. Fortunately, it didn't happen.

She carried on regardless for a few moments, suddenly grinding to a halt. She scanned the kitchen. I had no idea what she could possibly be looking for.

She gestured toward the two kids, who had thankfully returned to their Lego. "Watch them for a minute, would you? I just need to—"

I watched bemused, as she almost ran out of the room without finishing her sentence. At least it brought the teasing to an end. Actually, I'd gotten away lightly. No doubt it would all flare up later when she'd relayed the whole conversation to my mum. I could hear Charlotte upstairs. At one point, her footsteps were directly overhead.

"Charlotte, are you in my room?" There was no answer. She might not be talking to me, but she was talking to someone. I could hear her muffled voice as the sound carried down the stairs. Either she was talking to herself, or she was on the phone.

A few minutes later, she strolled back into the kitchen with a funny look on her face. I eyed her suspiciously, recognizing that look from when we were kids. It usually signaled she'd been up to something. "What's wrong?"

"Hmmm...what?" She shot an innocent look my way. "Do you want another coffee?"

I nodded my agreement. "Who did you call? Don't tell me you called Mum already?"

Spooning instant coffee into the mugs, she shook her head.

I frowned. "Who then? Were you trying to track down your missing husband?"

"He's not missing. He's just escaped. He'll come home when he's hungry."

I laughed at the grumpy expression on her face. We were always winding her up about how mean she was to her husband, but we all knew they adored each other.

It was another two hours before my parents came home, their familiar voices drifting down the hallway. I stood to greet them, my smile freezing on my face when I caught sight of the man entering the room behind them.

Oblivious to my shock, my mum swept in looking considerably cold and windswept.

"Guess who we bumped into outside, Dominic? He just happened to arrive at the same time as we got back. Isn't that a coincidence? We didn't even know you'd invited anyone."

I blinked, convinced I must have started hallucinating. There was no way Tristan could be in my parents' living room. This wasn't an address he could have gotten from my employee file. There was no possible way he could know it. When I looked again, he was still there, looking sexy and rumpled. He held his hand up, waggling his fingers in a small wave.

Suddenly, it all clicked into place. Ignoring Tristan completely, I swung around to face my sister. Any doubts I might have had disappeared at the guilty expression on her face.

"You took my phone, didn't you? When I heard you talking to someone, you were calling him. I'm right, aren't I?"

She shrugged, but it was less than convincing. I flicked another glance at the subject of our conversation. My parents were eagerly ushering him inside and encouraging him to take his jacket off. I turned back to Charlotte, speaking to her between gritted teeth. "I'm going to kill you, sister dear. You've pulled some stunts in your time, but this one really takes the bloody biscuit."

Charlotte smiled sweetly. "You'll thank me later."

"I seriously doubt that."

"We'll see." She inclined her head in the direction of the small group. "Look how well they're getting along. Isn't that sweet?"

I followed her gaze toward my parents. They seemed completely oblivious to the simmering antagonism between their son and daughter. Seeing me looking their way, my mother shot a chastising look in my direction.

"Why haven't you introduced us, Dominic? Where are your manners? I brought you up better than this. Tristan is your..."

"Boss."

"Boyfriend."

I glared at both my sister and Tristan as they simultaneously contradicted my story.

They shared a smile. I wanted to throw both of them out of the house. That's all I needed: the two of them colluding against me.

My mum's brow wrinkled with confusion. "Which is it, boss or boyfriend? Because they're very different things. You didn't tell us you were seeing anyone, Dominic. Although we suspected you might have had some sort of breakup." She directed her next comment at Tristan. "He's been so sad all Christmas. He tried to hide it, but a mother notices these things."

Tristan gave her his most charming smile. "We're sort of on a break. Dominic's idea, not mine."

My mother nodded understandingly. I was miffed when she didn't even bother asking for my side of the story. Since when did she take a complete stranger's word over her own son's? My dad disappeared out of the room, seemingly already bored by the whole thing. At least that was one less witness to this whole awkward situation.

Shaking my head, I sought to bring some sanity back. "That's an interesting interpretation of the facts, Tristan."

At the mention of the familiar name, Thomas suddenly raised his head from his coloring, the Lego having finally lost its fascination an hour ago. To my absolute horror, he picked up the chant from earlier. "Dominic's in love! Dominic loves Tristan!"

Tristan's eyes widened comically while Charlotte giggled. She covered her mouth with her hand. "Oh, that's funny. He's got a great memory. My boy's a genius."

"I never said that. *She*"—I pointed at my sister—"said it. I have never said any such thing."

I took a step back, inadvertently knocking the computer mouse on the table. I saw the moment Tristan's eyes dropped to something behind me, looking greatly amused. Confused, I turned to see what was so interesting. The laptop, now woken from hibernation, displayed a full-screen image of Tristan: the picture Charlotte had pulled up earlier and obviously hadn't bothered to close down.

"And that's got nothing to do with me either!"

I looked around the small group. My mum appeared stunned into silence, Tristan simply raised an eyebrow, and as for Charlotte, it was clear she didn't intend to take ownership of any of this. In fact, she seemed to be finding everything hilariously amusing. I tried again.

"It isn't!" Even to my ears, my denial sounded weak. "Tell them, Charlotte." She simply shrugged. I ran my hand through my hair. "Oh, for God's sake."

There was a long, awkward silence while nobody said anything. It was only broken when Tristan suddenly spotted the plate in the middle of the table. "Are they brownies? They look great. Can I? Is that okay?"

Trust Tristan to have homed in on the food. Actually, it was nothing short of amazing it had taken him this long. At the mention of the brownies, my mum suddenly found her hostessing skills again. She had Tristan sat down, coffee poured, and had brought the Christmas cake out to accompany the brownies before five minutes had passed. I groaned. There was no chance of getting rid of him for quite some time now. He literally had his feet under the kitchen table. He looked like he was in heaven.

Charlotte sidled over.

"Go away! I don't want to talk to you. And don't think that just means today. I probably won't speak to you ever again." I threw my hands up in a helpless gesture. "Look what you've done."

Ignoring me, she leaned closer to whisper in my ear. "Why don't you take him to your room? Have a proper—and I mean proper—conversation with him. Without all the witnesses you've got in here."

"I thought you were enjoying the show."

Charlotte attempted to school her face into a serious expression. She failed miserably, another giggle escaping from her lips.

It wasn't even worth the effort of glaring at her. It would just bounce off her, like she was made of Teflon. "I'm glad you find my life so amusing."

"Oh, come on. You've got to admit it is funny, what with the singing, and"—she gestured toward the laptop—"the picture coming up at that exact time."

"The picture that you'd Googled. Yet you didn't bother to mention that fact. You just let me look like an idiot."

Another giggle. "You didn't." She got a good look at my face. "Okay, so, not ready to find it funny yet. Maybe later." She placed a hand on my arm, leaning closer and lowering her voice even more. "I've got to say, though, the picture doesn't really do him justice. In real life, he's much more...he's so—"

I interjected, unwilling to listen to my sister drool over him. "Yeah, yeah. I don't need you to tell me that. I'm well aware."

"So are you going to?"

"Going to what?"

She sighed, as if I was being deliberately dense. "Take him somewhere private. Talk to him."

I looked over to where Tristan was deep in conversation with my mum, a brownie in one hand and a piece of cake in the other. God only knows what they were talking about. I just prayed it wasn't me.

"I can't. He's eating. Food is his number-one priority. There'll be no moving him until he's finished."

"Tristan?"

I shot her a sharp glance as she called his name. Tristan turned with a smile to find out what she wanted.

"You'd be happy to go for a private discussion with Dominic, wouldn't you?"

Tristan swallowed a mouthful of cake, casting a quick, unreadable glance in my direction. I kept my face purposely blank.

"More than happy! That's why I came here."

Charlotte nudged my arm. "There you go."

Tristan placed everything back on the plate and got up from the table before I could find an excuse. He cast one last, longing look at the contents of the plate before following me up the stairs.

Chapter Thirty-Four

I led Tristan into my room. Thankfully, it showed little evidence of having been my childhood bedroom. I went and stood by the window, staring out over the surrounding fields while Tristan stayed near the center. I watched from the corner of my eye as he surveyed the small space.

"I only stay here at Christmas. That's why it's kind of bare."

Tristan nodded but didn't make any comment. It figured that this would be one of those rare times where Tristan wasn't chatty. Maybe he was resenting the fact I'd dragged him away from his feast.

"Look, I'm really sorry my sister asked you to come here. I don't know what was going through her head. It's not fair of her to waste your time."

"She didn't ask me to come here."

"Oh!" I wasn't sure what else to say to that.

"She called me for...a chat. After our talk, I asked for the address, and she gave it to me." He held his arms out to either side. "And here I am." He paused as if carefully considering his next words. "Still waiting for a hello."

"What?"

"Is it too much to ask for a simple greeting or even a smile? It makes me think you're not pleased to see me." He paused. "I've missed you, Dominic."

I turned back to the window. "Nothing's changed." I listened to the silence behind me. Maybe he'd just leave?

Finally, he broke it. "What if I said I had absolutely no interest in having children? Would that make a difference?"

I spun around so quickly, it was a surprise I didn't give myself whiplash. "She told you about that?" I found it hard to believe Charlotte had so readily disclosed information from our private conversation.

"Yes, she did. And thank God for your sister. I don't think I would ever have got the information out of you. At least now I know what prompted you to make such a stupid decision."

"It wasn't stupid!"

Tristan crossed the bedroom in three strides, grabbing me by both shoulders and giving me a small shake. "Yes, it was. You didn't even talk to me about it. You didn't even ask me if it was true. You just decided what would be best for both of us. I didn't even get to have a say in it."

"Maria said…" I stopped. In the light of everything he was saying, it suddenly seemed ridiculous.

He gave me another shake. "Go on."

"Stop bloody shaking me, and I'll tell you."

He let his hands drop down to his sides but made no move to step back. "Well, that would be progress."

"She said she'd agreed to risk her modeling career to have a baby."

The look on Tristan's face could curdle milk. "Big of her. Especially seeing as we'd never discussed it. In fact, I'm pretty sure she knew I wasn't that bothered. I always thought that was one of the big attractions of marrying me. Did she say anything else?"

"She said your mum was desperate for grandchildren."

Tristan let out a long breath. "She probably is. But seeing as I have two younger sisters, one of them recently married and extremely broody, I don't think she'll have to wait that long."

I stared at him incredulously. "You have two sisters? You never mentioned them."

"You never asked. I'm sure there's an awful lot we still don't know about each other. If you'd stop running away for two minutes and stop coming up with bullshit reasons we can't be together, we might actually get to find out."

Several thoughts raced around in my brain for a few moments. Could I have really been that stupid? "I thought I was doing the right thing. I was doing it for you. That's why—"

"Why what?" Tristan lifted my chin with one finger, ensuring I had to look at him.

"That's why Charlotte decided I was in love with you. You know, noble self-sacrifice and all that…shit."

Tristan's gaze took on a greater intensity. "And are you?"

I took a deep breath, knowing if I was honest, there was no going back from it. "I think I am. I'm pretty sure I am. But—"

I caught a quick glimpse of a beaming smile before I was bodily lifted from the ground and spun around. I beat ineffectually at the arms encircling me. "Put me down, Tristan!"

It's true what they say, that you should be careful what you wish for. Unfortunately, I found this out the hard way as I was dropped from a great height onto the bed. Winded, I struggled to get my breath back.

"Jesus, Tristan! I'm not a sack of potatoes," I protested weakly as he threw himself on the bed beside me, the biggest smile on his face. "Parents' house. We can't do anything."

He leaned over me. "I know that." He perused me slowly, grimacing as he took in the fact I was still clutching my ribs. "Sorry, I got carried away. But you just told me you love me, so what did you expect?"

"I said I might."

Tristan rolled onto his back, his head making a sizeable dent on the pillow. "You do. I know you do."

I copied his position, rearranging myself so we were lying next to each other. As it was a single bed, it left us pressed together from ankle to shoulder. I could feel the heat of his body burning through the layers of our clothes. "You're like an overexcited puppy."

His voice rumbled from right next to my ear. "But you love me anyway."

I ignored him. The more I thought about the analogy, the more it fit. "You really are. You're drawn to food. You certainly eat a lot. You need plenty of exercise."

"But you love me anyway."

"You even try the forlorn puppy-dog expression when you want to get your own way. Either that or the pouting. I guess dogs don't pout, so that part doesn't work."

Tristan threaded his fingers with mine. "But you love me anyway."

Exasperated, I turned my head sideways to meet his gaze, only inches away. It felt like I'd been fighting this for ages: months, rather than weeks. I was tired of fighting it, tired of building a wall around myself and hiding behind sarcasm and cynicism. A burst of optimism hit me. Maybe this could actually work? Maybe it *was* possible for a supposed straight man to fall in love with another man—to fall in love with me. Who was I to decide what could or couldn't happen?

I stared into his beautiful eyes. "But I love you anyway."

Tristan's whole face lit up. "I love you too."

Before I could feel self-conscious and say something snarky out of habit, I found myself rolled so I was sprawled on top of Tristan. "Still at my parents' house."

Batting his eyelashes, Tristan played innocent. "I'm just trying to fit us more securely on this very narrow single bed. I don't know what dirty thoughts are going through your head."

"Right. Of course you are." I dipped my head, brushing my lips briefly over his. "So you wouldn't be interested in kissing me."

Tristan's nose wrinkled, while his hand came up and his fingers tangled in my hair. "I wouldn't be completely averse to the idea."

Zeroing in on my target, my progress was halted halfway by the firm grip on my hair. I winced. "Ouch. That hurts."

"Sorry." Tristan gave me a narrow-eyed look. "We're together, right...a couple? You're my boyfriend?"

I held back a smile. Given my previous U-turns, it was hardly surprising he felt the need to clarify. "Yes, Tristan. We are together. I'm done with denying my feelings for you. You're stuck with me." Saying the words sent a warm glow through me.

This time, Tristan used the grip on my hair to drag me nearer. Our lips met in a mutual show of need and desperation, his tongue tangling with mine. Our legs entwined while our hands searched for gaps in clothing. I needed oxygen, but right now, with no barriers left between us, I needed Tristan more.

He shifted underneath, bringing his erection in line with mine and starting a slow grind. I shuddered, my fingers gripping his biceps before they began an exploratory foray down to the zipper on his jeans.

Gasping, I pulled away. Resting my forehead against Tristan's, I fought for some self-control. There was nothing I wanted more than to rip off his clothes and have my wicked way with him. I rolled off him, creating what little distance I could within the confines of a single bed. "Parents' house."

Tristan chuckled. He turned sideways and leaned up on one elbow. "Sorry. Almost forgot. You turn my brain to mush. When are you coming home?"

"Couple of days."

Tristan groaned dramatically. "As soon as you're back, you're calling me and I'm coming round, and we're fucking until we're both too exhausted to move."

My flagging erection perked up at the visual images Tristan's words put into my brain. "I promise."

We were both silent for a few moments. I glanced across.

"Just to think, I almost got you to give up on us."

He laughed. "You really think that? I wasn't even close to giving up."

"You stopped sending messages." He'd sent one message wishing me a merry Christmas, and when I hadn't responded, I hadn't heard anything else from him.

"You were getting a brief respite over Christmas, and then I would have come up with some sort of plan. And don't think running away from the company would have made the slightest bit of difference. I know where you live." His brow wrinkled as he saw my face change. "What? What's wrong?"

I sighed wearily. "I forgot for a minute that I need to find a new job."

Tristan fixed me with an intense look. "Do you still want to leave?"

"Not really. It just felt like the only option at the time." I gestured between us. "You know after I—I didn't want to have to see you every day when..." I ran out of words.

"Then we'll sort it."

I looked at him hopefully. "Yeah?"

Tristan nodded. "Yeah. Don't worry."

A loud hammering at the door interrupted our conversation and made both of us jump. Charlotte's voice echoed through the closed door. "Can I come in?"

I answered immediately, raising my voice so she could hear me. "No."

There was a long pause before she responded. "Why? What are you doing?"

"Mind your own business."

The door handle moved slightly, as if Charlotte was fighting the urge to burst in. "Only, if you're doing *that*, it means you've sorted everything out." Her voice got louder, like she'd pressed herself against the door. "Have you?"

Poised to repeat my demand for her to keep her nose out of it, I was beaten to a response by Tristan.

"Yes, Charlotte. We've sorted everything out, thanks to you. You have earned my eternal gratitude. Your brother will thank you as well, once he's had a chance to think about it."

My grunt of displeasure was all but drowned out by the high-pitched squeal of joy from my sister outside the door. I rolled my eyes to disguise my secret pleasure at Charlotte clearly liking Tristan so much.

"Dominic?"

"Yes, Charlotte?"

"Mum wants to know if Tristan is staying for dinner. What shall I tell her?" At least she was asking me rather than him. I'd seen Tristan's eyes light up as soon as the word dinner was mentioned.

I thought for a minute. "Tell her yes, he's staying for dinner." There was another, more muted squeal before her footsteps clattered down the stairs. I poked Tristan in the chest. "You can stay for dinner, but then you have to go home, or else I won't be able to keep my hands off you. Understand?"

I'd really missed the smug smirk I received in lieu of a response.

Chapter Thirty-Five

Tristan drummed his hands impatiently on the steering wheel. I peered cautiously at the ominous red door at the end of the driveway. Since I'd returned after Christmas, things between us had been great. Actually, more than great. Practically perfect. True to his word, Tristan had quickly and efficiently convinced Human Resources to accept the retraction of my resignation. John Stone had been relieved. I'd been relieved I didn't need to find another job. Paul had shrugged and claimed it didn't make any difference either way, but I'd known he was secretly pleased.

As for the fact everyone in the company now knew Tristan and I were a couple, the jury was still out on how I felt about that. If anything, the whispers had increased. Paul kept reassuring me they'd eventually get bored and find something else to gossip about. When I eventually mustered enough courage to ask what they were saying, I wished I'd never asked. Apparently, Russell was running a book on how many days or weeks we'd last before Tristan got bored and went back to women. The maximum time anyone had bet on so far was five weeks. Tristan's response had simply been to laugh and say they were all going to be disappointed before spending hours in bed making me forget all about it.

I peered at the door again. This, though, was the thing I'd been dreading. I'd managed to put it off until now.

"What if your parents don't like me?"

Tristan sighed. "We've had this conversation. Why wouldn't they like you?"

"I'm a man."

Tristan plastered fake shock on his face. "Oh, my God, are you? I hadn't noticed." He laughed while reaching for the handle on the door. "I tell you what. I'm going to go inside. If they ask where you are, I'll tell them you're at the end of their driveway, refusing to get out of the car. They can come and peer at you through the window. If you wind the window down a bit, my mum can poke bits of dinner through the gap."

I grabbed his arm before he could get out of the car. "Wait! I'll come with you...just...what are the rules?"

Tristan turned, a frown on his face. "Rules? Rules about what?"

"You know, physical contact and stuff. I don't want to upset anyone."

He cocked his head to one side, regarding me with a long-suffering expression. "You're really overthinking this, Dominic. Unless you're planning on us getting down and dirty on the kitchen table while everyone's eating, then don't worry about it. My parents aren't ogres, and they're not particularly uptight, so do whatever *you* feel comfortable with."

I stole another glance at the door. I half expected to see someone in the doorway, trying to work out why their son's car had been parked there for the last ten minutes, yet their son hadn't actually arrived. Fortunately, it remained shut.

"And it's just your parents? Your sisters aren't going to be here?"

"Not for dinner. But they're desperate to meet you. I can't promise that one or both won't just happen to drop by before we leave. But again, they're both really nice. They'll wind *me* up. You know what sisters are like. But they'll be sweet as pie to you."

Taking a deep breath, I reached for the door handle on my side of the car. "Okay. I can do this. It's just your parents. I suppose I can't avoid them forever."

Tristan led the way down the driveway. I hung back as he entered the house. The first person to greet us was a very handsome man in his fifties. I would have recognized the man as Tristan's father even if we'd met somewhere else. If this was what Tristan was going to look like at that age, it was well worth hanging around for.

While we were still shaking hands, a petite lady bustled out of the kitchen. After the introductions, she hugged Tristan. Her attention then turned to me. I wilted under her silent scrutiny, looking to Tristan for help. He was far too wrapped up in an in-depth conversation with his dad to notice.

She looked over at her son. "Tristan, sweetheart. Do you mind if I borrow Dominic for a few minutes? I need some help in the kitchen."

I tried to signal desperately with my eyes for him to say no, without making it too obvious. I probably just looked constipated. He remained oblivious, not even glancing in my direction. He smiled at his mum, telling her of course I'd be glad to help.

She inclined her head toward the kitchen, communicating that I should follow. Reluctantly, I did as she asked. In the kitchen, a multitude of pots and pans bubbled and simmered away, producing an aroma that immediately caused my stomach to rumble. She gestured toward a seat at the kitchen table. Confused, I hovered nervously without sitting down.

"I thought you needed help, Mrs. Maxwell. I can—"

"Call me Patricia, please. I just said that so we could have a chat. You look really freaked out. There's really no need to be."

I sank into the chair, surprised by her directness. "I wasn't sure how you and your husband would feel about—"

"Tristan being with a man?"

I nodded. "I realize it must be weird for you. One minute he's meant to be marrying a beautiful model, then suddenly he's not, and he's with me."

Patricia opened the oven door, bending down to peer beneath foil. Seemingly satisfied by what she saw, she re-covered it and closed the oven door, swinging around to face me. "A couple of months ago, Tristan became much happier. We didn't know why. I thought through every possible scenario: him splitting up with Maria, Maria possibly being pregnant, business doing particularly well. Nothing seemed to fit. When did you take over as Tristan's personal assistant?"

"A couple of months ago." I gave the information automatically before belatedly getting the point she was trying to make. "But nothing was going on. If anything I was pretty awful to him. I didn't really want to work for him."

A small smile played around her lips. "It doesn't matter. Whatever you were doing, you made him happy. Much happier than Maria ever did." She paused to lift a pan lid and stir something. "Let me tell you about Tristan. He has this work persona, which is fine. He runs a large company, manages a lot of staff, so he needs to keep it all separate, and then there's the real Tristan."

"The over-excitable, yet adorably persistent nutcase." I immediately blushed, partly at the fact I'd interrupted her, and partly at the fact I was calling her son names. "Sorry, I didn't mean—"

She was shaking her head, a smile still on her face. "Don't worry. He takes after his dad, and I assure you I call his dad much worse. But the thing is, you know that. He's completely himself with you. The worrying thing with him and Maria was, he never seemed to completely drop that work persona when he was with her. You can't marry someone if you can't be yourself with them, warts and all."

This conversation was proving to be quite enlightening. "So you were never that happy with him marrying Maria?"

She seemed to contemplate the question for a few seconds. "If he thought it was going to work, then I'm sure he would have made it work. Tristan's always known his own mind. I remember when he was nine. We said he could have a pet. It was the usual conditions: he'd have to look after it; we weren't going to be left with the responsibility. We expected him to choose a dog or a cat. We took him to the pet shop. What did Tristan want? A big, fluffy white rabbit. We refused to get it for him. We took him home and tried to persuade him that another type of pet would be much more suitable. We even pointed out that his school friends would probably make fun of him. But he had his heart set on that rabbit."

"What happened?"

She smiled fondly. "He wore us down. We got the rabbit, and no one has ever looked after an animal more carefully or more fastidiously. Mr. Whiskers was the most spoiled rabbit you could ever imagine. When his friends or anyone else made fun, he just ignored them. He didn't care what anyone else thought."

Much as I'd enjoyed the story, I pondered for a moment what her purpose in telling it to me was. "So you're saying I'm the fluffy white rabbit?"

She laughed. "Maybe. I don't know. We talk a lot, probably more than most mothers and sons, and I know you've doubted his feelings."

I opened my mouth to object and defend myself. She held a hand up to stall me for a moment. "It's understandable. I guess what I'm trying to say is, I've never known my son to change his mind about anything he's got his heart set on, so you shouldn't doubt him."

I nodded, incredibly grateful for her honesty and the fact she was taking the time to put my mind at ease. She'd turned back to the stove, so it took me a moment to catch the next words she spoke.

"Can we get the horrible bit out of the way now?"

"The horrible bit?"

She swung around, hands on hips. For such a petite woman, she still managed to make herself look pretty formidable. "I don't want to ever see my son as miserable as he was over Christmas. If you can promise me that, we'll get along fine. I know Maria had a hand in it, but still."

It was funny how someone I'd met less than ten minutes ago could make me feel so terribly guilty. Maybe it was because she'd softened me up first by saying nice things. I found myself apologizing profusely and promising always to talk to Tristan first. I made promises to her I hadn't even made to the man himself.

It was another hour before we were seated for dinner. I found myself seated next to Tristan at the dining room table with his parents opposite. After the earlier chat, I felt quite relaxed with his mum. His dad, however, had barely said two words to me. I surreptitiously watched him from beneath my eyelashes, trying to gauge where he stood with his son's new relationship.

Tristan leaned over to whisper in my ear. "Can you stop eyeing my dad up? He's married. Not to mention the fact that he's way too old for you." His smirk gave away the fact he was only teasing.

I snorted before returning the whisper. "I'll keep the younger version, thanks. Reckon you'll look that good at that age?"

He winked. "Stick around, and you might get to find out." A warm glow suffused my body at his intimation we could still be together in twenty to thirty years' time. After the conversation with his mum, it suddenly didn't seem so ridiculous.

I gave my thanks as a plate was deposited in front of me. Spearing a forkful of food, I managed to get it halfway to my mouth before Tristan grabbed my wrist, preventing me from moving it any closer. I attempted to tug it out of his grasp but Tristan held firm, interrogating his mum as she eased into the seat opposite.

"Mum, I told you Dominic was allergic to fish, didn't I?"

Patricia struck an exaggerated thinking pose. "Hmm...let me think. You told me when you'd first got together. You gave me a complete rundown of your hospital visit." She paused to offer me a reassuring smile at that point before continuing. "Then you told me again when I mentioned that I hoped you'd be bringing him to dinner so we could meet him. Then you reminded me again when you managed to talk him into coming. Then you rang me last night and told me again. So yes, darling, I think we can safely say you have made me fully aware that Dominic is allergic to fish."

His dad let out an amused snort. Assuming the matter was settled, I made another attempt at steering the fork toward my mouth. Tristan still didn't let go. He was still looking intently over at his mum.

"So it doesn't have any fish in it?"

Patricia met his gaze steadily. "It's a roast dinner, darling. I don't think I could manage to get any fish in it if I tried."

Seemingly placated, Tristan finally relinquished my wrist, allowing me to finally eat the baby carrot on the end of it.

My concern at how little Tristan's dad was saying during the dinner grew. Apart from insisting I call him Grahame when we'd first arrived, he'd barely spared a glance in my direction or said two words to me. Tristan didn't seem unduly worried, but it still bothered me. I noticed Patricia's scrutiny. I offered her a smile but the woman was far too perceptive for her own good. She turned toward her husband.

"What was the name of that boy at college? The one you were obsessed with before you met me."

Tristan suddenly went still next to me. He stared at his dad like he'd suddenly grown two heads. Grahame put his fork down, his forehead wrinkling. From Tristan's reaction I expected him to dispute it.

"Miguel. He was Spanish. He played the guitar." His face took on a wistful expression. "He had lovely...hands. I could have watched him play the guitar for hours."

I slapped Tristan on the back as he started to choke.

Tristan might be struggling with the information, but I wanted to know more. "What happened?"

Patricia answered for her husband. "I lured him away. Miguel was no match for me."

Grahame nodded in agreement. Tristan sat with his head in his hands. Patricia winked at me. He may have gotten his looks from his dad, but it was becoming clear that the teasing personality and directness I was used to from Tristan were inherited from his mother. This became even more apparent when she fired a question at her son after a quick glance my way.

"Has he asked you yet?"

Tristan shot his mum a clear look of warning. "Mum, don't."

Intrigued, I had to ask. "Have I asked him what?"

Tristan was shaking his head. Amused, I watched as she completely ignored him. She leaned across the table, giving the impression that the two of us were in a private space where nobody else could hear us. I obliged her by leaning closer myself.

She spoke in an exaggerated whisper. "Tristan was hoping you'd ask him to move in with you."

I rocked back in my seat, trying to get my head around the information.

Tristan crossed his arms defensively. "You're going to end up scaring him off. I've only just managed to convince him we're actually in a relationship. I don't need interference."

Patricia leveled her gaze on me. "Are you that easily scared off, Dominic?"

I shook my head, feeling like this was some sort of test. Tristan looked less than convinced. I took a moment to imagine what living with him would be like.

"Why would you want to move in with me? Your apartment's bigger." I'd spent the night there last week. Tristan hadn't been joking when he'd said it wasn't very homely. It looked like he'd only moved in a week ago. "Surely you should be asking me to move in with you?"

"Yours is nicer. And your shower is better."

"Yours could be nice. If it had my things in it, then—" I stopped short. I was one step away from agreeing to move in with him when I hadn't actually been asked.

Patricia helpfully filled the gap. "You could always get a new shower."

Tristan nodded thoughtfully. "That's true."

There was a long, awkward silence. Now if he didn't ask me, it would feel somewhat like a rejection.

Tristan glanced my way before quickly looking away again. Was he nervous? I guess having this conversation in front of his parents wasn't exactly ideal, but he could thank his mum for manipulating it perfectly.

Patricia coughed, none too discreetly. "Oh, for God's sake, Tristan. Just ask him."

Tristan sighed, obviously completely irked he'd been put in this position. Feeling sorry for him, I laid my fingers comfortingly on his arm. He glanced down at them before meeting my gaze.

"Dominic, I know we've not been together that long, and there's been lots of misunderstandings, but I would very much like it if you would agree to move in with me. Whether that's my apartment, your apartment, or somewhere else entirely. I don't really care where it is, as long as you're there, because I know how I feel and—"

"Yes."

"If you don't want to, well that's fine as well. I'll probably keep asking you. You know what I'm like, but—" He suddenly caught himself. "Did you say yes?"

I nodded, and then I had three people all beaming at me with matching smiles.

Epilogue

hree months later

When the shadow fell over my desk, I knew who it was without having to look up. The cologne was a dead giveaway; I'd given it to him myself as a birthday present.

"Have you escaped from your office again, Tristan? I'll have to have a word with Matthew about increasing the barricades."

He waited for me to look up. I finally did, taking a moment to admire the gorgeous man. It may have only been a few hours since I'd last seen him, but I never got tired of looking at him. Today's suit looked particularly good on him. He could have passed for a model, fresh off the catwalk.

"What do you want, Tristan?"

"I need your help with something."

Checking his hands revealed they were empty. Obviously, the "something" wasn't anything he could have brought with him. I raised an inquisitive eyebrow.

"I need your help with something in the office upstairs."

The last time he'd claimed that, I'd found myself backed against the desk with him huskily insisting he couldn't wait until we got home. "I'm not falling for that one again."

Tristan smirked at the memory. "It's not that. I promise."

"What is it then?"

He suddenly looked uncomfortable. "I can't go in there. There's a...you know...one of those things, on the desk."

"Oh, I see!" I frowned. "Where's Matthew? Get him to deal with it."

"At his desk." Tristan trailed his fingers along the back of the chair. "I haven't...I mean, that is to say...I don't really want to—"

"You don't want him to know you're scared of spiders?"

"I'm not scared!" Tristan looked genuinely indignant. "But there's no need for Matthew to know that I'm...not keen on them."

I sighed dramatically for effect. We both knew I was going to agree to go with him. I rose to my feet, making a big show of checking my watch. "I can spare you ten minutes."

We found ourselves alone in the elevator. Predictably, Tristan took the opportunity to move in close, trapping me against the wall. I spread my fingers over the surface of his shirt, enjoying the feel of the warm skin beneath and laughing as he nuzzled my ear. He pulled back slightly, both of us keeping an eye on the elevator display, ready to separate if anyone else got on. I plucked at his tie. "Remember you've got to take Snow to the vet's after work."

Snow was our cat, named of course after Jon Snow from *Game of Thrones*. The fact it was a black cat, Tristan claimed, was ironic. The cat had still fared better than the lizard when it came to names. The poor lizard had to put up with being called Littlefinger, a result of having one toe slightly shorter than the rest.

Tristan nodded. "I still think he might be lonely."

I knew what was coming next. "No."

"But—"

I pushed him away, partly to show I was serious and partly because in about five seconds flat, the elevator door was about to open on the top floor. "We are not getting another cat."

I briefly caught the familiar pout before I turned on my heel to exit the elevator. Matthew didn't seem particularly surprised to see me when I entered the office. Funny, that. It was almost as if I spent nearly as much time up here as I had when I'd worked here.

He waved a hello. "Is Tristan with you?"

I pointed behind me. I'd left him behind in the elevator. No doubt he was formulating his dastardly plan to convince me to expand our menagerie. "On his way."

Marching straight into Tristan's office, I half expected to find there'd never been a spider in the first place or it had disappeared. There was a spider, but it had to be a close call as to whether it was the smallest one I'd ever seen. Shaking my head, I opened a window and flicked the unwanted visitor outside, hearing the expected sound of the door closing and locking behind me.

I let myself be drawn into Tristan's arms, locking my arms together behind his neck. His arms tightened around my waist. "Has it gone?"

"I think so. It's hard to tell, given that it was so small I could barely see it."

He buried his face in my neck, and we swayed together. "Yeah, well, it was still a you-know-what."

I closed my eyes, enjoying the feel of our bodies locked together. "If I didn't know you better, I'd think it was an excuse to lure me up here."

I felt the smile against my neck. "Nope. But now you're here, I'm going to make the most of it."

"Matthew's outside."

"No, he's not. I sent him for lunch." Tristan's hands moved downward, cupping my ass and pulling me against him more firmly. "Have I told you that I love you today?"

I undid a button on his shirt, sliding my hand between the gap. "Twice. Once during breakfast. Although, to be fair, I wasn't entirely sure whether you were talking to me or the scrambled egg."

Tristan undid the button on my trousers, enabling him to slide his hand inside and curl his hand around my cock through my underwear. "Oh, it was definitely to you. I like scrambled egg but not that much. And the other one?"

I gasped as he started a firm rub. "You sent a text, mid-morning." I undid three more buttons on his shirt.

"Doesn't count. Not unless I say it." He licked the tendon on my neck, heading for the place he knew drove me absolutely wild. "Have you told *me* that you love me?"

"Not yet. I like to keep you waiting. It keeps your ego in check."

"Tell me." His teeth scraped over the sensitive skin behind my ear.

With great reluctance, I extracted his hand from my trousers, pulling away slightly. He protested, as I knew he would. I dropped a brief kiss on his lips in apology. "I'm not spending all day sticky."

He pouted before strolling over to his desk and leaning against it, his fingers fumbling with his shirt buttons. "You just wait until next week when we're on holiday and I've got you all to myself."

"You mean the holiday I haven't agreed to go on."

"I signed off on your annual leave."

"You were the one who handed the form in. I never saw it."

"But you are coming?" For a moment there was a flicker of unease. Keeping him on his toes was all very well, but sometimes I had to be careful I didn't push it too far. I walked over, cradling his head between my hands and staring intently into his eyes.

"I love you, Tristan. Of course I'm coming. You're stuck with me for the rest of your life."

"I don't believe you." Tristan's smile was devilish. "You need to do something to convince me."

"Like what?"

Tristan took a step forward so I was forced to take a step back. I suddenly felt the edge of the desk against my thighs. He leaned in farther, the position forcing my back down onto the desk.

"I'm not making love in your office."

Tristan came down on top of me, his hands making short work of the buttons until he'd peeled the sides back to reveal my naked chest. "Why not?"

"Tristan!" I really tried to put a note of warning in my voice, but we could both hear the smile in it.

He continued to play along anyway, as he returned to nuzzling my neck. "You can't get fired. You're immune to being fired because the boss is head over heels in love with you, and you can do no wrong in his eyes. If you're worried about getting sticky, then just take all your clothes off first. I've got wet wipes in my drawer."

I brought my hands up, burying them in his hair and pulling him more firmly on top of me, his erection burning like a brand through both of our pairs of trousers. "Why have you got wet wipes in your office?"

He smirked. "Just in case. For emergencies."

"And Matthew's really gone for lunch?"

He nodded slowly, a smile spreading across his face. He knew I was wavering. I decided to try and wrest back some control from the situation. "You know you'll owe me, right? If I give in to you and let you have your wicked way with me over your desk, you're going to have to make it up to me."

Tristan eased off me but only far enough to start shrugging his way out of his own clothes. "Anything." He grinned wickedly, his hands moving to the fastening of my trousers.

I gave in. It was always inevitable that Tristan would get his own way in the end, but seeing how long I could hold out on him was all part of the fun, and I knew he wouldn't have me any other way. It was clear we were never going to get bored of each other.

Thanks, from H.L Day

Thank you so much for choosing to read this book. You've made me really happy. How could you make me even happier? Well, you could leave a review. Then, I'd be ecstatic. :)

About H.L Day

H.L Day grew up in the North of England. As a child she was an avid reader, spending lots of time at the local library or escaping into the imaginary worlds created by the books she read. Her grandmother first introduced her to the genre of romance novels, as a teenager, and all the steamy sex they entailed. Naughty Grandma!

One day, H.L Day stumbled upon the world of m/m romance. She remained content to read other people's books for a while, before deciding to give it a go herself.

Now, she's a teacher by day and a writer by night. Actually, that's not quite true—she's a teacher by day, procrastinates about writing at night and writes in the school holidays, when she's not continuing to procrastinate. After all, there's books to read, places to go, people to see, exercise at the gym to do, films to watch. So many things to do—so few hours to do it in. Every now and again, she musters enough self-discipline to actually get some words onto paper—sometimes they even make sense and are in the right order.

Finding H.L Day

Where am I? I often ask myself the same question.
You can find me on Twitter[1].
You can find me on Instagram[2]
You can find me on Facebook.[3]
Send me a friend request or come and join my group -Days Den[4] for the most up to date information and for the chance at receiving ARCs
You can find me on my Website[5]
Or you can sign up to my newsletter[6] for new release updates.

---

1.   https://twitter.com/HLDAY100

2.   https://www.instagram.com/h.l.day101/?hl=en

3.   https://www.facebook.com/profile.php?id=100010513175490

4.   https://www.facebook.com/groups/2214565008830022/?ref=bookmarks

5.   https://hldayauthor.co.uk/

6.   https://wordpress.us18.list-manage.com/sub-scribe?u=e4815ef5cc09451a6bcd7aaa4&id=1875e83c44

More books from H.L Day

A Christmas Situation (Temporary Series; Tristan and Dom #2)

Love conquers all. But can it survive Christmas?

Dominic and Tristan have been together for almost a year. So everything's got to be plain sailing, right? Not quite. Not if you ask Dominic. Tristan's a bundle of energy and crazy ideas at the best of times. Add in Christmas, and it's a recipe for disaster.

That's not the only issue. There's also Tristan's mysterious absences and secret phone calls to contend with. Dominic might be insecure, but he's not crazy. His boyfriend is definitely up to something, and neither family nor friends seem interested in listening to his concerns. He won't jump to conclusions this time though. He'll talk to Tristan. Only what do you do when you can't get a straight answer out of the man you love?

When Tristan's secrets are revealed, will their first Christmas together also be their last? Or is Dominic about to discover that all his worries have been for nothing?

Only time will tell.

A story containing Christmas snark; a drunk Tristan; snow; and absolutely no mention of spiders—well alright, maybe a few mentions.

Buy now from Amazon

Read the excerpt at the end of this book

Time for a Change

What if the last thing you want, might be the very thing you need?

Stuffy and uptight accountant Michael's life is exactly the way he likes it: ordered, routine and risk-free. He doesn't need chaos and he doesn't need anything shaking it up and causing him anxiety. The only blot on the horizon is the small matter of getting his ex-boyfriend Christian back. That's exactly the type of man Michael goes for: cultured, suave and sophisticated.

Coffee shop employee Sam, is none of those things. He's a ball of energy and happiness who thinks nothing of flaunting his half-naked muscular body and devastating smile in front of Michael when he's trying to work. He knows what he wants—and that's Michael. And no matter how much Michael tries to resist him, he's not going to take no for an answer.

Sam eventually chips through Michael's barriers and straight into his bed. But Michael's already made some questionable decisions that might just come back to haunt him. He's got some difficult choices to make if he's ever going to find love. And he might just find that he's too set in his ways to make the right ones quickly enough. If Michael's not careful, the best thing that's ever happened to him might just slip right through his fingers. Because even a patient man like Sam has his limits.

Buy now from Amazon

Kept in the Dark

Struggling actor Dean, only escorts occasionally to pay the bills. So, his first instinct on being offered a job with a strange set of conditions is to turn it down. No date. Don't switch the lights on. Don't touch him. I mean, what's that all about? What's the man trying to hide? Dean certainly doesn't expect sex with a faceless stranger to spark so much passion inside him. It's just business though, right? He can put a stop to it whenever he wants.

When Dean meets Justin—a scarred, ex-army soldier unlucky in love. Dean's given a chance at a proper relationship. He can see past the scars to the man underneath. He's everything Dean could possibly wish for in a boyfriend: kind, caring and sweet. All Dean needs to do is be honest. Easy, right? But, Justin's holding back and Dean can't work out why. But whatever it is, it's enough to give him second thoughts.

They both have secrets which could shatter their fledgling relationship. After all, secrets have a nasty habit of coming out eventually. The question is when they do, will they be able to piece their relationship back together? Or will they be left with nothing but memories of bad decisions and the promise of the love they could have had, if only they'd both been honest and fought harder.

Buy now from Amazon

Refuge (Fight for Survival #1)

If you no longer recognise someone, how can you possibly be expected to trust them with your life?

Some might describe Blake Brannigan's life in the small Yorkshire village of Thwaite as bordering on mundane. His job in a café doesn't exactly set the world alight. But, he's got his own house, a boyfriend, and a close-knit group of good friends. For him, that's more than enough to lead a contented life.

Then in one fell swoop, everything's ripped away when he's forced to flee the village with only his boyfriend for company. He doesn't know why they're leaving. He hasn't got the faintest clue what's going on, and he's struggling to understand the actions and behaviour of a man he thought he knew. A man that it soon becomes clear knows far more about what's happening than he's letting on. A man hiding a multitude of secrets.

When the true extent of what's happening comes to light, Blake is rocked to the core. Peril lurks around every corner. The smallest decision suddenly spells the difference between life and death. If Blake's to have any chance of survival in this new and frightening world, he's going to have to unearth buried secrets, figure out whether love really can conquer all, and face emotional, physical, and mental challenges the likes of which he could never have imagined.

One thing's for sure, when life suddenly boils down to nothing more than the desperate need to find refuge, priorities change. Blake's certainly have.

Buy now from Amazon

Taking Love's Lead

Zachary Cole's new personal shopper is stunning in more ways than one. Gone is the staid, professional Jonathan. In his place is sexy, whirlwind Edgar, whose methods and lifestyle are less than orthodox. Still reeling from the experience, Zack can't get him out of his head. He needs to see him again. Even if it does involve dragging his heavily pregnant sister and her dalmatian into his cunning plan.

Sick of being dumped yet again, dog walker Edgar's pledged to stay single and put energy into finding a career more suited to an adult instead. Zack might be extremely tempting...and just happen to pop up wherever he goes, but that doesn't mean he's going to change his mind. He's got bigger priorities in life than a website designer who's after a brief walk on the wild side. Edgar's heart has taken enough of a bruising. He's not prepared to get dumped again.

Zack wants love. Edgar only wants friendship. Can the two men find common ground amid the chaos of Edgar's life? Or is Zack going to find that no matter what he does, there's no happy ending and he'll have to walk away?

Warning: This story contains dogs. Lots of dogs. Big ones. Small ones. Naughty ones. Ones that like ducks, squirrels, and lakes and ones that like to be carried. No dogs were harmed in the writing of this book.

Buy now from Amazon

Edge of Living

Sometimes, death can feel like the only escape.

It's been a year since Alex stopped living. He exists. He breathes. He pretends to be like everyone else. But, he doesn't live. Burdened by memories, he dreams of the day when he can finally be free. Until that time comes, he keeps everybody at bay. It's been easy so far. But he never factored in, meeting a man like Austin.

Hard-working mechanic Austin has always gone for men as muscular as himself. So, it's a mystery why he's so bewitched by the slim, quiet man with the soulful brown eyes who works in the library. The magnetic attraction is one thing, but the protective instincts are harder to fathom. Austin's sure though, that if he can only earn Alex's trust then the two of them could be perfect together.

A tentative relationship begins. But Alex's secrets run deep. Far deeper than Austin could ever envisage. Time is ticking. Events are coming to a head, and love is never a magic cure. Oblivious to the extent of Alex's pain, can Austin discover the truth? Or is he destined to be left alone, only able to piece together the fragments of his boyfriend's history, once its already too late?

Trigger warning: Please be aware that this story deals with suicidal ideation and other dark themes. If this is a subject you find uncomfortable, then this book is not recommended.

Despite this, there is a guaranteed HEA.

Buy now from Amazon

Excerpt from A Christmas Situation
Chapter One

July

The familiar strains of my mobile ring tone drew my attention away from the urgent e-mail I was writing. My boss, John Stone, had stressed that it needed sending as soon as possible. Eyes still fixed on the screen and one hand still trying to type, I reached inside the pocket of my suit to answer it on autopilot.

The silken tones in my ear, bearing a hint of confusion, were all too recognizable. "How long has there been a yucca plant in the corner of my office?"

Tristan. That would teach me not to bother checking the caller ID first. Mind, ignoring him would only ever have provided a temporary reprieve. Failure to answer the call would have triggered a flurry of text messages, or a personal appearance. Sometimes, it felt like a miracle that either of us got any work done. In moments of severe weakness, I even wondered whether it might have been better to have given in and stayed as his PA. I'd never have admitted those thoughts to him, though—even under the duress of extreme torture.

I loved the man to absolute pieces, but we'd been a couple for six months and I still couldn't say I was any closer to figuring out how his brain worked. I was beginning to doubt I ever would. "It was there when I was *forced* into being your personal assistant, so that means it was there months ago."

There was a long pause. "'Forced' is a strong word, Dom, and also blatantly untrue. Are you sure about the plant?"

I decided to skip the conversation, that having no choice in the matter, not being given prior notice, and being manipulated into staying there a lot longer than I was supposed to, did equate to being forced. It wasn't anything we hadn't already disagreed on hundreds of times already. "Quite sure."

Tristan made a noise as if he was considering something. "Did you put it there?"

I paused to offer a nod as John Stone left his office, cringing at the realization it was my mobile I had pressed to my ear during work hours. Not that I could get fired when it was the CEO of the whole company on the other end of it, but I hated being made to look anything less than professional. I forced my mind back to the apparently crucial conversation that couldn't wait until we'd gotten home. *What was it? Right, plants.* "Why would I put a plant in your office?"

Tristan groaned as if I'd asked a stupid question. "I don't know. It's like cushions, isn't it? You're a cushion-type person."

I refrained from asking for an explanation as to what he meant by that. Or how plants and cushions were the same thing. We'd have been there all day. "Tristan, what's the problem with the plant, exactly?"

Another long pause. I could picture him in his office. I'd have bet anything that he was stood in the middle of it, staring at the plant with obvious animosity. How he'd failed to notice it before, I had absolutely no idea. It was at least four foot tall and very green.

Finally, he spoke. "It's very leafy."

I pressed "send" on the e-mail, hoping I'd managed to write it without inserting the word plant anywhere. "It's a plant. If it didn't have leaves, it would just be a stick in a pot."

Another considering noise. "Won't it attract...you-know-whats?"

I tried, and failed, to keep the huge smile off my face. So *that's* what he was stressing about. It also explained why I was the one having the conversation with him, instead of his PA, Matthew. He still refused to confess his fear of spiders to him. I played dumb. "Botanists?"

"No."

"Other plants?"

"No." He made a noise in this throat, clearly intended to demonstrate his disgust. "You know what I'm talking about."

I laughed silently. "You could just say it, you know. The word itself can't grow legs and crawl all over you."

His shudder was audible even over the phone. "You're really mean to me. I have no idea why we got a place together, just so you could be mean to me for more hours of the day."

With a quick glance toward the door to check whether John Stone had closed it, I lowered my voice. "I don't remember you complaining last night when I was sucking your cock."

Tristan gave one of his throaty laughs. The sound never failed to make my cock twitch. "You were too busy to notice."

I fiddled with a pen, wishing that there was a lot less of the day left until I could get Tristan home and have him all to myself. I could always go down to his office, but I'd never managed to quite get past the point of feeling completely and utterly unprofessional. "Hmmm...weird. I remember an awful lot of 'oh Gods,' and you saying my name over and over again, but I don't remember any complaining. I'll try and listen more carefully next time." I closed my eyes at the moan that came down the line in response. I guessed I wasn't the only one replaying last night's blow job in my head. "I remember hearing that a lot, too."

I took a deep breath. Any more of this and I was going to be pulling my cock out under the desk and urging Tristan to talk dirty to me. The knowledge he wouldn't hesitate to oblige did nothing to cool my ardor. I needed to change the subject before John Stone returned to the office and got a huge shock. I coughed. "So...anyway...the plant. Get Matthew to put it in his office, or if that's too close for your peace of mind, get him to put it somewhere else in the building. Or get rid of it altogether."

"Good idea!"

I shook my head wearily, but with a smidgeon of fondness, and resisted pointing out that the solution was obvious to anyone with half a brain. Left to Tristan, he would have spent the next few months, eyeing it suspiciously while expecting an army of spiders to burst out of it at any time. "Now that's sorted, can I get on with my work?"

"I didn't call you to talk about the plant."

"Of course you didn't. Stupid me for not realizing that. You know, considering the fact all we've talked about is a plant." I heard the sound of Tristan's office door open and imagined poor Matthew being dragged in to be subjected to the world's weirdest mime act based around the offending plant.

"I called to ask what time you'd be home."

Strange question! "What do you mean? Aren't you taking me home?"

"Not today. I need to leave early."

"Why?" I hated myself for asking the question. I sounded exactly like the suspicious, insecure boyfriend I was. Why would Tristan need to go somewhere on his own, though? We always went home together. Even if I was working late, which happened a couple of times a week, he grumbled, but he still waited. I normally lasted about an hour before caving to the face-pulling, the pouting, and his rumbling stomach because he hadn't eaten for at least ten minutes.

"It's a surprise. I need to prepare...something. What time will you be home?"

I shrugged, even though he had no way of being able to detect the action. "I don't know. Six."

"Exactly six?"

I frowned. "Hopefully. Depends if the bus is on time and how much traffic there is on the way."

"Okay."

He hung up, and I was left staring at the blank screen of my phone. It rang again about thirty seconds later, Tristan's name flashing on the screen. I answered it without speaking, his voice coming straight through. "I forgot to say something."

"You mean like, goodbye."

"That as well. But, I was thinking more along the lines of telling you I love you."

The words had the same effect they always did, no matter how many times a day he said it: they stole my breath and reduced my insides to mush. I finally regained the ability to speak, the words being pushed out through the huge smile on my face. "I love you, too."

"See you later. Six. Don't be late."

I was halfway through saying goodbye when the line went dead again.

Buy from Amazon

Printed in Great Britain
by Amazon

65267191R00149